MW01596015

# SAGAMORE

## JACK SONNI

# SAGAMORE
## BY JACK SONNI

Copyright 2025 by The Estate of Jack Sonni

Published 2025 by Cool Dog Sound

P.O. Box 454 • Water Valley, MS 38965

COOL DOG SOUND
that little rock n' roll book label from Mississippi

www.cooldogsound.com

For more information contact dozens@cooldogsound.com.

ISBN 979-8-218-72364-4 (paperback)

*One Horse Town* lyrics used by permission
of Charlie Starr/Blackberry Smoke

Cover art by Jared Spears
Book design by Susan Bauer Lee
Author photo by Sonia Farnsworth

*For my family.*

*In the tiny town where I come from*
*You grew up doing what your daddy done*
*And you don't ask questions, you do it just because*
*You don't climb too high or dream too much*
*With a whole lotta work and a little bit of luck you can*
*Wind up right back where your daddy was*

— Blackberry Smoke, *One Horse Town*

*"Let every state and province in America look out sharply for the bird-killing foreigner; for sooner or later, he will surely attack your wildlife. ... If you are without them today, tomorrow they will be around you."*

— William T. Hornaday, President,
New York Zoological Society,
***"Our Vanishing Wildlife" 1913***

*Sagamore, Pennsylvania*
*March 1932*

The sheriff crouched by the dead man. With the back of a gloved hand, he patted the outside pockets of the man's coat and found them empty. He picked up a stick and flipped the shredded opening of the blood-soaked coat back. Poking at the inside pockets, he found a leather billfold that contained a badge engraved "SPECIAL AGENT."

Johnson studied the dead man's ashen face, the eyes popped as if he'd been surprised. His chest lay open in a bloody pulp of shredded shirt and skin, the work of a close-range shotgun.

A playing card stuck to his forehead, the Jack of Spades, with a neat, round bullet hole near dead center. *Someone wanted to make sure you were very dead,* Johnson thought and used two gloved fingers to close the eyes, then peeled the card loose.

*Bersaglio.* The word the young Italian woman, the young hunter's widow, used. Target.

*Where the hell did those Colts go?* Johnson wondered, remembering the game warden's reputation for fancy gun handling and thinking the man probably slept with them.

Johnson glanced over his shoulder to see his deputy coming back from his truck with a tarp. He slipped the billfold and the card into the pocket of his own coat and stood. Long-legged and rail thin, Johnson appeared taller than his 5'8" frame. He was muscular, strong at 50 and unafraid to step to bigger men.

"Get him covered up. I'm heading back." Johnson said. "You wait for the ambulance to get here."

The deputy, Johnson's nephew Dennis, was farm boy big at 6-foot-4, pushing close to 275. He towered over most, and his bulk stretched his uniform shirt to the material's limit. The deputy's intimidating physical presence was often enough to deter confrontations and give pause to any troublemakers who thought of escalating a situation.

"How long you think that man's been out here?" Dennis asked.

Johnson's gaze went from the body skyward where a trio of turkey vultures circled high above the scene.

"Can't be all that long," he said. "Couple hours tops. Birds haven't gotten to him yet. Conductor saw the body when the train passed this morning about daybreak."

The deputy watched the vultures and tried to chase the image of the ugly birds feasting on the game warden. Johnson pointed to the holsters still strapped to Markle's thighs. Both empty. "Man went about with those two pearl-handled Colts of his," he said. "You come across them in the truck or anywhere around here?"

"No sir, nothing in that truck but a couple pair of handcuffs."

Johnson looked to the game warden's truck. "You sure about that? You look around these bushes, around that tree?"

"Yes sir," the deputy said. "Before you got out here, I walked all up and down here. Like you taught me about a crime scene. When will the meat wagon show up, you think?"

"They'll get here when they get here," Johnson said. "Tell you what. You occupy yourself while waiting. Take another look around and in that truck. See if those guns turn up."

He walked back to his patrol car, a grey Ford Model T Tudor sedan, got in and looked back to watch the deputy cover the game warden's body. There might be someone, family or friend, somewhere who would mourn the man's death, but Johnson was not going to be joining them.

The sheriff drove away thinking about the violence the game warden brought with him when he arrived in Indiana County. How the game warden hid behind his special agent badge and used the governor's mandate of reining in unlicensed hunters to instead wage a private war on immigrant Italians who shot songbirds as they did in their homeland. Shooting doves and pigeons almost made sense to Johnson but it was the hunting of robins, finches, nuthatches, blackbirds and blue jays he didn't understand. But these were men scratching out a living working the mines in Sagamore, hunting to survive. He shook his head and muttered himself.

"All this trouble over a bunch of little birds."

2

*Three weeks earlier*

The boy woke to the same black of his sleeping. He lay in the deep dark of early morning, knowing the time without needing to check the watch ticking on the bedside table. The sound of his father entering the back door leading to the kitchen told him the time.

Corky Trunzo was christened Eugene but only his mother called him that, and only when she was displeased with him. His father used the Italian *Eugenio* when he wanted the boy to pay attention. To everyone else, he had forever been known as Corky, a nickname his grandmother gave him when he was an infant. To ease his teething pain, the woman had dipped wine corks in the fiery grappa she made and rubbed them on his gums. She also allowed the baby boy to suck on corks soaked in her homemade wine, her belief that *vino* was a curative for everything from colic to upset stomachs to a child's unwillingness to sleep.

The family story was that "cork" was the first word the boy said.

Corky rolled from his bed and turned on the small bedside lamp before his feet touched the cold wooden floor. He was not tall but compact and muscled from playing first string varsity basketball throughout his high school years. Handsome, with warm, brown eyes, he wore his hair slicked back in a tall pompadour. Wearing the long johns he slept in, Corky hop-stepped into a pair of heavy canvas trousers. He buttoned a long sleeve flannel shirt, then pulled a too-large wool sweater over his head. Frayed at the edges, a hole at one elbow, the sweater was a hand-me-down from his older brother, and the boy wore it like a uniform. He made a halfhearted attempt at straightening his bedclothes. The shelf above the head of the bed still contained the books his brother read from to him each night. *Treasure Island, Robinson Crusoe, The Count of Monte Cristo, The Adventures of Huckleberry Finn*. Corky fell asleep to the sound of his brother's voice every night of his life. His own dreaming fueled by the older boy's stories.

The boy turned off the light, left his room and made his way downstairs.

He was six when Rudy enlisted in the Army. He had just turned seven when two servicemen in dress uniforms appeared at the front door and delivered their much-regretted news and presidential gratitude. His mother wore her grief like armor and if Corky hugged her, she stiffened and felt so brittle, he believed if he squeezed too tightly the woman would shatter into a million pieces. Her death came less than a year later.

At the bottom of the staircase, he could see into the kitchen. In a cloaking darkness broken only by the single match struck to light the stove and the soft blue flame of the burner, his father made his morning coffee. He watched the old man slide a chair from the table and lower himself into the seat, in the slow motion of a man worn to the bone and with no memory of a body that didn't carry a boxer's battered ache.

His father was an old man now, having passed through middle age giving half a lifetime to working the coal mines in the Appalachian hills and Allegheny Mountains of western Pennsylvania. Every morning since arriving in America, depending on his shift, Thomasso Trunzo left or returned home at 4 a.m., the soft groaning of the floorboards the only betrayal of his presence as he moved like a ghost through his own home.

Corky stepped into the kitchen where his father sat, drinking coffee in the blue shadows cast by the lit burners under two large pots of water on the stove.

"Morning," Corky said in a whisper.

His father raised his cup in return.

"You going to sleep ok after having that coffee?"

The old man shrugged his shoulders. "Eh, *mezzo mezzo*," he said.

"You need your sleep, Pops," Corky said.

The old man shrugged again, sipped his espresso and lifted his chin at Corky. "*Che fai?*"

"I'm going hunting with Sonny," he said. "Meeting him near the mines."

The response was a silent nod as his father bent to untie his boots. Corky switched on the overhead lamp that cast a weak, yellowed light and crossed the kitchen, dragging a large, galvanized tub to the stove. He opened the oven door, lit the burner, and moved the tub in front of the growing heat.

His father returned home after every shift encased in black. Coal dust covered his clothing, his face, and hands, rimmed his eyes, his nose and mouth. The boy watched as the old man stood, removed his coat, and placed his boots near the back door. He hung his coat and then stripped off his shirt and pants and socks, dropping the dust-caked work clothes in a basket by the door. He unbuttoned his union suit, the neck and cuffs of the sleeves and ankles blackened, shrugged out of the top half that hung from his waist like a second skin, soaked in sweat and grime. His back and chest mottled with the black dust that masked his face and sat in the deep creases around his eyes.

Coal dust had wormed its way into his skin and his lungs and clung on his breath. Seeped into his muscle and swam in his blood as the mine claimed his body, turning flesh and bone into the same bituminous rock he pulled from the earth. To Corky, the dust hung in a powdery veil over his father, dulling the sight of him as if he walked in a faded tintype of earlier times.

He watched in silence as his father skinned out of the union suit bottom, tossed it into the basket and stepped into the tub, lowering his still-muscular frame until he sat submerged to the chin, soaking the ache that ran to his bones. When the man waved him over, Corky would lift the pot from the stove and pour more hot water into the tub.

Corky walked out of the kitchen into the hallway. He opened the closet and took his heavy coat off the hanger and slipped it on, then reached for the long-barreled 12-gauge shotgun leaning in the back corner. He went back into the kitchen, slinging a canvas game bag across his shoulder to hang at his back. It was a good day of hunting when he returned home, the bag heavy and bouncing off his hip, keeping time with his stride. He was filled with pride in doing his part to put food on the table.

He leaned the gun near the back door and, seeing his father lathered in a dingy foam, pulled a pot off the stove to pour over his head and shoulders. He set the second pot next to the tub.

"Alright, Pops," he said with a smile. "Uncle Benny's picking me up on his way to work. I'll bring back something for dinner."

His father nodded and lifted a watery hand, shooing his only living son to the door and into the dark morning.

Corky went out and down the back stairs into the yard. He ducked under the porch to where his dog waited, chained to a small doghouse, tail wagging in anticipation of the hunt. The boy dropped to his haunches and let the dog off the chain, giving the beagle mutt a two-handed neck scruffing. He reached inside the doghouse, groping in the near corner and pulled out two small Mason jars. He tucked one in his bag, the other in his left coat pocket. Backing out from under the porch, he trotted up the hill along the house, the dog at his side. The pair stood by the road for only a few minutes before the headlights of Uncle Benny's truck appeared, then came to a stop in front of them. His uncle sat behind the wheel and greeted him with a smile.

"Morning," Corky said.

"*Buon giorno,*" his uncle said. He was a small, swarthy man, his mouth hidden by a bushy mustache, a newsboy cap tilted back on his head. Corky tapped the tailgate and the dog leapt into the bed. The boy slid into the truck.

"*Come stai? Va bene?* Oh, wait," Benny said as he clamped his hand on his nephew's leg and shook it. "In *L'Merica*, we speak Engleesh." Straightening to sit taller, Benny spoke with practiced formality. "How... are ... you ... this morning?"

"I am well, sir. How are you?"

"I am, *come si dice?*" he shook his head, then raised his forefinger. "Fine!

The two shared a laugh. Benny pointed to the shotgun. *"Dove"*? Where you go hunting?"

"I'm meeting Sonny at the trail that goes up behind the mines towards Salt Lick."

His uncle's smile disappeared. He turned and gave Corky a questioning arched eyebrow. When the boy gave no answer, he shook his head and returned to his driving. Both knew of the corrupt game warden Markle and the danger he posed to Italians hunting in the local hills.

The lights of the coal yard rose above the trees. Corky pointed to a truck parked just beyond a rutted dirt turnoff that cut into the woods. His friend Sonny and Sonny's father, Walt, a mine foreman, stood leaning against the tailgate. They each raised a hand to shield their eyes as Benny edged off the road and pulled to a stop. Walt Johnson walked to the driver's side and bent down.

"Morning, Benny," he said. The Italian nodded, tipping his hat. Bending farther, Walt looked across the cab. "Won't get much hunting done sitting in this truck, Corky. Your uncle needs to get to work, too."

"Yes, sir," Corky said, smiling. Waiting for his friend's father to move away from the truck, Corky pulled the jar from his coat pocket and tapped it against his uncle's hip. Without glancing down, Benny's hand found the jar, which he slipped into his own coat. Corky gave his uncle a sideways glance and got a wink in return.

Outside the truck, Corky called to the dog and motioned him to follow. The mutt jumped from the bed and began sniffing the ground.

"Benny," the foreman said. "I told Sonny they should go on out to hunt his Uncle Carl's farm. Won't be any trouble out there." The two men exchanged glances. A silent acknowledgment of Corky having no hunting license and the threat the game warden posed.

"*Eugenio.*" Benny called to his nephew, who was standing with his friend checking their guns.

Corky looked up, saw his uncle raise his forefinger to his right eye and tap his cheek.

"*Capisce'*?" A command more than a question. Listen to what this man says.

Corky nodded and waved. He whistled for his dog and the trio walked into the woods.

It was early afternoon and the rain had picked up again. When Indiana County Sheriff Albin "Buzz" Johnson crossed over the creek north of town, the water was slapping against the bottom of the bridge. Another hour or so, he figured, and the bridge would be washed out. He would organize some men to set up a roadblock when he got back to his office, but he had one quick stop at Mazzoni's market. When the clapboard building appeared out the rain, Johnson pulled into the gravel lot in front of the market.

He parked next to the only other vehicle. A truck. In the open back, two men sat, huddled against the wet. As the sheriff walked by, he could see the men were Italians. Their clothes muddied and soaked through. Both were handcuffed and one man's face was bloody and bruised purple.

He entered the store and shook the rain off his coat and did the same with his Stetson. Mazzoni, the owner, was behind the long counter.

"*Ciao*, Sheriff. *Come stai, bene?*"

"Doing alright, Angelo, Thanks," Johnson said. "A bit wet out there, though."

"*Si*. I think it's now forty days and forty nights. No? I think maybe I should be building a big boat, eh?"

Johnson laughed. "Well, just make sure you leave room for me and the missus, if you do."

The grocer smiled. "*Si, si*, we won't leave without you both."

Another voice joined the conversation.

"No Mazzoni, you cannot leave Sheriff Albin Johnson to drown in these rising waters."

Johnson turned to see the game warden.

Ed Markle stood just a bit over six feet tall, his height crowned by a broad brimmed Stetson with a gut that hung over his belt. He wore knee high boots, a waistcoat underneath his waxed cloth field coat. As he came to stand at the

counter, a shotgun crooked in his arm, Johnson took note of the pair of long bar-
reled Colt 45s in twin holsters strapped to his thighs like an Old West gunsling-
er, an affectation carried further by Markle wearing the guns handles forward.
Something the sheriff had seen in a photograph of Jesse James.

"I'm surprised to see you out this way. I mean, you're Indiana County, right?"
The game warden waved his hand in a circle. "But isn't this Armstrong County?"

"Just coming out a few extra miles to get some of Mr. Mazzoni's pastries,"
Johnson said.

"What you got that's so good the sheriff travels all the way out here?"

"I make *biscotti*," Mazzoni said.

"Biscuits?"

"No, *signore*, *biscotti*. A cookie."

"Why can't you just call it a cookie?

Mazzoni stammered and looked to Johnson.

"Angelo, make up a box, same as mine," Johnson said. "My gift to Mr.
Markle."

"Don't bother, Angelo," Markle said. "Not much of a cookie person. I'm a
bit particular about my desserts. More of a pie man. Hey, pie-zahn, you got any
apple pie?"

Mazzoni shook his head. "No apple pie."

"No? How about cherry? Or maybe peach. You got to have some peach pie,
I bet."

"No pies, *signore*. *Mi dispiace*."

"Forget it," Markle said. He swung the shotgun up and admired it. "You
ever see one of these, Sheriff? Made over in Eye-Ta-Lee someplace." He turned to
Mazzoni. "Ain't that right, pie zan?"

"His name is Mr. Mazzoni," the sheriff said.

"Oh, I know his name, Johnson," Markle said. "Hell, it's on the damn sign
out front. No reason we can't be friends, just because the man don't make pies."
Markle turned and scanned the shelves behind the shop keeper. "So, Mister
Piezan, you got some 12-gauge shells?"

Mazzoni called toward the stockroom. A boy appeared and greeted Johnson
with a wave. The smile on his face vanished when he saw the game warden.
Corky looked at his boss, who tilted his head towards Markle.

"*Accudire*," Mazzoni said to the boy. "Take care of *Signore* Markle, eh?" He
pointed at the gun the big man held. "*Calibro dodici per il fucile da caccia.*"

Johnson followed Corky's gaze as it bounced from his boss to the shotgun,
to the game warden's grinning face. Something in the man's eyes betrayed the
grin. Something wolfen. A predator's eyes. The boy remained where he stood.
In defiance or fear, Johnson wasn't sure. When the boy looked his way again, he
gave him a slight nod.

With his eyes on Johnson's, Corky said. "Twelve gauge. Buck, slug or…" He turned and looked straight at the game warden. "Bird?"

Markle burst into a laugh. "Now, my young wop, why in the hell would I want birdshot? You know shooting birds is against the damn law, now, don't you?"

"No law against shooting pheasants," Corky said, his voice rising, his fists clenched at his sides. "Or turkeys, neither. Right, Sheriff Johnson? Or all the quail around here? Tell him, sheriff."

"*Eugenio,*" Mazzoni hissed. "*Piano, piano, eh?*" He shooed the boy towards the storeroom entrance. Corky glared at the game warden then at his boss. Johnson signaled Corky towards the stockroom with a tilt of his head. The boy stepped through the doorway and disappeared.

"Those men," Johnson said to Markle. "Out in your truck."

Markle gazed at the shotgun, he fingered the swirling circles of the engraving. "I only get paid half of the fines they collect when I bring poachers in," he said. "Most of the time, they got no money to pay."

Corky returned and set two boxes on the counter then moved back to stand in the stockroom doorway.

Markle slid open one of the boxes, pulled two shells out and loaded each barrel. "So, of course, that means I don't get paid a chunk of what's owed to me for doing my job." He snapped the gun closed. "But I can make some extra selling these guns. One this nice, I just might keep for myself though. And those men in the truck broke the law. Laws they know about. Like needing a license to hunt any damn thing in these counties. So what would you do?"

Johnson said nothing.

Markle scoffed, shook his head. He pocketed two boxes of shells Corky had placed on the counter. "Come on outside, Johnson. Let me show what I'm dealing with here." He walked to the door, swung it open, holding it wide. "Come on."

Johnson stepped through the door but Markle stopped. "Hold up, sheriff, I forgot something. Give me a deck of them playing cards you sell, Mazzoni," he said. "Wait, make it two."

The rain had stopped but the sky remained the color of lead. Markle walked past the sheriff and opened the door to his truck. He laid the shotgun on the seat. Johnson saw another shotgun, not as fancy, along with a pair of revolvers inside. The game warden slammed the door and waved Johnson towards the back of the truck. The two hunters sat bent forward, their faces buried in their knees. Neither moved until Markle pounded on the side of the truck bed. Both heads jerked upright, and they leaned back, cowering at the big man's looming presence.

"Let me show you what these two were up to, sheriff. Right in your back-yard." He pulled a canvas bag out of the truck, flipped it opened and dumped the contents. A dozen small birds spilled out onto the ground. Johnson saw they were all songbirds of one kind or another - doves, robins, nuthatches. "You see any pheasants?"

He toed the pile with his boot. Johnson was silent. Markle leaned back and called out to Corky, who had come out of the store along with Mazzoni and stood watching from the porch. "How about you, young wop? What's that they call you? Corky? You see any pheasants?"

Corky just stared at the big man.

"How about turkeys? No? Not so loud now are you, boy?"

He waved at the men in the truck, motioning them to move to the end of the bed. "Get your asses over here," he said, pounding the side. When neither moved, he slapped the hat off the head of one, grabbed his coat collar and pulled him to the tailgate.

"Alright, Markle," Johnson said. "That's…"

"Alright what?" the man snapped. "That's what? Enough?"

Markle faced the hunters. "Now, which one of you dumbass wops is going to explain this to me." He nudged at the dead birds with the toe of his boot. "Shooting goddamn birds." The game warden shook his head, spat again. "That's what they send me out here to stoop. They got the whole U.S. Congress going crazy over what you are doing out here. Got all kinds of experts saying you are killing all the birds that eat the insects and if they ain't no more birds, the trees gonna get et up by the bugs and when the trees get all et up, we won't have no more air to breath because that's why we got them in the first place. Making air. And won't be no more if all the trees are gone. They say you wops is going to bring the end times on us all."

Markle laughed. Shook his head.

"I don't believe that shit for a second. But you know who does? The god-damn Governor's wife. And she is all up in that man's ass about saving the precious birdies. And he ain't getting no peace and he sure as hell ain't getting no wiggle on 'til that woman of his is happy. You know what I'm saying?" He winked at Johnson and rocked his hips back and forth in mock intercourse.

"So they send me out here - the Governor his own damn self-calls me and says, Ed Markle, you got to get on out to western PA and do something about this." He stopped pacing and looked down, gesturing at the two Italians. "About you fucking wops shooting that nice lady's birdies."

"Markle," Johnson started. The game warden raised his arm, pointed at the sheriff and wagged his finger. He brought it to his lips, shushing the man like a child.

One of the Italians looked up and met Markle's glare. In a low voice said, *"Mi dispiace, signore. Io non capisco."*

Markle bristled. "Fucking speak American."

In one swift move, he pulled his Colt and swung the gun down on the man's forehead. Shocked, Johnson reached for his own revolver. Before Johnson could get his gun out of the holster, Markle had the Colt leveled at his chest. Wolf eyes blazed behind the gun.

"No, no, no," Markle said, smiling. "Do not get in the way of me doing my job, Johnson. Hand off that iron?"

Johnson hesitated. Markle cocked the Colt with his thumb. Johnson brought his hand away from his side. Markle kept the gun steady as he reached inside his coat with his other hand. He brought out a leather billfold and flipped it open to reveal a badge. He held it out alongside the Colt.

"Not sure if your eyesight is good enough to read that, Sheriff," he said. "So allow me." He turned it back towards himself. "It says, 'Special Agent.'" He faced it towards Johnson. "Not sheriff." He grinned. "No sir, Special Agent. That's me. And I am not bound by any county lines or such nonsense. The whole damn state is my jurisdiction, and nobody is to try and stop me from doing my job in the manner I see fit. Understand?"

The question was met with silence.

"And, believe me, I was to shoot you, right now?" Markle said. "Put one right in that star you got pinned over your heart? Tell them you obstructed, impeded me in my sworn duty to enforce the law? Not one goddamn thing anyone would say or do about it."

Johnson knew the man was right. With the governor's backing, there was little if anything he could do to intervene. As much as he wanted to shoot Markle where the man stood, he couldn't.

Stepping back, Markle took a deep breath, and exhaled in an exaggerated act of calming himself. He started pacing and began to spin his Colt on his trigger finger, back into the holster, drawing again, spinning, high, low, crossing in front of his body, raising the gun over his head, low again, tossing and catching… a well-practiced routine done without once looking at the spinning revolver.

Johnson's eyes grew wide at the display. He turned and looked over his shoulder to the store front. He saw Corky turn and go inside.

"I don't give a fuck about no birds, Johnson. But you're going to keep your nose out Ed Markle's business? Or are you just some wop lover?"

The question hung in the air.

Johnson watched as Markle, gun still in his right hand, took a couple long strides and grabbed the pistol-whipped hunter by the hair. The game warden leaned into the man's face until their noses almost touched. Blood oozed from the split skin of the Italian's forehead and streamed from his torn lips and cracked teeth.

"Now you listening?" Markle said, still gripping the man's long black hair. "You ca peeshy, you dumb wop?"

Markle shoved the man's head back and let go of his hair. He looked at the palm of his hand, then wiped it on the man's coat. He brought the Colt up, pointed at the hunter's head and cocked the hammer back with his thumb. "How 'bout now you piece of - "

He was cut off by the sound of a shotgun being racked. Both Johnson and Markle turned to the porch where Corky stood, the gun raised to his shoulder, pointing down at the game warden.

"Corky," Johnson said, raising his hand. "Don't."

Corky held his aim.

"Sheriff," Markle said. "I suggest you tell that welp to get that gun off me."

Johnson seethed as his finger twitched above his gun. His mind racing in search of a single legal exoneration for putting a bullet in the man. When he came up empty, he steadied the twitching finger above his gun.

"Corky," Johnson said, without taking his eyes off Markle. "Put it down."

Mazzoni reached out and put one hand on Corky's shoulder and used his other to lower the shotgun.

"That boy's just vermin like these two here, Johnson. World will be a better place when we're rid of them. And you know what? I think I'm going to take these two here and play some cards. Yes sir, do a little gambling, give them a chance to win back their guns. Hell, they beat me, maybe Ed Markle will let them go home instead of jail."

"Markle, what the hell?" the sheriff began. The game warden ignored the question. Johnson saw him reach to his side and reflexively his own hand pulled back towards his gun. But when Markle turned to face him, he saw that the man held, not his Colt, but a deck of playing cards that he fanned with his thumbs. Johnson lifted the brim and pushed his Stetson back. He studied Markle's face.

"Tell you what. Let's play a quick little hand. One card. High card wins," He held the fan out to the hunters, cards face down, his thumbs riffling the backs. "Pick a card, pyzahn," The pistol-whipped hunter urged his friend to go first. The man reached out and made his choice.

"Show me."

The hunter turned the card.

"Eight of Clubs to the young pyzahn. Not too bad." Markle said, pushing the cards towards the hunter he'd laid the pistol on. "This man's luck is due for a change, don't you think, Sheriff?"

"Cut the shit, Markle," Johnson said. "Just let these two go and we can be done here."

"Ease up now. Ed Markle's trying to give this man a chance to win his freedom. Now pick a card. They won't bite you."

The bloodied hunter touched a card in the middle of the spread.

"You sure?"

The man's eyes narrowed at Markle and snatched the card. Without looking at it he held it up.

"Jack of Spades," Markle said, "Now it gets interesting." He turned to Johnson, lifting the cards towards him. "How about you, sheriff? You in on this? Maybe you can win that fancy shotgun."

Johnson shook his head.

Markle shrugged and riffled the cards with his thumbs, stopping once or twice, then pushed one card out of the fan. He pulled it free and snapped it face up.

"Well, look at that," he crowed. "Ace of Diamonds. Looks like I got me a new shotgun."

He walked around the truck and opened the door. He looked at Johnson and touched the brim of his Stetson. "You enjoy them biscuits now," he said and got in the truck.

Johnson watched as Markle drove away, the two hunters staring back at him. Corky came down off the porch to stand at Johnson's side.

"That man needs to die," Corky said.

Johnson sat in his office with his feet up on his desk, coffee mug in hand. He stared out the window, wondering if his nephew deputy could possibly make a worse cup of coffee. He set the half-finished cup on his desk, stood and pulled on his coat.

"I'm heading out," he called.

Dennis appeared in the doorway, coffee pot in hand.

"Where are you going?" he asked.

"Out to Sagamore," Johnson said.

"What's out there? That's not our jurisdiction," Dennis said.

Johnson eyed his nephew. He wasn't sure what it was that annoyed him so much about the kid's constant questions. Why he took it as an intrusion, when it was probably motivated by the young man's desire to be included in on what was going on. But it annoyed the hell out of him.

"I'm going out to see Gina Ferraro," Johnson said.

"What's she need to see to you about?" the deputy asked. "I mean, not like the Italians want us out there."

Johnson bristled but knew that to be true. Beyond the fact it was another county and not his jurisdiction, he had no obvious reason for driving out to Sagamore. Not as a lawman. None of the Italians would talk to him beyond a polite, obsequious hello. Few besides a child or two would even wave to acknowledge his presence as he drove by. They didn't trust him or any sheriff or the law they represented, the justice he was sworn to uphold.

He also knew that whatever Gina Ferraro wanted to talk to him about must be important. To her at least. When a young man came to his house last night with a note from Gina asking for him to come to Sagamore, he could not refuse.

"Not sure if I'll be back later, but I'll check in with you," Johnson said.

"Everyone knows she's connected to that mobster Dino Crocetti, in Pittsburgh," his nephew said. "Folks say he's part of the Black Hand and runs everything in western PA and most of Ohio, too. All the gambling, prostitution, bootlegging. Nothing moves on the barges on the three rivers past Pittsburgh without him collecting a fee. Like he's carved out his own kingdom here."

"Seem to know a lot about him," Johnson said. "Thought he just owned that jazz club in the Hill District down in Smoketown."

"Everyone knows his reputation. And that Ferraro woman is in deep with him. Besides, what we got going on that she knows anything about?"

"One thing she knows?" Johnson said. "Is how to make a damn fine cup of coffee. Calls it a *cappuccino*. She makes an espresso then puts some warmed-up milk in it and a little bit of sugar, too. One of the best things I've ever tasted. Might just send you out there so she can teach you how to make it cause you sure as hell don't know what you're doing."

Gina Ferraro lived in Sagamore and ran her home as a boarding house for Italian miners. The local *paesani* regarded her as a resource, a "fixer," someone they could go to for help of almost any kind. She made things appear - a much-needed job for a neighbor's cousin newly arrived from the old country, a suitable match for a daughter, a small loan until payday. And she made things disappear, like a pestering landlord or an unwanted pregnancy.

Or, if any of the stories were half-true, her husband.

Johnson came to know the woman well and relied on her from time to time when a rare problem led him to the Italian community. Often, the trouble disappeared without his involvement. He never inquired about the methods used. Just as he turned a blind eye to Gina's selling whiskey from the still in the laundry shack at the back of her property. But, as his deputy said, he was aware of her connection to Crocetti and his being the source of her power. Not something to take lightly.

Knowing he would find her in the kitchen, Johnson went to the back door of her house. Gina greeted him warmly as always, with a hug and a kiss on each cheek. She waved him to take a seat at the table and, without asking, went about making a cup of espresso with warm milk for him. Gina brought the coffee along with a plate of small cookies heavily dusted in powdery white sugar that she set on the table.

"*Grazie'*," Johnson said, as he took a cookie. "*Come stai?*"

Gina faced him, wiping her hands on her apron. She rolled her eyes to the ceiling and crossed herself. "I'm old."

"You'll outlive us all," Johnson said with a wink.

He expected Gina to join him at the table but instead she disappeared into the living room. He heard a soft knock on a door and two voices speaking in Italian. A moment later, Gina reappeared, ushering a young woman into the kitchen. Johnson guessed her to be in her early 20s. She was dressed in widow's black, her hair pulled back in a tight bun. Gina directed her into a chair and the woman sat, her hands folded in her lap, her head down. She looked up at Johnson when Gina introduced the two, and he noted the mix of sadness and anger in the young woman's coal-black eyes.

She greeted him in heavily accented, broken English, then looked to Gina, who motioned her to begin. The widow held an envelope out to Johnson. He placed the remainder of his cookie on the plate, dusted the powdered sugar from his fingers, took the envelope from her hand. He opened it and pulled out four cards. The one on top was a funeral card, an illustration of an angel yielding a sword. The others were from a deck of playing cards, each with a small circular hole punched in the center. A chill riffled the back of his neck at seeing the hole in the Jack of Spades was caked with cordovan smudges he knew to be dried blood.

He turned the funeral card over and read the back. A man's name along with the dates of his birth and death. Johnson did the math. The man was barely twenty-two when he died.

"Your husband?"

The woman nodded.

He pointed to the playing card. "What is this?"

"*Bersaglio*," she answered.

Johnson shrugged. "I'm sorry, I don't know this word."

The widow looked to her older friend.

"Target," Gina said.

"Target? You mean, for shooting. For practice?"

"*Si*, target." Gina repeated and raised her hand making a gun of her fingers.

"I don't understand," Johnson said, and his gaze went from Gina to the young widow, who spoke in a snarl.

"*Il bastardo* shoot Antonio like *bersaglio*. Tar-get," she said.

"What bastard? Who?" Johnson said but felt certain he knew the answer.

"Markle," the widow spit the answer. "*Figlia il puttana*." She picked up the pair of unbloodied cards and stood. She held them in her fingertips, arms straight out to the sides, and glared at Johnson.

Johnson sat without moving for a moment, the young widow's eyes boring into him. He raised his own hand as a gun and pointed his finger to each card. The woman gave him a nod. He looked down at the bloodied Jack, then back up at the woman. She tossed the pair she held on to the table and snatched up the third card. The widow brought the card to her face and pressed it onto her forehead. The card stuck and she stood, hands at her side, the hole in the card dead center of her forehead.

"*Bersaglio*," she said, her face a stone, washed of emotion, but Johnson saw her eyes brimming. She ripped the card from her forehead, slapped it onto the table and rushed from the room. Johnson heard a door slam.

He sagged against his chair at the realization at what Markle had done. Even after witnessing the encounter in the parking lot at Mazzoni's, he had wanted to believe the stories he'd heard were just that, stories. Exaggerations that grew with each telling of the game warden's tactics but seemed so outlandish as to not possibly be true.

"How does she know this is what happened?" Johnson asked Gina.

"There were two men," she said. "Her husband and a friend. And after this *bestia ferrocia* killed Antonio, the friend was let go, instructed by Markle to tell what he had seen. And to warn all the Italians to stay out of the woods. That was not the word he used for us."

Johnson stared at the cards. "When did this happen?" knowing the answer. He had no doubt that it was Antonio and his friend in the back of Markle's truck. The cards from the game Markle played in front of him. His chest tightened with guilt.

Gina sat at the table across from Johnson.

"Albin," she said. "The friend said that you…"

"Yes, I saw them."

He looked at Gina and dropped his eyes at seeing the sadness there. The disappointment. He thought about trying to explain, to tell her that Markle had pulled a gun on him, threatened him and that this man had been given a special license and was beyond Johnson's control. But he knew there was no excusing his lack of action. "There was nothing I could do, Gina."

His comment was met with the "look" he dreaded seeing. The band around Johnson's chest tightened further. He gathered the cards and slid them all back into the envelope. When he held them out to Gina, she shook her head.

Johnson sighed and stood, tucking the envelope into his coat pocket. Gina walked him to the back door and out onto the porch. Johnson stared out across the back yard with its small vineyard, as if the right thing to say was hanging on the winter-bare vines. He knew better than to offer the well-rehearsed and equally worn proclamation of doing his best to help. To bring swift justice to the young widow. He knew the promise would be empty. Even if he could bring Antonio's friend in as a witness, someone to stand in a courtroom and testify against the game warden, he knew in his heart that no judge would convict Markle. Not on the word of an illiterate immigrant. Markle had been hauled into court on an assault and battery charge for beating an Italian fisherman. The game warden walked free.

Johnson felt her hand on his arm. He turned to his friend.

"That man must be stopped, you know this, *si?*" she said. "And *capitano mio*, if you cannot stop him …" There was no need for her to finish. Both she and Johnson knew her words held no idle threat. She had not gained the respect of her community by not delivering on promises, especially those that brought swift judgement and punishment. There were well-established lines that were not to be crossed, and this tiny woman had shown both the means, through her connection with Crocetti, and the resolve to administer justice as she saw fit.

Johnson knew the stories that trailed her in the years since the disappearance of her husband. She refused to wear the black of a widow, which only fueled the rumored reasons the man – whose reputation for gambling, philandering and abuse of his wife was well known - had suddenly vanished. She met the questions - *where is your husband, signora? Is he visiting relatives? Has he gone back to Italy? When will he return?* - with nothing more than a shrugged shoulder or a glance towards heaven as if to say, God only knows. Gossips filled the vacuum of her silence with answers of their own. He'd run off with another woman. He was murdered by a jealous husband. Killed by the Black Hand for his gambling debts. Gone back to Italy, leaving his wife and son with another child on the way to struggle on their own. She let the talk swirl around her and went about her business, renting rooms, raising her children, doing what she could to make ends meet, which included making whiskey. All the while establishing herself as a powerful force in the community of Italian immigrants.

"Give me a bit of time," he said. "I'll take care of it."

Gina turned and gave him a weary smile. She patted his forearm, turned and went inside.

He shoved his hands in the pockets of his jacket and looked past the neat rows of gnarled vines to the trio of fat hogs rolling in the slop of their pen. The one story he refused to acknowledge was that Gina had killed the man herself and, according to legend, fed his body to the hogs. He ignored the rumor at hearing it mentioned and replied, giving the reason for her raising pigs was for the spicy sausage she called *salsiccia* that she made. But he also knew it was to mask the smell of the fermenting mash in the stills.

Johnson went down the steps and kicked at a stone on his way to his car. As far as he was concerned, Markle deserved to be dealt with in the harshest possible manner. He glanced back at the now-closed door and then out to the hog pen. His history with Gina told him she was capable of anything.

The land surrounding the Sagamore mines was a maze of thickly wooded steep hills and hollows. Winter-bare oaks, maples and birch grew tightly packed, stripped of leaves. Thickets of briars and scrubbed underbrush lay in wild patches. Clouds moved across a half-moon spilling a pale frozen light down into the narrow cut of the road. Corky and Sonny walked through the sparse slashes of luminescence and caught flickering glimpses of each other and the dog – there, then not there – and did their best to sidestep the rainwater-filled ruts. The road narrowed to a single track that began to rise out of the bottomland and curve up the hillside with a tree line edged in a glow as if dawn had arrived in the wrong sky.

At the crest, the sky opened as the hill fell off in a steep rock face and the boys stood high above the coal yards that lay bathed in a bowl of light. The giant tipple jutted from the opposite hillside and coal gave a guttural roar as it spewed from the chute, filling car after car. The trains stretched for almost a mile and a half along the tracks and when the last car was filled, it rolled out of the mine, heading for the coke plants up north in Jefferson County or the steel mills in Pittsburgh. As soon as one train pulled away from the tipple, another mile of cars rumbled into place behind a new set of double engines.

The sounds of the mines ricocheted through the hollow, the discord born in the industry of robbing the earth of coal. The instruments used in the gutting of the mountains - a cacophony of machine, man and animal - reverberating and echoing, amplified a dozen-fold in the hard-walled chambers of the tunnels to float from the fissures and yawning maws of the catacombs mazed beneath the hills of Sagamore. The sound was constant, an ever-present humming like the haunting ring of tinnitus that rose out of the shafts, carried up from the tunnels to sing in the black dust that coated everything in their world.

Corky and Sonny squatted and watched the black rock flood the open train car and rise in an obsidian mound. The thick dust plumed into the night, obscuring the floodlights like clouds across the moon. What Corky saw was a future no different than that of his father and uncle. A certainty that, if he stayed in this place, he'd be doomed to a life spent a half-mile underground in a six-foot-high tunnel, swinging a pickax at a wall of black rock. He was determined to escape not just the preordained misery of the mines, but the whole damn place. The suffocating, soot-filled world of Sagamore.

They both knew the mines held death. In their short lives, they'd known men from their small town who had been lost. That's what they called it when the mines caved, or the gases exploded, or the air turned to poison. They'd been lost like a misplaced sock or toy.

They'd been to funerals, heard the crying and wailing, witnessed wives and mothers dressed now forever in black and watched other children, some their own age and younger – their father, brother, uncle, grandfather now gone – stand at the grave, staring at their own doomed future in the dark pit at their feet. And there was always the priest, saying to rejoice rather than mourn for these souls had been lost to God. Both boys knew otherwise. These men were not lost. They were taken in exchange for black rock. And the money that filled the coffers of the mining companies.

"You bring something to keep us warm?" Sonny asked, his head cocked, eyebrow raised in question.

"It ain't that cold out here," he said.

"You didn't answer the question." Sonny elbowed his friend. "I know you brought some. Always do."

"A little early don't you think?"

"Just a nip to get the blood pumping. No big deal."

Corky shrugged and brought out the jar. Sonny reached into his own bag and pulled out a cup and held it out.

"You brought your own cup?"

A sly grin spread across Sonny's face. "Boy scout. Always be prepared."

Corky tipped a bit of the 'shine in. Sonny frowned and pushed his cup forward.

"Come on. Don't be a piker."

Corky relented, splashed a bit more into the cup.

"That's right," Sonny said and took a sip. He coughed and laughed at the same time. "Goddamn," he said, eyes watering. More coughing and laughing. He raised his cup at Corky. "Hard to believe my best friend is an honest-to-god moonshiner. I was born lucky, I guess."

Corky was the one who convinced his grandmother to start making whiskey instead of the grappa she made in a still hidden in the laundry shed. The truth was, Corky was now the one making it after learning the process from first watching, then helping Gina make the fiery liquor she sold to boarders and neighbors. As a young boy, he'd helped his grandmother around the boarding house, spending most Saturday afternoons cleaning, stripping beds, hauling the linens out to the laundry shed. He pumped water to fill the wash tubs and tended the fireboxes and, under the watchful eyes of his grandmother, learned how to tend the copper pot still that sat in the opposite corner of the shed. His curiosity became a passion and, by the time he turned twelve, he was making batches on his own. He took over the process from beginning to end, always eager to clean the still and begin a new batch. He did the bottling but never bothered to ask his grandmother or seemed to care what became of the crates he stacked by the door, that were gone the next day. Corky was certain his father knew about his mother-in-law's still, but as far as he knew, he'd managed to keep his part of the bootlegging from him.

Corky raised his gun to his shoulder and sighted down the barrel, aiming at the spotlight hanging above the spout of the tipple, his finger resting on the trigger. "Tell you one thing," he said, lifting his chin in the direction of the coal. "I am never going down in that hole."

"What are you going to do?"

"*Nonna* talks about leaving me her place so I can take over running a boarding house," Corky said. "It's like a done deal in her mind. My life is spent here renting rooms to miners and making 'shine."

"You could make some real money if you stayed," Sonny said. "Doing what she says. You know that, right?"

"Any money I can get is for a damn train ticket," Corky said. "Or to buy a car and drive straight down Route 22 until I hit New Orleans and then who knows where. Which you are more than welcome to come along and get out of here, too. We can travel around just like Rudy said."

"Corky," Sonny said, putting the cup in his bag. "I don't go work the mines, my daddy'd probably shoot me his own self."

Corky studied the side of his friend's face. He knew what Sonny was saying was the truth. His friend's father chose to work coal even though he'd lost an arm to the mines. The man preached union and worker's rights like a religion, believing his crusade to be a calling, a righteous battle that, if he had his way, his son and son's sons would carry on. It saddened Corky to think of his friend doomed to that life. He turned back to his aiming.

Sonny laid a hand on his friend's shoulder. "Come on," he said. "We got hunting to do."

Corky nodded, still aiming. He whispered the sound of a gunshot and smiled.

"Yeah," he said, "let's go kill something."


They made their way towards home in the late afternoon. The pair kept a brisk pace, joking and not caring about the noise they made, having finished hunting for the day. The trail wound down a hollow and emptied out on the train tracks near the mines.

"I have to piss," Sonny said, stepping off the trail and leaning his gun against a tree. He waved his friend on.

Corky walked to the trailhead and had just stepped out of the woods onto the gravel rail bed when a low growling came from the dog. The boy looked up to see a man leaning against a truck parked at the crossing. He wore knee-high boots and a long coat held closed by his arms folded across his chest. Corky's eyes widened at seeing who had to be Markle, the game warden. The man smiled and casually parted his coat, pulling it back to reveal the twin pearl-handled, long-barrel revolvers holstered on his hips. Corky and the dog, still growling, stood frozen.

"That bag looks heavy, boy. Good hunting out there today?" the warden said. "Let's see what you got."

Without moving from his leaning, Markle raised his hand and crooked a beckoning finger. Corky took a half-step forward, then stopped, eyes locked on Markle.

Markle pushed off the truck and reached into the bed, pulling out a pair of handcuffs on a length of chain bolted to the wooden rail.

"Just bring the damn bag over here," Markle said. "And get in the fucking truck, because I know you ain't got no license. And I'm betting that bag is filled with those little birds you wops keep shooting."

Corky's grip on his shotgun tightened. The dog stopped growling and lowered into a tight-muscled crouch.

When Markle lay a hand on one of his Colts, Corky spun and dove for the woods. A bullet smacked a tree above his head. He heard the dog barking, another pistol crack and a choked yelp followed by silence. Scrambling to his feet, Corky ran in a low crouch along the path towards where he'd left Sonny.

"Better stop, boy," Markle said and let off another shot, the bullet slapping leaves overhead.

Sonny looked out from behind the tree to see Corky running towards him, waving him away. He shouted "Markle" as he passed and jerked a thumb over his shoulder. Sonny, bug-eyed, fumbled to close his pants, grabbed his shotgun, and ran after his friend.

Pointing Sonny towards a copse of pines further up the trail, Corky broke off the path in the opposite direction, ducking branches and weaving through the underbrush, moving swiftly but as quietly as possible. He made the way towards a sharp rise leading to a ridge and an outcropping of rock. Scuttling up the steep hillside, he tucked behind the rock, and sat, breath held, listening to pinpoint Markle's movement through the woods. He edged out enough to see the game warden standing in the trail, both guns out, scanning the woods.

"Alright, boys," he said. "You run. I got your dog. I'll get your dago asses. Keep hunting. Markle will be waiting." He spat on the ground, holstered his Colts, turned and began walking back towards the railroad tracks and his truck. He made no effort to hide his movements, stepping heavily, shuffling leaves, swatting at branches as he moved down the trail.

After the man's crashing through the brush faded, the sounds of the woods slowly returned. Corky came off the ridge. Leaping and sliding down the steep slope to the path, he broke into a run toward the railroad tracks. He slowed nearing the trailhead and moved into the brush.

Corky stumbled out of the woods onto the rail bed. Sonny came to the trailhead, slid down the embankment to stand beside his friend. The boy's eyes widened at the sight of his dog laying on the ground where Markle's truck had been parked. The two friends, shocked and silent, crossed the tracks. Corky crouched, laying his shotgun on the ground and, tears streaming down his cheeks, stroked his pet's side. Tucked in the dog's collar was a playing card. Corky lifted the card and stared at the design.

"What's that?" Sonny asked. Without a word, Corky handed him the card. Sonny studied the blood-smeared face of the Jack of Spades. "What is it with this asshole?" he said and slipped the card into his shirt pocket.

Corky swiped his sleeve across his eyes, and stood, grabbed Sonny's pump-action shotgun and walked in the direction of Markle's departing truck. He fired round after round until the trigger clacked on the empty chamber, but he racked and squeezed the trigger again. And again. And again. His vision blurred behind a river of tears. When Sonny dropped a hand onto his shoulder, Corky turned and looked at his friend in confusion, as if waking from a dream, puzzled to find himself standing in the road, holding his friend's weapon. Sonny took the gun and turned Corky around, guiding him back.

Without a word spoken, the two buried Corky's dog.

Corky arrived at his grandmother's house after leaving Sonny at the mine gate. He sat in the kitchen and told her what happened in the woods. The tears had stopped as waves of rage rolled through his body. He punched his thigh with a balled fist, eyes fixed on a knot in a floorboard near his feet.

His grandmother listened without remark and rose from her chair to cross the kitchen. She opened a cabinet and withdrew two small glasses and a tall bottle, then returned to sit at the table. She poured a double finger of clear liquid into each glass, pushed one across to her grandson and, raising her glass, motioned for the boy to drink.

Corky took a sip, winced, then threw back the rest, slamming the glass onto the table. A shudder racked his shoulders as the heat slid into his chest.

"He is a bad man, this game warden," Gina said. "And *pazzo*." She tapped her forehead.

"I'm going to kill him," Corky said, and tears came again.

The old woman snorted and shook her head slowly.

"No," she said. "You will not kill him."

He straightened in his chair and glared. "Why not? You don't think I can? That man needs to die."

"*Si*, he does, but this is not for you. Killing. This is not what you do." She waved her hand at Corky. "Believe me, this *animale*, Markle. He will have a problem one day. But he is dangerous and not for you to deal with."

Corky shook his head. "He shot at me. And Sonny. He killed my dog, *Nonna*."

"There are more dogs," she said. "There are no more grandsons."

The boy held his grandmother's gaze. Gina Ferraro was a small woman, barely five feet tall, but anyone who took the woman's stature and delicate features as signs of frailty was a fool.

Corky knew all the stories, but he found it near impossible to conceive of his grandmother as a killer. But when she was angry, his fleeting thought was that maybe an act such as murder wasn't so far-fetched. Right now, in this moment, full of rage and pain, he hoped it was all true and she would be able to fix this and make one more problem disappear.

"His time will come. *A presto*," she said. "Go home. Tell your father what happened with this *animale'* game warden. Tell him about your dog. Tell him not to worry or get involved. And you hunt someplace else and stay away from that man. Believe me, his time will come soon."

Corky sat up, rubbed his face briskly, then ran a sleeve across his eyes, drying the remaining tears. He pushed himself from the table, stood, gathered up his shotgun and slung the game bag over his shoulder.

"All right, *Nonna*," he said. "I hope you're right." He moved around the table and bent to kiss his grandmother's forehead. Gina reached up and gave the boy's cheek a pat that ended with a pinch. She pressed a finger to her lips and winked. "You don't tell him about the grappa, *capisce*?"

Corky smiled and, with a wink, turned and went out the back door, stepping into the dark.


Gina stood on the back porch, watching the boy walk the road towards home and disappear in the night. Returning inside, she crossed the kitchen to the stove and brought a box of wooden matches and a small plate with her to the table. From a drawer in the sideboard, Gina drew a prayer card with the image of Michael, the avenging angel. She sat, holding the card. As her lips moved in a whispered malediction, she struck a match and touched the flame to the edge of the card. She watched it burn, repeating the curse, until she could hold it no longer and dropped the blackening paper onto the plate. With the smoke curling upwards, Gina closed her eyes and, conjuring a vision of the game warden's painful end, knew she could not wait for Sheriff Johnson to act. There was no choice other than to make a phone call in the morning to Pittsburgh.

Housed in a large two-story building, a nightclub named Nootsy's sat just across the Indiana County line in Armstrong County and operated as a speakeasy on the ground level and bordello on the upper floor. The office in the rear of Nootsy's was paneled in dark wood and dimly lit. Thick curtains covered the windows and held the smell of countless cigars enjoyed by the owner, Seb Lisitano. He was a short, fat man, dark-complected, with a neatly trimmed moustache. An Italian Oliver Hardy. A Victrola sat in a corner; the long golden horn gave off a warm glow. Silent now, the office was usually filled with the sounds of Lisitano's favorite Italian operas. Lisitano was seated at his large desk; behind him on the wall hung a large painting of a woman reclining on a lounge, naked except for the jeweled necklace around her neck.

"You killed his fucking dog?" Seb Lisitano asked, shaking his head in wonder.

Markle sat opposite the rotund Italian, slouched down in the wooden chair, his ankle propped on his knee. He studied the toe of his Western boot, then licked his thumb and rubbed at a scuff mark, ignoring the question.

"Hey *stronzo*," Lisitano said. "What's wrong with you? You kill the boy's pet?" The man stroked the head of the monkey, Nootsy, sitting on his lap. The monkey was glaring at the game warden through hooded, jaundiced eyes.

Markle raised both legs and brought his boots up to rest on the corner of the desk.

"It's a fucking dog," he said and picked a piece of lint off his pant leg. "You wanted these dagos scared, right? Seems you care more about the animals than your own people. Yeah, I killed the kid's dog and left a message they can understand better than English, ok? So now you go get your protection money and stop busting my balls."

Lisitano lifted Nootsy from his lap, giving the monkey's chin a scratching before setting him on the desk. The primate hissed at Markle and leapt to the credenza behind the desk to sit in a small chair, furtively watching Markle from his perch.

"That thing gives me the creeps," the game warden said, meeting the monkey's stare over Lisitano's shoulder.

"I don't think Nootsy cares much for you, either," Lisitano said. He turned and spoke to the monkey. "Do you, Nootsy? No, eh?" He brought his body back around in his chair. "Yes, scaring these hunters is what I told you to do." He reached across the desk and slapped at the boots, shooing at Markle to get them off his desk. The game warden smiled without moving but after brief stare down, dropped his feet to the floor.

"Frighten. Not kill them, as I've now heard you've done," Lisitano said. "There is no money to collect from a dead man. Arrest them, take their guns. Get your cut of the fines. Sell the guns. And pay me the money you owe, *capisce'*?" The fat man rose, walked around his desk to stand beside Markle. He smiled and clasped his hands together, looking down at the game warden. Markle looked away, glowering like a sullen schoolboy.

"Do the job as I asked, ok?" Lisitano said. "No more with the killing and this cowboy stuff with shooting the cards. It's a good business we have, no? So please." He dropped his hand onto the game warden's shoulder. "Let's stick with the plan and it's all nicey nice, everybody happy."

Markle brushed the hand away. "Not sure how much money you think you can continue to squeeze out of all these poor fuckers," he said. "This kid? With the dog? He's how you and I are going to make more than we'd ever make pinching these dumb bird killers which is getting to be more work that it's worth, if you ask me."

The Italian rolled his eyes. Markle pointed to the chair behind the desk. "Sit," he said. "You're going to want to hear this."

The club owner sighed and sat down. He waved his hand in the air. "I'm listening."

"The day after I chased this kid …"

"And killed his dog."

"Yes, I killed his dog. Seb, for Christ's sake. Can we move on about the damn mutt? I was pissed off, chasing those kids through the woods, little fucker's not listening, ok? You want to hear this or not?"

Lisitano opened a cigar box on his desk and went through the ritual of cutting and lighting one. Once satisfied it was drawing nicely, he waved his hand for Markle to continue.

"Next day, I go out a bit north of Salt Lick," the game warden said. "I don't figure this kid is coming back to that same spot, but I know the Italians like to hunt up past the mines in Ernest."

"You going to give me a report of your whole day? *Che fai?*" Lisitano said. "Get to the making big money because that's where this story better end."

Markle's jaw tightened.

"I nab this greaseball hunter out by himself," Markle said. "No license, a bag full of those damn little birds they keep killing. He's got a shotgun, one of those Italian makes with all the fancy inlay on the stock. Nice gun. Looks new so I tell him to hand it over to me. He refuses so I have to skin my Colt, show him who's in charge and he gives it up. And I'm looking over this gun, adding up the money I figure to get for such a fine gun, and he asks if I'm the warden who killed the Trunzo boy's dog."

"He knew about that?" the club owner asked. "He knew his name?"

"Word travels fast, don't it?" A proud smirk came to the game warden's face.

"Didn't seem to scare this particular hunter much, did it?" Lisitano said.

Markle glared at Lisitano, the smirk gone.

"Oh, he was scared," Markle said. "He knew he was fucked three ways to Sunday. Cause I'm thinking if he can afford that beauty of a shotgun, he's no broke-ass miner and I'm going to get all the money coming my way finally. Maybe more out of him if I scare him good enough. I asked him about this Trunzo, where he lives, told him how that information could be worth something and, if he tells me, maybe I'll let him go, won't arrest him, hell, he can even take his itty-bitty birds with him. Well, this dumb dago starts motor-mouthing about the kid, how he lives with his old man, a widower coal miner down in Sagamore. Tells me which house and everything. And then he keeps yapping, tells me about the kid's grandmother runs a boarding house out that way."

Lisitano stopped following the smoke floating through the room and leaned forward.

"She has money?"

"She does," Markle said, a crooked smile coming to his lips. "But not from letting a few coal miners dirty the sheets of her spare rooms, that's for sure."

"*Che cozzo*, get to the point," Lisitano said with exasperation.

"The wop told me the old woman's got a still out back of her place," Markle said.

"He must be making a joke," Lisitano said. "Just some story to get away from you."

"Thought the same at first," Markle said and reached into his coat pocket. He placed an ornately engraved pewter flask on the desk. "The man was kind enough to share this with me and, got to say, it's damn good 'shine," he said, and slid the flask towards Lisitano. "Have a nip, see for yourself."

Lisitano opened the flask, brought it to his nose and sniffed. His eyebrows rose and he nodded slightly then took a sip. He smiled and took another, longer one.

"Smooth, isn't it?" Markel said. "No burn. Damn near sweet, you ask me."

Lisitano nodded his agreement and said, "This hunter told you this Trunzo woman has a still in Sagamore and making this?"

"Her name's Ferraro, she's on the boy's mother's side," Markle said. "And yes, she's got a still but that's not the best part."

Lisitano sighed. He rolled his hand in a circle. "Can you get to it, ok? I have a train to catch Tuesday and I'd like to hear the end of this before I leave, *capisce*'?"

"Where are you going?"

"*Que cazzo de mincia*. I'm not going anywhere," Lisitano said. "It's a joke, *stunad*. I was being – *qual e la parola? Sarcastico*, eh? A figure of speech." He turned and spoke to the monkey. "*Questo è molto stupido,* eh, Nootsy?" There was a blur of motion from across the desk and when the fat man looked around, he saw Markle had his Colt out and cocked, the barrel pointing at the monkey's head.

"Hey, I know enough wop speak to understand when I'm being called stupid to a fucking monkey, ok?" He said and shifted the gun to Lisitano. "This is all getting on my tits, understand me? I can even this up another way if you like. And be done with you, that ratty little beast and this whole goddamn place, right now."

"*Piano, piano,* Edmund," Lisitano said, his mouth dry. "It was a joke. We're friends. We do business, no? I want you to make money, like me. With me. Ok? Please tell me."

Markle sucked on his teeth, eyeing the fat man, assessing his choices. He eased the hammer down with his thumb and lowered the revolver.

"The still's on the old lady's property but according to this dago hunter, she's not the one making this whiskey."

Lisitano's eyebrows lifted.

"He says everyone knows it's the boy," Markle said and rose from his chair, talking as he walked to the office door. "I think you know what to do with that bit of information, right?" he said. "Go put the squeeze on the old lady to make whiskey for you. Then you can make money on all the bootlegging in three counties." He paused before opening the door. "You can thank me later by giving me a cut off the top," he said and left.

Lisitano stared at the closed door. A rising anger turned his ears red.

"Thank you?" he said. "You do foolish things like killing dogs and hunters. You bring attention to my business with this nonsense. You threaten me? You threaten my Nootsy? And you want me to thank you? *Stupido*. This *agita* I don't need." He waved his hand, shooing at the door.

"So you tell me, Mr. Special Agent big shot," he said. "Why do I need you?"

# 10

The road to Sagamore wound through the rolling north Appalachian foothills
of western Pennsylvania. The asphalt ribbon spooled out of the country dark by
scant yards in the wobbly light of the car's headlights. The night held a dozen
variations of darkness. Black sylvan thickets gave way to shadow-blanketed
stretches of farmland, rising to a tree line silhouetted against an obsidian night
sky curtained in black storm clouds, billows edged in white, lit from a lurking
full moon. The car slowed as it approached the scattered houses at the edge of
the small town and came to a stop on a rise. No lights glowed in the windows at
this hour and, when the driver killed the headlights, the night turned black as the
mines that tunneled beneath the surrounding hills. Salvatore Gentile sat behind
the wheel, the idling engine a low rumble in the otherwise silent dark.

Sal got out and, closing the door without a sound, leaned against the black
Nash Ambassador. The car was discreet and fast, perfectly suited to his work.
The wind shifted, parting the clouds, and the full moon shone brightly for a few
moments, but he felt no urgency to hide.

He was a young man, in his mid-twenties, Italian, finely dressed in a dark
grey three-piece suit with a silk tie. His boots were handmade, buffed to a
high shine that glinted in the moonlight. Sal wore an overcoat draped on his
shoulders, like a cape. The garment was light in weight and made of a shimmering silk blend. His thick raven hair, cut in one length slicked straight back
underneath a black beaver felt fedora with a band striped in thin lines of red,
gold and grey. His clothes were expensive, custom-tailored with a classic cut.
He pulled a Parodi from the pack tucked in his pocket. The match flared as he
lit the small, thin cigar, the glow like a small spotlight on his face. With his aq-
uiline nose, full lips and coal black eyes, he was movie-star handsome. Anyone
who happened by could easily have been forgiven for thinking that Rudolph
Valentino had risen from being recently dead to appear on a rural roadside,
enjoying a solitary smoke.

Beneath his suit jacket, Sal wore shoulder holsters that held twin nickel-plated Colt 1911 semi-automatic pistols under each arm. He carried a razor-edged stiletto. Resting on the passenger seat was a *lupara* - a sawed-off, double-barreled shotgun with the stock cut to a pistol grip. The weapon was common in the hills of his home in Calabria and all throughout the *Mezzogiorno*, used by shepherds to protect their flocks against wolves.

These were the tools of his trade.

Sal took a long drag on the Parodi and streamed smoke into the damp night. Wind sieved the tall pines, a murmuring of ghosts rising in the needled branches. Sal thought of the winters of Calabria. Wet and cold as what he'd found here, but this air stung his nostrils. The acrid smoke from coke ovens and steel mills, borne on the wind, mixed with a fetid sweetness that rose from the mines and strip pits and left a metallic taste on his tongue. He thought the place smelled like an open grave. Or the air that wafted from the edge of Purgatory. The last resting place of damaged souls.

A dog barked somewhere in the hills, and another joined, then another. The three calling to each other, then rising in a chorus of howls that ended as quickly as they'd started. No lights appeared in any windows or doorways along the row of houses.

The assassin did not question his being sent to Sagamore. He was unaware of the brutal treatment the Italian immigrant hunters had endured the past few months at the hand of a corrupt game warden. That this man had used his badge as a license for extortion, beatings, and murder. Sal would never ask to be told the "why?" behind his instructions. He knew the details were none of his concern. If he was called upon, a problem existed that his skills were the only solution. He performed his duties as directed, and it was enough knowing that his presence was at a request made by the *'Ndrangheta capo* Crocetti, who controlled Pittsburgh. His allegiance was sworn by blood to this *famiglia*. Sal was the embodiment of the spiritual guide of the Calabrian "*Societa' Secreta,*" Michael the Archangel, the Avenging Sword of God. His initiation rite was concluded by blood dripped from his cut finger onto a funeral card with the image of Michael, sword raised and aflame.

All he had been told was the address of a boarding house run by a *Calabrese'* widow. He was also unaware of the wheels that had been set into motion. The unintended consequences of his actions. Or by the widow's phone call.

The only thing he knew for certain was, that by the time he left Sagamore, the problem would no longer exist.

He waited. Four mornings in a row, he stood among the trees with a view of the clearing and waited for the game warden to return. This place where Markle staked out immigrant hunters. The place where he shot at Corky and Sonny. Where the dog was killed.

Dawn broke in a sky streaked of red, rose and purple. The trees cast long shadows across the clearing. An hour passed before he heard the sound of a vehicle's approach. The game warden's truck appeared out of the tree tunneled gravel road and came to a stop at the edge of the clearing opposite the trailhead. Markle stepped from the driver's side, glanced at the sky, and lit a cigarette. He watched the game warden lean against the front fender, smoking, and surveying the tree line.

Songbirds called to one another, the melodies floating in the air through the trees, carried on a gentle breeze. Standing in the woods, he could smell the coming of spring. When he stepped from the trees, the morning sun was at his back. He knew Markle would only see his silhouette, his face hidden in shadow. He held the shotgun at his side, along the back of his leg. When the game warden noticed his approach, Markle pushed off from his leaning and pulled his coat back, exposing his twin Colt revolvers holstered at his hips.

"Nice morning to be out hunting," Markle said, his right resting on the Colt. "Let's take a look at your license now. Bring it on over here."

He closed the distance between them, keeping his head down as he approached. They were five yards apart when Markle reached out his hand, motioned to have the asked for license to be handed over. He took one more step, swung the shotgun up and pulled the trigger. The blast caught Markle in the stomach, knocking him back, in a shocked stumble. His arms outstretched seeking balance before he dropped to his knees and brought his hands to the bloody hole in his guts. His eyes raised to his assailant, in disbelief, seeking an explanation that would never come.

Locking eyes with the dying man, he leaned down, lay his shotgun on the ground and, from the game warden's holster, lifted one of the Colts. He admired the revolver with its pearl handle inlaid with a silver disc engraved with the letter "M" in a filigreed script. From his shirt pocket, he pulled a playing card, the Jack of Hearts and turned it so Markle could see it. The game warden moaned, his breath wet, choked with blood. His body swayed but remained upright.

He pressed the card against Markle's forehead, stood and walked off several paces. He turned and raised the Colt, pulled the trigger once. The bullet tore through the center of the card and Markle's skull. The game warden slumped, dead before hitting the ground. With the toe of his boot, he turned the dead man on his back and took the second revolver, tucking it in his own belt.

Silenced by the gunshots, the songs of the birds returned and without another look, he returned to the woods, a broad smile on his face as his soft whistle joined the birds melodies.

# 12

The news of the game warden's killing spread quickly and, by the end of his day, Johnson had heard from several community leaders expressing concerns and pushing for answers he didn't have. After enduring months of Markle's campaign of brutality, the Italians told Johnson they felt the man got what he deserved. They also worried about repercussions if the murderer was found to be one of their own. Others, mainly the mine bosses and town folks of Indiana, many of whom quietly - and some not so quietly - condoned the warden's brutal methods, were outraged that a lawman had been cut down in the line of duty.

Johnson knew Markle was a vicious bully with a badge and disliked him from the first moment their paths had crossed. His patience was tested by those who clamored for "justice," which sounded more like vengeance to him. He felt as the Italians did and was glad to have the man gone.

The phone call from the governor's office surprised and upset him the most. The governor wanted this wrapped up immediately, the man's chief of staff said, and if Johnson couldn't make that happen, they would send someone from Harrisburg who could. The sheriff was about to remind the governor's man that his was an elected position and not an appointment, so he didn't answer to the governor, but the line went dead.

He left the office and stopped by his older brother's house. He sat across from Walter at the kitchen table discussing the murder, coffee mugs steaming in front of both.

"The man got what he had coming to him," Walt said. "Most of the time they're hunting land the mining company owns. Who gives a shit? Company only cares about what's under the ground. Hell, if I ran the place, I'd let the miners hunt the lands as part of their salary. Make it a benefit for killing ourselves in the mines. But they like the control."

"The company wants you all buying food from their store, not getting free meat."

"That's right, little brother," Walter said. "Keep us working against a debt we'll never pay off."

This was not a new conversation. Walter had worked the mines since childhood and had become a union organizer. The brothers both knew the mining bosses saw all the workers as nothing more than indentured servants. After the accident that took Walter's arm, Johnson felt certain his brother's days as a miner were done and he was secretly relieved. But the accident only served to cement Walt's determination to prove he was no less of a man, and he returned to work the mines a foreman.

"Ok, Walter," Johnson said. "I hear you, but we're not going to solve the plight of the working class today. Right now, my job is to find out who killed Markle."

"Got your work cut out for you there, sheriff," Walt said. "I've heard at least a dozen men, white and Italian, even some Polacks, say they wanted that asshole dead."

Johnson drummed his fingertips on the table. He turned to look out the window over the sink, staring into the fading sunset, and nodded. Plenty of people with motives, he thought. Doesn't make them killers.

"Hell, after what he did to my boy, Sonny, your own damn nephew," Walter said, taking a sip of coffee. "I have my own reasons for doing that piece of shit. You should, too."

Johnson looked at his brother and leaned across the table, his voice tight. "The hell you talking about. After he did what to Sonny?"

"That maniac took some shots at him," Walt said. "Him and that Italian kid he runs with, Trunzo's youngest, the one they call Corky. They were out hunting together and ran into Markle, I guess. They got a few rabbits and Corky had some of those birds them Italians like and everyone's all up on their high horse about making them stop hunting the damn things. Markle threatened to arrest them both and they ran. Who wouldn't? And that crazy jackass shot at them. You believe that shit? Shooting at a couple boys?" Walter's face was a mix of disgust and anger. "Then he goes and shoots the dog."

"What dog?" Johnson asked.

"He shot Corky's dog," Walt said. "That man ain't right in the head."

Johnson rubbed his face with his hands and sighed. "When was this?"

"A couple weeks back, I guess," Walt said.

"Jesus, why didn't you tell me about this?"

"I ain't seen you, Buzz, so I'm telling you now," Walt said. "I told the boys to stay away from those woods. I know Corky doesn't have a license. So, I figured they got away with one and better to just let it be. Told Sonny they need to stick to hunting his uncle's farm and avoid Markle all together."

"Where's Sonny?" Johnson asked. "I'll need to talk to him and Corky."

"They're both at basketball practice," Walt said. "He doesn't want to talk much about it. All he said was Corky took it bad. He's had that dog since his brother died. Mutt was old but Sonny always said it ran like a pup when they took him out to hunt. Both were pretty torn up and angry. I don't blame them at all. I'd personally like to thank whoever gave Markle what he deserved. Honestly? The thought of putting that mad dog down myself crossed my mind more than once."

Johnson eyed his brother and read the seriousness of his statement in his face. "You say this all happened out near the crossing at Salt Lick?" he asked.

"That's what he told me," Walt said. "Sonny said the dog was laying across from the trailhead that comes out at the tracks. Why's that so important?" Walter asked.

"It's where they found Markle's body," Johnson said. "Laying at that crossing."


Lisitano cradled the phone on his desk and dropped back in his chair with an exasperated groan. He knew it was inevitable, really, the crazy things the game warden had been doing. His methods had gone way beyond what was necessary to work the racket they had put together on the hunters.

"I told you, *testa durra*," Lisitano said aloud. "Didn't I?" The fat man leaned back in his chair, rubbed his face with both hands and sat staring at the ceiling. Nootsy, the monkey, lounged back in his small chair, mimicking the fat man.

"Now what, Nootsy?" he said. "What are we going to do now?" He sat in silence, eyes searching the ceiling for answers he seemed to believe lay hidden in crazing plaster.

Opportunity. This was the word that Seb Lisitano always kept in his mind. *Opportunità*. It was what he sought and, although the search didn't always lead to the end he hoped, each had presented another opportunity. This was his gift, as he saw it. Being able to see what others did not. He toyed with the silver flask Markle had left on the desk. He unscrewed it, sniffed and took a swig. Two bottles of whiskey sat on his desk as well and he set the flask down between them. He studied them with the same intensity he had the ceiling. As if the answer would be conjured in the flask's designs or the labels of the bottles.

Opportunity.

He picked up the flask.

"Boy," he said, setting it down in the center of the desk.

He slid one of the whiskey bottles over next to the flask.

"Dog."

He brought the other whiskey bottle over.

"Markle."

He looked at the three objects and saw the puzzle coming together. He opened the desk drawer on his right and brought out a revolver and laid it on the desk.

"Sheriff." He pulled the cigar box from the corner of the desk, opened it and laid the flask inside and dropped the lid.

"Jail," he said, a lilt of satisfaction in his voice. "*Opportunità*, Nootsy, can you see it now?" The fat man opened the center drawer of his desk, brought out a small notebook and, licking his finger, began flicking through the pages. He ran his finger down the list of names and numbers on each page, muttering to himself, until he found the name he sought. "Yes, Nootsy, opportunity." He lifted the phone and tapped the cradle until the operator came on. After a brief conversation, Lisitano stood and put his coat on. He picked up Nootsy and called for his man, Cranio, who appeared in the doorway.

"Let's go for a ride," the fat man said. "And bring the girl."

# 13

Corky sat at the table watching his grandmother move about the stove. The kitchen was warm, heated by the burners where large pot of sauce simmered and water for pasta boiled. Music from his grandmother's large radio in the living room drifted on the air. He recognized the melody of "*Sweet Georgia Brown*," one of his grandmother's favorites. Another blast of heat filled the room when she opened the oven and removed two loaves of freshly baked bread. The boy took in a deep breath, savoring the smells. He guessed that half his life had been spent in this kitchen. More than in any other room in her house or his own. His grandmother sliced a large piece off one of the loaves and set it, hot and steaming, along with a small dish of olive oil on the table in front of him.

"*Mangia,*" she said and turned back to her stove, stirring the sauce. "*La pasta sarà pronta per un minuto.*"

The boy dipped the bread in the oil and took a large bite. He closed his eyes and moaned in approval. He heard the back door opening and, turning in his chair, saw a man standing just inside the doorway. Expecting it be one of his grandmother's boarders, he was surprised to see it was not a miner. This man was dressed in a tailored dark suit, vest, and tie. He wore a long overcoat draped around his shoulders and, removing his fedora, nodded at Corky.

"*Buono notte,*" he said. "*Mi chiamo* Salvatore Gentile." He then turned to Gina at the stove. "*Mi scusi, signora. Mi dispiace per apparire non invitati.* If I may, it's important that I speak with you."

Gina glanced at the man, her eyebrow raised and nodded, tilting her head towards the table. "*Siedi a mangiare prima.*" Her attention turned back to the pot of sauce.

"*Grazie, signora,*" Sal said as he moved to the table.

"Where are you from, *Signore* Gentile?" Gina asked.

"New Orleans, now," he said. "But I am *Calabrese* like you. And Signora Ferraro, *Signor* Gentile *non è necessario, per favore, chiamami* Sal."

Gina smiled and pointed towards the table. "*Buono,* Sal." She reached for the man's overcoat which he slipped off and hung on the back of the kitchen door.

"You live in New Orleans?" Corky asked, studying the man.

"*Si,* but I travel for my business," Sal said.

"What's your business?" Corky asked.

"I work for my uncle," Sal said. "He is a businessman in New Orleans with many responsibilities and partnerships from there to here in Pittsburgh."

"But what do you do for him?"

Gina appeared at the table, two bowls of pasta topped with sauce, a large meatball in each. "*Mangiare prima,* eh?" She said, wagging a finger at Corky. "Questions later."

She returned with a small bowl of her own and a bottle of red wine. She sat, uncorked the bottle and, after filling her glass, filled Corky's and passed it to Sal.

"*Grazie,*" he said and poured a half glass for himself, which he raised, nodding to his hostess. "*Cent d'anni.*" Corky and Gina both raised their glasses in return.

Beyond Corky and Sal praising the meal, the three ate in silence. When they'd finished, each using the fresh baked bread to scoop the remaining sauce, leaving the bowls practically spotless, Gina motioned for Corky to clear the table. The boy rose and gathered the bowls but when he reached to remove the wine bottle, she playfully slapped his hand away. Corky placed the bowls in the sink and returned to sit at the table. His grandmother had refilled her glass but did not pass the bottle, instead parked it near her elbow. She took a long sip, licked her lips as she eyed the deep red liquid, then turned to her guest.

"Now, *Signore* Sal," Gina said. "You may tell us what is so important that you must visit this evening and cannot wait until morning."

Sal drained his glass and set it on the table. Corky thought he saw a slight shake of the man's head. "As you know, Signora," Sal said. "I was sent here by my uncle as a favor to your friend, Signore Crocetti, who you asked for help in taking care of a problem here."

"What problem?" Corky asked.

Sal smiled and drew a circle with his finger on the white checkered table-cloth. He looked at Corky.

"It is not my place to ask or know the nature of the trouble," Sal said. "I am only told to make the trouble go away."

Corky realized what the man was saying and turned to his grandmother.

"Wait," he said. "You asked for help? To have Markle killed?"

Gina was about to speak when lights swept the windows, accompanied by the sound of a car coming to a stop in front of the house.

Sal and Gina's eyes met. Corky's head swiveled from his grandmother to Sal, who asked her. "Are you expecting anyone?"

Gina shook her head. "No."

Corky had never seen a monkey. When he answered the door, he thought at first the man - short, fat with a droopy mustache - was carrying a small child in his arms with its face nestled in the man's overcoat. It wasn't until the head turned to reveal the simian's hairy face that Corky realized his mistake. Along with the monkey, the fat man was accompanied by a man so thin and cadaverous Corky thought it might be a skeleton in a suit and long overcoat. The skin on the man's face was stretched so tight and his eyes so deep set – little more than black holes – that it appeared that his fedora was resting on a skull.

His grandmother appeared at his side and Corky felt the tension rise off the woman at seeing the strange trio standing on his porch. The boy was surprised when, without a word, she pushed open the screen door and stood back to allow the visitors inside. Gina motioned for him to close the door, then walked past the guests into the living room and sat in an armchair. The fat man sat on the small sofa and set the monkey beside him. The animal leaned back, lounging against the throw pillows, turning his languid gaze about the room, assessing his surroundings and, as if finding them uninteresting and pedestrian, shook his head, closed his eyes and went to sleep.

Corky sat on the arm of his grandmother's chair. The skeleton man lingered in the doorway, his hands shoved into the pockets of his rain-streaked overcoat. His eyes were hidden by the brim of his fedora, but Corky sensed the man's cold stare.

The fat man fussed over the monkey, shifting the pillows, straightening the animal's white shirt and trouser leg.

"This weather is not good for Nootsy," he said. "I hate to bring him out when it is this cold, but ..." He paused and looked to Corky. "Do you have a small blanket?"

Corky began to rise when his grandmother's hand touched his thigh. Gina sat silently, staring at the fat man.

"No?" The visitor said, then waving to a shawl draped on the back of a small, cushioned chair next to the fireplace, nodded to the skeleton man. The man moved across the room and pulled the shawl off the chair and handed it to the fat man.

"Ah, *grazie*, Cranio," he said and covered the monkey. Satisfied that his companion was comfortable, he turned his attention to the old woman. He motioned to Cranio, who crossed the room to the large wooden radio to turn the music off.

"You know who I am?" Lisitano said.

Gina replied with a barely perceptible nod.

"*Buono*," Lisitano said. "Signora Ferraro, I come here tonight as a friend, to help you."

The old woman raised an eyebrow.

"Your grandson," the fat man said, pointing to Corky. "He has some recent trouble, no? With the game warden?"

Corky's face paled. His grandmother's was a blank.

"It's no secret what this man…*come si dice*'?" He waved his hand, glanced at the skeleton, who replied in a raspy whisper, his black eyes locked on Corky.

"Markle."

"*Si*, Markle. Everyone knows Markle was *animale*. What he did to our *paesani*. To this boy. His dog." Lisitano shook his head. "To be honest, I was intending to visit Signore Trunzo." He looked at Corky. "And offer my help to him."

"What help?" Corky asked. "Nonna, what's he talking about? What kind of help?"

Gina raised her hand, wagged her forefinger. "Signore Lisitano is in the business of taking money from his *paesani*."

Lisitano sighed and the obsequious smile returned. He spoke to Corky.

"I make it my business to protect my friends," he said. "I use my associations to reach mutually beneficial agreements, let's say. In your case, as I was planning to explain to your father, it is possible, with my help, to make the trouble with the game warden go away. Make it so you can hunt without being arrested … or worse." Lisitano read the questioning look on Corky's face. "There is, of course, a fee for my services. To arrange your protection. Which I was intending to discuss with your father."

"Fee?" Corky said, his voice rising. "Pay you with what? My father has no money."

Lisitano waved him off. "It no longer matters, does it? Now that the game warden is dead, no?" He waited but no response came.

"Your trouble," he said, pointing at Corky, "is not with being able to hunt, so there is no reason to speak with your father at all." He leaned back, crossing his legs. "No, your trouble is much, much greater because the sheriff believes that you are the one who killed Markle."

Corky leapt to his feet, his voice loud. "What did you say? I didn't kill him. Who said that? You're a liar."

The monkey woke with a shriek and leapt to its feet, then onto the arm of the sofa, and sat hunched, eyes darting around the room, the air filled with its high-pitched screaming. Lisitano reached for the animal and pulled him into his arms. "No, no, Nootsy," he said. *Piano, piano.*"

Cranio stepped towards Corky, his gloved hand raised for a backhand strike. Gina pulled the boy by the shirt sleeve, stood, held her hand up at Cranio and shook her head. The skeleton man stopped, arm cocked back, holding her gaze. Lisitano waved at the man to stop. Cranio dropped his hand, sneering at Gina as he stepped back.

Lisitano spoke quietly to his monkey, stroking the patched fur of its head, trying to calm the animal. Without lifting his eyes from his caressing, the fat man spoke in a soft voice.

"No, there is no doubt the sheriff is looking in your direction," he said. "Sheriff Johnson knows about your dog and why you would be angry and have reason to kill this man."

"I didn't kill that game warden," Corky said.

Lisitano raised a finger to lips then pointed to his ear.

*"Tranquillo, ragazzo,"* he said. "It does not matter. This is what you must understand. The sheriff must solve this immediately because the game warden worked for the governor himself. They will need to punish someone quickly. *Capisce*?" The man smiled. "The sheriff, the governor, they do not care if you killed this Markle or not. They simply need someone to blame. They will make their own truth in their courts. They will find you guilty because you are Italian." He paused and locked eyes with Gina. "And they will hang you."

Corky sank onto the arm of the chair. Gina placed her hand on his forearm, patted it gently.

Lisitano turned his attention to the monkey again, scratching under his chin. "Yes, they will, won't they, Nootsy? Blame him and hang him."

The room fell silent other than the fat man's cooing over his pet. After several moments passed, Gina spoke and asked.

"And how is it you can help us?"

Lisitano smiled. "You see, Nootsy?" he said to his pet. "Now they understand the terrible situation they are in and they are curious about how we can help." He looked up, turning to Cranio and jerked his head towards the front door. The man nodded and went out. Lisitano lifted the monkey off his lap and set him on the sofa, plumping a pillow for the animal to lay against. He turned and addressed Gina and Corky.

"It is quite simple, really" he said. "The boy needs an alibi. Someone who will say he couldn't have killed the warden because he was with them." He paused. "Of course, signora, you could say your grandson was with you. Or his father could say the same. But no one will believe you. Or him. They will know you are just lying as anyone would to protect their son, or grandson, from hanging."

"So, what?" Corky asked. "Are you saying you will tell them? They would believe you?"

Lisitano shook his head. "No, no. Not me. What would I say? That you were with me? The sheriff would find that very hard to believe."

"Then how can you help?" Corky asked.

"Let us say that I can provide someone," Lisitano said, "who will say you were with them at the time of the murder. And several others who will swear to the same story? While the sheriff is under great pressure, he would have a very difficult time, even if you were put on trial, to find you guilty with a story told by so many."

The front door opened and Cranio stepped inside. With him was a young woman who appeared to be not much older than Corky. A cascade of long red hair fell to her shoulders in waves of curls and framed a pretty face sprinkled with freckles. Eyes of glistening emerald darted about the room, and she frowned at seeing Lisitano.

"Look who's here, Nootsy," he said. "Your friend, Christina." The monkey hissed and the girl flinched, taking a step back. "Oh Nootsy, be nice. Come in," he said waving the girl into the room. "Come, sit."

When she hesitated, Cranio grabbed her by the upper arm and pushed her forward.

"That's right, sit here with me and Nootsy," Lisitano said and patted the sofa next to where he sat. The girl perched on the edge of the cushion, an arm's length from the fat man. She stared at the floor.

"Christina," Lisitano said. "I'd like you to meet Signora Ferraro."

The girl looked up at Gina, nodded and her eyes dropped back to the floor.

"Of course, you know her grandson," Lisitano said and gestured towards Corky.

"What?" Corky said. "I don't know her."

"No?" Lisitano said. "That's not very kind of you, *ragazzo*. I know perhaps you are embarrassed in front of your grandmother, but ..." He turned to Christina. "Please, *ragazza*. Tell the *signora*."

Her green eyes lifted, then darted away from Gina's stony gaze.

Lisitano grunted. "Tell them."

"I was with him," the girl said. "We were together."

"That's a lie," Corky, stunned, said, his voice a whisper. His eyes wide, locked on the girl, his voice rose. "I don't know her." He turned to his grandmother. "Nonna, I've never seen her." Gina raised her hand to silence him as she nodded at the girl to continue.

"He came to see me at the club," she said. "He got very drunk and stayed the night. He had a terrible hangover and slept until late in the afternoon."

Corky shook his head slowly. "No, no, no, I didn't. I wasn't there."

"And what day was that, Christina?" Lisitano said.

"The day that game warden got killed." She said.

Lisitano smiled at Gina and Corky. "You see now?" he said. "How could your grandson be guilty of this crime if he was asleep when it occurred?" He turned to Christina and patted her arm.

"And the sheriff is to believe your little *putana*?" Gina asked. The girl's freckled cheeks flushed as she glared at the old woman, who only smiled.

"Well, there were other girls there," Lisitano said. "They will all agree with her, that they saw the boy at Nootsy's, and they will tell the sheriff the same story."

"But it's not true," Corky said. "I don't know her. I've never been to your club or bar or whorehouse." He stopped, embarrassed when his eyes met Christina's and he saw her expression, a mix of hurt and anger. "Sorry," he said. "I don't know what it is, because I've never been there."

"None of that is important," Lisitano said. "It will be the truth as far as the sheriff is concerned. And you will not hang. That is what is important. What we all want." His smile was wide and false.

"And there is a cost for your help." Gina said.

"*Sono un uomo d'affari,*" the fat man said. "And you are a businesswoman, no?" He waved his hand at the room. "We both need to earn from the services we provide. But I'm not interested in taking money from your boarding house. I know there's little to be made renting rooms to a few miners."

Gina shrugged. Lisitano shook his head, his face a mask of sympathy. "No, I'm interested in your other business."

"I have no other business," she said.

Lisitano raised his hand. "Please, *signora.*" He clasped his hands in prayer, shook them then held them wide. "*Scuzi,* but we all know about Gina Ferraro's laundry shed."

Gina's face remained expressionless.

"There's nothing to know about my grandmother's shed," Corky said.

"Oh, it's no secret, *ragazzo,*" he said. The smile left his face, and he raised an eyebrow at Corky. "It's no secret who makes what comes out of that shed, either."

Corky's jaw dropped.

The fat man spoke to the monkey. "You see, Nootsy? They think what they do is a big secret, *un gran misterio! Ma non siamo stupidi, eh?* No, we are not. *Sei molto intelligente, eh?*" He tapped the side of his head. "*Molto, molto intelligente.*" He turned back to address the woman and her grandson, his face serious.

"Enough nonsense, signora. Here's what's going to happen. Your grandson will work for me, now, and make whiskey for my club and for me to sell to my associates. *Capisce*?"

Gina's eyes narrowed, her anger simmering.

"You can't do this," Corky said. "I won't make whiskey for you."

Lisitano kept his eyes locked on Gina. "Oh, *si, ragazzo*," he said. "You will."

"*A van culo*," Corky shouted. "I won't work for you. Nonna, tell him."

"*Rispetto*," Lisitano said and raised his finger at Corky. "Never again curse at me, *capisce*? It will be the last words you speak, eh?" He paused, his face stone. "Here's why you will work for me. Christina, tell them what you saw." He patted the girl's thigh. The girl stiffened, her eyes widened in fear.

"No," she said, shaking her head, looking from Gina to Corky.

Cranio stepped to her side and gripped the back of her neck. She closed her eyes and spoke in a whisper. "I saw him."

"Speak up, Christina," Lisitano said. "Please, so they can hear you."

"I saw him at the club," she said.

"Where at the club?" Lisitano asked.

"He was hiding on the back porch."

"When was this?"

"It was in the afternoon," Christina said.

"What day was this?"

"Tuesday," she said.

"The day the game warden was found dead?" Lisitano asked, pressing his case. The girl nodded, her eyes dropping to the hands she nervously worked in her lap.

"And what else did you see?" Lisitano said. "When you found this boy hiding on the porch?"

She shook her head and Cranio tightened his grip. She sighed, closing her eyes again and said, "He had blood all over his clothes and his hands."

Corky leapt to his feet. "Liar. Lies!" he said. "*Nonna*, stop them. This isn't true."

"It is as true as the other story, *ragazzo*," Lisitano said. "The sheriff will hear one or the other. Which of the two depends on you." He locked eyes with Gina. "And your *nonna*."

Lisitano stood as Cranio grabbed the girl by the upper arm and yanked her off the couch. As he swung the front door open, she glanced over her shoulder at Corky, her eyes filled with tears and sorrow. Cranio looked at Corky, a twisted smile gave way to a low cackle, and he pushed the girl through the door and out into the night. The club owner paused at the door.

"*Signora* Ferraro," he said, his smile made false by the dark eyes above it. "I expect an answer in the morning, although I'm sure you realize as I do, you have little choice now. It's business, no? And it will be *buono per te*." He pointed to the old woman then tapped his finger on his chest. "*E buono per me.*" He twirled his finger. "*Buono per tutti, eh?*"

Corky searched his grandmother's face but could read nothing there. Lisitano shrugged. "You let me know by tomorrow when I can expect to pick up my first load." He shifted the bundled monkey in his arms and spoke to it. "What time, Nootsy?" He said and bent his head, turning an ear to the drowsy simian. "Ah, *si, buono* Nootsy. *Perfetto.* We will tell her to call me by noon."

He tipped his hat to Gina. "*Ciao, signora,*" Lisitano said, and looked at Corky. "*Ciao, maestro.*" He went out the door, across the porch and started down the steps. Cranio stood by the Cadillac and held the rear door open.

"Lisitano," Gina said, stepping out onto the porch. "*Scuzi.*" Lisitano stopped and turned. "You can have my answer now."

The fat man raised an up-turned hand, gesturing for her to speak.

"*Ascoltami,*" she said. "From me, you get no whiskey. You get *niente, eh? Meno di niente.*" She wagged her finger then brought her hand up and flicked the underside of her chin with the back of her gathered fingers. Cranio, eyes blazing, stepped towards the porch. Lisitano stopped him with a shake of his head. The fat man laughed.

"*Tu Calabrese',* eh?" He tapped his knuckles on his forehead. "*Testa dura.*" The smile vanished from his face as he glared at Gina. "No, *signora,* this is too important to make a decision so quickly," he said. "Without truly … what's the new English word we learned, Nootsy, the one that means to think about?" He brought a finger to his pursed lips, his face screwed in mock concentration then his face brightened. "Ah yes, ruminate. Roo-mee-nate. You need to roo-mee-nate a bit more, eh, signora?" He turned abruptly and slid into the back seat of the car. Cranio smirked at the two standing on the porch, closed the door and got in behind the wheel. The car started, the headlights came on, and lit the long driveway against the dark. The rear window came down as the car began to roll forward, Lisitano's fat face appeared. He smiled broadly and lifted the monkey in his arms until the furred face could be seen. "Say *Buonosera,* Nootsy." The fat man brought the monkey's arm up and waved the paw. "*Ciao, ciao.* Bye-bye." The faces disappeared and the fat man's laugh trailed from the window as the car slowly rolled down the drive.

Corky broke away from the door and raced back into the house through the living room and pushed the kitchen door wide.

Sal stood, leaning against the sink, his arms folded across his chest.

"Pack a bag," he said. "A small one and only take what you absolutely need."

"Why?" Corky asked.

His grandmother walked into the kitchen and, standing in front of Corky, took his hands in hers.

"You must go away," she said, looking into his eyes. "Leave Sagamore."

Corky jerked his hands out of his grandmother's grasp.

"What? No," he said, eyes widening in disbelief.

"There is no choice, *mimmo*," Gina said. "You must leave until things can be arranged and you can come back."

"Arranged? Who's going to fix this?" Corky said.

"I will speak to Mr. Crocetti," Gina said and glanced to Sal. "He will know what to do."

"*Si*," Sal said, then paused, looking first at Corky then the widow, holding her gaze. "But I must tell you, truthfully, this will take time. It is not as simple as working an arrangement with the local sheriff or even a judge in the usual way. I think it best to go directly to my uncle to handle this with Signore Crocetti. He can reach into much higher places. Markle was taking orders from the governor. Worse, my understanding is that it is the governor's wife who is behind the crusade to save the songbirds and stop the Italians from hunting them. But he can be convinced. All men can be persuaded to change their mind. Even his wife can be persuaded."

"How? Money?" Corky asked.

"That is usually the first step," Sal said.

"I don't have any money," the boy said.

"There are other, more persuasive, means." Sal said, his voice edged with menace. Corky straightened, his eyes narrowing. Sal read the question on the boy's face.

"Yes, this trouble will go away," he said. "But this is not your problem. The concern is time."

"Where am I supposed to go?" Corky said.

"You come with me," Sal said. "To New Orleans."

Corky's breath caught at the sound of the two words, his mind a mix of fear, relief and excitement at getting out of Sagamore.

"It's a long trip," Sal said. "But no one would think of looking for you there. My uncle will take care of you. And you will be safe with me."

"*Buono*, Sal," the widow said. "This is good. Someplace faraway with you." She reached out and patted the man's hand. "Corky, you go with Sal. You'll be safe as he says. You can trust him."

"Trust him? He's a killer," Corky said. "I'm just supposed to go a thousand miles away with him?"

The old woman held her grandson's gaze and nodded her head.

"*Si*," she said. "This is exactly what you will do."

"Listen to your nonna, *fratello mio*," Sal said. "She's correct."

"Don't call me that," Corky said, turning to glare at Sal. "You're not my brother. My brother's dead. I don't know you and all this craziness is because of you." The boy's voice rose to a shout. He pointed his finger at Sal. "You. You killed Markle. Now I'm the one who must leave or get thrown in jail? Or hang? *Va Fanculo.*"

"*Eugenio!*" his grandmother snapped. "Calm down, please. Do not blame him for something I began. He will help us."

"Us?" Corky said. "You mean me. He can just leave, go back to New Orleans or wherever and disappear. The sheriff has me to blame."

"*Si*, they do," Sal said. "And they are going to want to move quickly. Guilt has nothing to do with it. They have an Italian to blame and that's all they want and need for the public. There will be great pressure to solve this as soon as possible, regardless of who is guilty. And this fat man with the monkey will help them."

# 15

Close to midnight, Sal sat in the Nash Ambassador, parked at the bottom of the front porch steps, the powerful engine rumbling. Corky and his grandmother said their goodbyes without words. Gina released her grandson from a tight hug, then slid a prayer card into his hand. Corky glanced at it and recognized the image: an avenging angel with upraised sword. He gave his grandmother a questioning look. She turned his hand to expose the back side. Above the printed prayer for protection and guidance was written the word "Pittsburgh" and a string of numbers. She guided his hand to place the card in the breast pocket of his vest.

Corky tied his sweater around his waist, threw his bag into the back seat and got in the passenger seat. Sal leaned forward to meet Gina's gaze. The old woman tapped her forefinger on her cheek at the corner of her eye and Sal nodded his reassurance that he would watch out for the young boy. She turned and went inside.

Sal eased the car into gear and drove down the drive, stopping at the main road. He looked in the direction he'd watched Lisitano's car go. Without looking at his passenger, he asked, "Do you know where that *cazzo's* business is located?"

Corky jerked his thumb in the direction Sal's gaze was fixed. "About twenty minutes or so that way."

Sal nodded, pulled the car out on to the main road, driving towards the fat man's nightclub.

Lisitano cranked the handle of the Victrola and stood at the wooden cabinet, eyes closed, as the voice of Enrico Caruso rose from the curved horn. Nootsy slumbered in a small chair on the credenza behind the desk. When he heard to door to his office open, his eyes remained closed, but he waved a finger towards the sound.

"*Rispetto,*" he said. "Do not interrupt the maestro, Cranio."

"Cranio is not here," Sal said as he stepped out of the shadows into the office. He held the *lupera* at his side. Lisitano's eyes snapped open, confusion on his face.

"Who are you?" he asked, then shouted for Cranio.

"He will not come," Sal said. "He is gone."

"Gone?" Lisitano asked. "Gone where?"

"Gone," Sal said. "To hell, I'm quite certain. If you believe in such things."

"Who the fuck are you to come into my office?" he asked. "Do you know who I am? The people I am connected to?" His voice rose in anger as he edged away from the Victrola towards his desk.

"It is not important that I know who you are," Sal said. "Or who your connections are. What matters is I know *what* you are. Which is a *decerebrato* who threatens a child and an old woman."

"She sent you here?" Lisitano said. "To threaten me? This Ferraro *cagna* sends whoever you are to my place?"

"See, *cazzo*," Sal said. "You prove my point. You have no respect and, honestly, you are very, very stupid. Signora Ferraro is woman who is respected by important men. But she did not send me. I came on my own because I cannot tolerate such a threat to these people from the likes of you. *Capito?*"

"I'll ask you one last time. Who are you?" Lisitano said. "What business is any of this to you?"

"*Mi chiamo* Salvatore Gentile," Sal said. "Believe me, Signore Lisitano, there is no pleasure for you in making my acquaintance."

"*Avanculo*, Salvatore Gentile," Lisitano said and shouted, "Get the fuck out of my place."

The monkey, Nootsy, woke and began to screech at seeing the stranger. Agitated, the animal jumped up and down, hissing, teeth bared. Lisitano lurched to his desk, pulling open a drawer. Sal took two long strides into the room and raised the *lupera*. Lisitano, eyes wide in fear, pulled a revolver from the drawer. Before he could raise the weapon, Sal let go a blast from the shotgun. The buckshot tore Lisitano's chest open and slammed the fat man back into his chair, dead before he sat.

The monkey let loose an ear-piercing wail, as he leapt from his perch, scaling the wall, and jumped to swing from the light fixture above Sal's head. He ducked as Nootsy sailed past, dropped to the floor and ran out the door.

Corky was waiting in the car for Sal to return when he heard the shotgun erupt. He was halfway across the parking lot heading to the back porch when he saw Nootsy streak from the doorway and bolt into the woods. Sal came out and made his way towards Corky in fast walk. He grabbed his upper arm, spun him and pushing the boy towards the car. Neither noticing Corky's sweater slipping from where it was tied to his waist, falling to the ground. Both men got inside and, spewing gravel, Sal gunned the Nash into the night.

# 16

"The killer used a shotgun and by the looks of it, I'd say it was sawed-off."

Sheriff Johnson was half-listening to his Armstrong County counterpart, Jim "Mac" McNutt, as he took in the scene in the office at Nootsy's night club.

"It was no secret Markle spent time here," Mac said. "Word was he had a gambling problem. Had a hankering for the girls here, too. Owed Lisitano a heap of money. He'd be my number one for this, if the man wasn't dead himself."

Johnson knew Mac was right about the shotgun being cut down. It was the only weapon that had that kind of spread in close quarters and could cause the damage he was seeing. Lisitano, the owner, was seated behind his desk, a gaping hole in his chest, his head tilted back, his mouth open wide, and his dead eyes popped as if he'd seen something wondrous appear on the ceiling, or finally found an answer to an inscrutable question he had sought his entire life. Who knew, thought Johnson. Maybe in that last moment, he did.

Johnson moved around the desk, careful to not step in the thick, sticky puddles of blood. He nudged Lisitano's swivel chair with his boot and saw a revolver still clutched in his right hand. His eyes went to the credenza and saw the small chair on it.

"What's that all about?" he asked.

"That was for the man's monkey," Mac said. "Called it Nootsy, named this place after the damn thing."

Johnson's eyebrows arched He stood and tilted his Stetson back to scratch his head.

"A monkey?"

"You never heard about it? Thought everybody in three counties knew about that damn thing. Everyone hated it. The man had a small chair up behind the bar, too, like a throne. The little bastard would sit up there drinking whiskey."

"You're joking, right?"

"Dead serious," Mac said. "And it was a mean drunk, I'll tell you. Bit more than a few customers, but Lisitano wouldn't think about putting it down. Just kept giving it booze until the thing would pass out. Wanted to shoot it my damn self. Curious where Nootsy's gone."

"You a regular here, Mac?" Johnson asked. "You deal with him much?"

"I don't even bother coming out here when there's trouble," The Armstrong sheriff said. "I let Lisitano and his muscle deal with any of it."

"Why's that?"

"I shut this place down twice," Mac said. "Both times I had a judge tell me it'd be in everybody's best interest if I paid attention to more pressing matters in the county."

"Lisitano paid him off?" Johnson asked.

"Could be, but I think it'd take someone with a bit more juice to buy a judge," Mac said. "Word is the Youngstown Black Hand was behind Lisitano."

"That can't be making Crocetti very happy," Johnson said. "Having someone edging into his territory."

"You think he's behind this mess?"

Johnson shrugged his shoulders. "Where's the other one?"

Mac jerked his chin towards the open door at the rear of the office, and both men walked to where a body sat splay-legged, back against the wall, in a pool of blood. The dead man's head was tilted forward, a fedora covering his face. His overcoat was open to reveal a shirt front saturated crimson with blood. Sheriff Mac knelt, removed the hat, and used the stiff brim to lift the man's head. Johnson was taken aback at the cadaverous face. Below the man's bony chin was a wide gash across his throat, so deep the man had almost been beheaded. Mac let the head drop and stood, tossing the fedora on the dead man's lap. The bare head looked even more like a skull.

"They called him Cranio," Mac said. "Italian for skull, which seems fitting, no? He was Lisitano's man." Johnson pointed down at the revolver laying on the floor near the dead man's hand.

"That get used?" he asked.

"Nope," Mac said. "Didn't get a shot off at whoever came through that door."

"Killer come in this way?"

"Seems so," Mac said. "Hallway leads to the back door of the place. Door wasn't busted in. Sounds crazy, but I'm wondering if the killer knocked. I'm thinking the Skull here opened the door and got greeted by a very sharp blade to the throat before he knew what was happening."

"Let's see that back door," Johnson said.

The two men left the office and walked down the short hallway, passing a stairway leading to the second-floor brothel. A pair of young women, clutching their robes closed at the throat, stood at the foot of the stairs, watching the two lawmen pass. Johnson tipped his hat and followed Mac through the back door to the small porch, where a pair of men dressed in white stood off to the side with a stretcher leaning against the wall. Both men smoked cigarettes, their faces blank with boredom. Johnson turned to look off the porch to take in the parking lot. He watched his nephew deputy, Dennis, walking the edge of the parking lot along with Mac's man as they searched for signs of the killer.

"Thanks, Mac," Johnson said. "I think you're right about the killer's weapon but I'm just not sure how all this connects to Markle, if it does at all."

"Thought you had that kid from Sagamore for that?" Mac asked. "The one had his dog killed by Markle?"

Johnson arched an eyebrow. "Now where'd you hear that?"

"You'd be amazed at what you hear over coffee at the diner just up the road," Mac said. "News of any kind makes its way in there, so many folks stopping in from all over the area. Best coffee in the county and really gets the tongues wagging."

Johnson thought it best if he kept his opinion about Corky and the investigation to himself. "I've got my boss and a line of bosses' bosses all the way up to the governor on my ass, so let me know if anything else turns up here."

Mac nodded and motioned to the two men on the porch to take the bodies out. Johnson turned to see the rain had returned in a drizzling mist that hung in the air more than fell. He stepped off the porch, shoulders hunched against the wet, and made his way to his truck where Dennis now stood. A shout came from Mac's deputy from the far corner of the parking lot. The man held a piece of clothing that he brought to the truck.

"That's Corky's sweater," Dennis said.

Johnson looked at his nephew as he picked a leaf off the sweater's sleeve. "You sure?"

"Anybody knows Corky knows that sweater," his nephew said. "I ain't never seen that kid without it on or wrapped around his waist."

Johnson nodded, trying to recall an image of Corky dressed differently. Besides a baseball or basketball uniform, he could only think of two times he saw the boy without the sweater – both when he wore a suit at the graveside of his brother and his mother, barely a year apart.

"That the Sagamore boy you like for the game warden shooting?" Mac asked.

Johnson shook his head. "Don't like him at all for that," he said. "Or this mess here. Not sure exactly how those fools in Harrisburg got wind of Markle killing the boy's dog, but they sure seem to think that's enough motive."

"You and I have both seen killings done for a lot less," Mac said.

"True enough," Johnson said. "That boy just don't have it in him, is what my guts are saying."

"You think he's tied up with your killer? The one you don't know?" Mac smiled.

"Can't make sense of his sweater be laying out here otherwise," Johnson said. "Doesn't look like it's been out here long." He took the sweater and draped it over his arm. "Dennis, you help the sheriff here, see if you find anything else. I'm going to head back to town." He turned and shook hands with his counterpart. "See you, Mac. Thanks for the help."

"No problem," Mac said. "I better get back inside and make sure these deputies don't miss anything. Or get distracted by any of these employees." Johnson smiled and gave Mac's shoulder a playful punch. He got in his police sedan and turned onto the road towards Sagamore. As he glanced at the sweater, he thought, maybe seeing this would get Gina Ferrara to tell him what and who was behind all this trouble.

# 17

"Folks going to start talking about us, Gina, me stopping to see you so many times these days."

Johnson was sitting in the old woman's kitchen again, sipping a cup of espresso and warm milk. He realized that in all the years of coming to the woman's house, this was the only room he'd ever been in. His wet coat was draped on the back of chair that Gina placed next to the stove. The warm kitchen was a welcome comfort after the drive in the freezing rain.

Gina smiled as she placed a plate of cookies on the table, then reached out and pinched his cheek. "They talk because of trouble," she said. "Or *amore*?"

"Well, I do think Mrs. Johnson gets jealous when she hears I'm out here," Johnson said. "Especially knowing I'm getting some of these cookies."

"I will send you away with some for her, so we keep her happy, and not suspect our plans of romance," she said and tapped a forefinger on her temple. "*Capisce', bello*?" She took his hat from his head and set it on the chair to dry along with the coat, then returned with an espresso of her own. He watched as she twisted a sliver of lemon peel and ran it along the rim of the small cup before taking her first sip. In the entire county, he'd never come across a woman as resilient and resourceful as Gina Ferraro. He doubted half the men he knew could have carved out the life she did after being left by a spouse to raise two kids on her own. And if Johnson was being totally honest with himself, he had to admit that he was more than a bit fearful of the woman. He had seen the look that came over her face and the blackness in her eyes when she was pressed or displeased – a look he only had seen in men, one that never foretold good things. But with men he knew what to expect and how to deal with it. Always had, and was rarely rattled, even in combat. He was never certain what to expect from this tiny woman or knew for certain of what she was capable of doing.

As he reached into the canvas bag in his lap, he realized he was holding his breath, knowing that what he was about to confront her with would not make her happy. Johnson lay the sweater, neatly folded, on the table. He thought he caught her eyes widen but there was no missing the tightening of her jaw as she raised the espresso cup to her lips. She took a sip and, without lifting her head, gave Johnson a hard, half-lidded glare over the top of the cup. She straightened, setting her shoulders back and, placing the cup on the table, sat silent. Johnson closed his eyes and sighed. He ran his hand down his mustache and chin. When he opened his eyes, he kept them lowered and looked at the sweater.

"Gina," he said, and hesitated. "Please don't make this harder than it needs to be."

The woman said nothing.

"You know this is Corky's sweater," he said. "Gina, please. Tell me where he is. Help me find him and straighten out this Markle mess."

Gina waved her hand, sweeping the idea away.

"You think you can help Corky?" she asked. "How? Like you helped all our people this *animale* game warden hurt. Or killed?"

The rebuke stung and Johnson's anger rose. He met her gaze with a hard one of his own.

"You know where we found this?" Johnson said. He leaned forward and tapped the sweater with his finger. "In the parking lot of Nootsy's. Know what else we found? A man with his throat slit, and very dead Sebastian Lisitano."

Gina remained a sphinx, her lips tight, hands folded in her lap. Johnson slammed his hand down on the table, causing it to jump, but Gina barely flinched. Silence hung between them.

"Gina, you know me," Johnson said. "You know my brothers. Our families. I've never harmed any of your people. I don't care about the hunting or the birds. You know Italians hunt out on my brother Carl's land all the time, license or not. I don't bother with any of it. Not even what goes on in that laundry shed of yours." He pushed his cup away. Gina's lips moved into the slightest of smiles, but she said nothing. Johnson shook his head.

"Please, Gina, listen to me," he said, leaning forward, his elbows on his knees. "These assholes in Harrisburg have called out every lawman in this part of the state to find who killed Markle and they will put it on Corky because they need to blame an Italian. Any Italian, guilty or not. I can't keep the fact we found this," he said, touching the sweater, "a secret from the state police for long. Believe me, if they find him before I do, they will not care that he's innocent. It will not end well for him."

"And if you find him," Gina said, "This will end well for my grandson?"

Johnson looked away, rubbing his chin. "The only thing that will fix this," he said, "is finding the person really responsible."

"Do you know who is responsible? The one who set this in motion?" She asked and waved her hand. "That *animale* brought it on himself. Isn't it enough that an evil man has finally been punished for all he has done? Isn't that justice? You, of all people, know things are not black and white in this world."

The two friends sat in silence, their gazes locked on each other's eyes. An unspoken conversation passed between them, both knowing all too well the other's thoughts.

A dozen years ago, they sat in this same kitchen, in the same chairs at the same table sorting out a problem that would link them forever.

Around midnight, on this particular Saturday night, Johnson was called to the scene of a murder which took place in the rear room of the general store in town. During a card game, heated words were exchanged, accusations of cheating ended when the accused leapt from his chair and slashed the throat of his accuser with a straight razor. The killer ran, disappearing into the night. The card players were all Italians and knew the fugitive well. He was a drunk, deeply in debt from a never-ending losing streak. An unrepentant womanizer, Gaetano Ferraro, lived in Sagamore with his wife, Gina.

The sheriff drove to the small town, out of his jurisdiction in Armstrong county, but the murder happened in his county so felt justified in going after the killer. When Johnson arrived at the Ferraro home, the door was answered by the small woman with coal black hair and shining eyes the same color, set in a calm, but serious face. He introduced himself.

"I know who you are, Sheriff," she said and, answering Johnson's quizzical look, added. "I make it my business to know the important people in this area and I know why you're here."

She turned and walked towards the kitchen. Johnson followed and stopped cold in the doorway. A man lay sprawled on the kitchen floor, blood pooling from his broken head, obviously dead. Johnson crossed the room, skirting the body and sat in the chair opposite Gina. He knew from experience the law is not black and white. The man was a degenerate gambler and a murderer. He learned from the card players, he abused and cheated on his wife. Had Johnson found him alive and arrested him, the man would surely be found guilty and hung, dead just the same. Justice done. And this woman? What's to be gained by arresting her, he thought. An immigrant woman, killing her husband, even in self-defense would not be seen as innocent by a jury in this county or any others in western Pennsylvania. Sending her to prison or the more likely sentence of hanging would not serve justice. He was the only one who knew what she admitted to having done. There were no witnesses.

There was only a body.

What they did together that night was never spoken of again. Never alluded to by either of the guilty parties. Until tonight.

Johnson ran his hand across his face and sighed. He knew there was no answer coming from the woman, that she was busy calculating her options and working out how to save her grandson her way. Johnson stood, patted Gina's shoulder, and left her sitting at the table. He stepped off the porch and glanced toward the hog pen in the back yard.

No body. No crime.

The rain beat a steady counterpoint to the metronome clack of the wipers as Johnson drove through the dark, needing home, the company of his wife and the dinner he knew would be waiting for him. He'd left Gina's without another word spoken between them. The old woman had never turned her gaze from the sweater on the table to see him leave.

Eyes hard on the road, he recalled seeing the look on Gina's face, when it occurred to him that maybe he'd been mistaken. A shudder had rippled his spine when he realized he was looking into the boy's face. The same set jaw and tight smile, the heavy-lidded gaze with eyes that glinted with the same coal black light. He reached up to wipe away the condensation on the windshield and cranked his window down to help clear the fogging, as the tires hissed on the rain-slicked road.

Another shudder came now, convulsing his shoulders, as the thought that the boy had inherited more from his grandmother than looks. Something deeper, colder. Something in the woman that came dangerously alive when a line had been crossed. A line that only she knew existed. The shudder gave way to a tightening in his gut, brought on by the realization that maybe, given the boy was most certainly on the run with someone involved in all this, he'd been wrong about Corky being unable to pull the trigger of a shotgun aimed at the game warden or the fat club owner. And slice a man's throat?

His foot pressed heavy on the accelerator, pushing the car towards home, where dinner and his wife's company had fallen from his desire, now replaced by the solace to be found in several fingers of whiskey from the jar tucked on a top shelf in the kitchen cupboard. He was determined to do his best not to be bothered by the irony, the 'shine being one of the things Gina Ferraro could make appear.

# 18

They rode in silence. Sal at the wheel, smoking his small cigar, the window half opened. The Nash's powerful Advanced Six engine a low drone. Corky sat in the passenger seat, sunk into the rich leather, his knee bouncing, eyes wide as he stared shell-shocked at the road ahead in the jittering headlights.

"You killed Lisitano," he said. A statement rather than a question. Sal's face was lit by the glow of his Parodi cigar as he took a deep pull. He streamed the smoke towards the open window then spoke.

"He was a danger to you and your *nonna*," Sal said. "Men such as this *animale'* will never stop until they get what they want. To threaten *Signora* Ferraro, a woman of honor, who is respected by important men, comes with consequences, *Eugenio*. In my world and in my work, there are rules. It is strange, I'm sure, to hear that such rules exist amongst men of my business. Yet they do and, as difficult as it may be to understand, we are men of honor. Our word is our bond. We believe blood, *la famiglia*, is more important than anything, everything. Including the church. *La famiglia e tutti. Capisce'?*"

Corky nodded.

"As men of honor," Sal said, "we have rules and I tonight acted in haste, in anger, and without permission."

"Permission?" Corky asked. "You need permission to kill someone? This is something you go and ask someone? What do you say, please let me kill this person?"

"That is exactly what happens."

Corky sat up, rubbed his face.

"Our friends in Pittsburgh and my uncle are now in a situation with the *Napolitano* in Youngstown to which this Lisitano was connected," Sal said.

"How do you know that?" Corky asked.

"He thought telling me would save his miserable life," Sal said. "But without either Signore Crocetti or my uncle understanding exactly what happened, they will say I have to answer for my actions."

"What's that mean?"

Sal did not answer the question, but said, "There is something else. Another complication."

Corky turned, staring into the dark in the direction of Sal's disembodied voice. He waited and when Sal did not continue, he asked with an edge of disgust in his voice. "What is it?"

He heard Sal take a deep breath before the words came.

"I did not kill the game warden."

# MISSISSIPPI

# 19

*Rosedale, Mississippi*

She was beautiful by any measure, a face Michelangelo could have carved from the finest Carrera, flawless with exception of the thin scar that ran along her left jawline. Serafina Locatelli had blossomed into an early womanhood. At nineteen, she was long-limbed and coltish, slim-hipped with large breasts, taller than her peers in the Calabrian village where she was born. A cascade of raven tresses fell to the middle of her back and framed the high cheeked, olive skinned oval of her face. As if her stature and figure were not enough to ensure the impossibility of her going through life unnoticed, she was blessed with the rarity amongst the *Mezzogiorno*. Her eyes were the color of the Mediterranean sea's brilliant, crystal-line blue. Even scarred, she was a beauty envied by women and desired by men of all ages.

Serafina stood at the large window of the café, watching the rain fall in gray sheets that swept the flat, open fields across the road, battering a sign welcoming all to Rosedale, Mississippi, pop. 752. Dark ripples snaked the widening puddles that were turning the gravel lot that fronted the cafe into a lake. She had seen nothing but rain since entering the harbor in New Orleans. It had rained day and night without end the entire week of traveling north along the swollen Mississippi river and she began to wonder if this new country would drown.

The letter came from a father she had not seen since she was five years old and said nothing about endless rain. Serafina surprised herself at the depth of her anger at the man. A righteous indignation at his assumption of her acquiescence to leave her home without question served to ignite the long-buried rage and hurt at being abandoned, left in poverty with nothing but an unfulfilled promise. She railed against her mother's insistence that she go but knew behind her own loud protests that this was her way out. The longed-for escape she held onto as she grew from a child to a woman.

Serafina had long ago given up struggling to recall the man's face, her memory holding nothing more than her father's shadow in a doorway. It was the sound of his voice, the words of his promise to send for her, that remained. His answer to her question of when, a lullaby whispering in her ear that conjured dreams of a life beyond the barren hills of Calabria. *Presto, presto.*

Soon.

She was unmarried and had no long-lasting interest in the men, young or old, in her village or the surrounding towns who approached her at the *sagras* and festivals. Men who freely pinched the asses of other girls as they passed had learned no such liberty was to be taken with the tall beauty with the blue eyes. More than a couple of hands had been bloodied by the razor she carried. The catcalling and whistles gave way to curses and threats. On the night of her rape, the attacker came from a dark doorway, struck her and took the razor from her sleeve. As he forced himself on her, he dragged the steel edge from just below her left ear halfway down her jawline. Not deep enough to cut her throat but enough to open her skin, leave her alive but marked for life.

Serafina did not hide as her face healed. In the weeks afterwards, she walked the dust-caked streets of her village, head held high. The words echoing in her mind. *Presto, presto,* silently adding, I will be gone. Not to Naples or Rome, or further north to Milan or Torino but L'America. Away from this place and all of its doomed, desperate fools.

The letter was a lifeline, the ticket a rescue from the prison of her empty present and desolate future. The message was short and contained nothing other than the instructions of where to collect the ticket he'd purchased for the voyage to join him in New Orleans. How she was to get to the port in Naples was left to her. There was no inquiry as to her well-being or her life in Calabria. No questioning as to whether this was what she wanted or if even it was possible for her to simply pick up and leave Italy. Just an assumption that his absence was not an abdication of his patriarchal stature and that there was no acceptable objection or reason not to obey his command. The letter lacked any mention of her mother, the wife he'd left behind to cross the ocean in search of a vague notion of a better life. No fulfilling the promise of summoning the woman who carried his name to finally join him in that new land to share in the expected bounty he'd been so certain of finding there. No excuses given for his long absence.

There was only the one ticket for a daughter he did not know nor would be able to recognize but, for a reason known only to him, was needed in his life now.

There was no mention of Mississippi, a grocery cafe in a place called Rosedale or the deal her father had made. From the window, she could see the back of the road sign they'd passed that welcomed visitors to the small town in the middle of endless cotton fields, and she cursed it and God under her breath.

The battering of rain on the tin roof of the market mixed with the murmuring conversation of her father, Cossimo, and the market's owner. The thrum made it impossible to hear what they were saying, but it no longer mattered to her. She knew they were discussing details of their agreement, which she'd already heard from her father on the journey up-river. Cossimo was giving her to this man in trade for the market and cafe business. She was to travel with him to his new home in some place called Arkansas. A town where other Italians lived.

Serafina turned from the window and looked at both men sitting across from each other, in animated negotiation, neither paying attention to her. The owner, a Sicilian, named Palumbo, was a small man, dark-skinned and bald, with a walrus mustache shot with grey. He looked old enough to be her father, possibly even her grandfather. She had no intention of being part of this arranged marriage, bartered away like a cow. And no such man had ever appeared in the dream of her new life in *L'America*.

This turn of events presented her with a puzzle she felt confident of solving. She could go along and bide her time until she could escape. The man made it sound like it was a long journey to this place in Arkansas. Surely, she could find an opportunity to slip away while on the road or when he slept. He certainly didn't look able to run fast enough to catch her if she just jumped out of the car. She looked the two men over again, her fingers tapping on the handle of the straight razor stitched into the sleeve of her coat. The thought of killing them both flashed through her mind. Easily done she told herself. Neither was in any shape to move more quickly than a cow. She saw herself taking the razor to the Sicilian's throat first. This she decided would give the man who abandoned his only daughter, then called across the ocean only to barter her away a brief glimpse of his fate before she came around the table and opened his neck, as well. She would be out the door on her way back to New Orleans, disappearing into the city she had only glimpsed. If she only knew where she was.

*Presto, presto,* she said to herself and turned back to the window. Two cars appeared out of the dark grey downpour, headlamps fluttering weakly, the wavy, yellow light skittering the surface of the small lake of the parking lot to shine directly through the window bathing Serafina's face as the black sedans came to a stop. Doors opened on both, two men got out of the first car, A third man, larger than the others, stepped from the second car. They all wore waxed cotton raincoats, their trousers tucked into knee high boots, fedoras pulled low on their faces

The trio sloshed through the puddles and came up on the covered porch, shaking the water from their coats. Only one took off his hat and shook the rainwater off. Even in the dim porch light, Serafina could see he was handsome with a face of chiseled features. She watched as he pulled a comb out of his coat pocket and as he ran it through his brilliantined hair, looked up, giving her a half-smile and a wink. Surprised, she stepped back from the window and turned as the cafe door opened, the little bell ringing. The first man was skinny, swamped by his coat, ferret-faced, eyes blinking as if unaccustomed to the light.

He stepped inside and leaned against the counter. He fished a pack of cigarettes from his pocket, lighting one with shaky hands. The ferret was followed by a man who filled the entire doorway and stood a head taller. The big man was barrel-chested, with long black mutton-chop sideburns joined by a bushy mustache that was waxed and curled at the ends. He stepped into the cafe, moved to the side of the door and stood with his arms folded across his massive chest.

The handsome one stepped in next and set his fedora on the counter, his gaze sweeping the room as if taking inventory. He began to walk around, running his hand along the counter, looking at the floor, the tables, nodding occasionally. He stopped at the back counter, leaning across to see into the kitchen. Seeing no one there, he turned and walked to the table.

He spoke, addressing the two men while looking only at Serafina. She met his stare without expression then turned her gaze to the window.

"My name's Stallings," he said. "Larkin Stallings. Mind if I sit?"

Not waiting for answer, Stallings pulled a chair from a nearby table and sat across from the Sicilian and Serafina's father. "These other two fine gentleman work with me." He turned to point. "That skinny one is my Uncle Brother. That big man is Young Uncle, but we just call him Yunk."

Neither of the pair spoke.

"Now," Stallings said. "Which of you two is the owner here?"

The two Italians looked to each other, both waiting for the other to speak. Cossimo pointed his chin at Palumbo, who began to stroke his walrus mustache.

"This is my place," Palumbo said. "Was."

"Well, which is it? Is-ah or was-ah?" Stallings said.

"I have just made a deal with *Signore* Cossimo," Palumbo said. "He is the new owner."

"Just now?" Stallings asked.

"Yes," Palumbo said. "I mean, no."

"Yunk, you hear this?" Stallings asked without taking his eyes off the nervous Italian. "Sounds a bit confused, right? Yes-ah. No-ah. Let's make-ah up-ah your mind-ah."

"No. I mean to say," the former owner said. "We made the deal some time ago but have just now concluded our business."

"Man just made a deal and here's the new owner."

Cossimo gave the Sicilian a bug-eyed stare to ask what was happening and got a shoulder shrug in answer.

"*Scuzi, signore*," Cossimo said, addressing the newcomer. "I don't know why you ask or why it's a concern of yours."

The man turned back in his chair and leaned across the table on his elbows.

"Cos-ee-mo? That your name?"

Cossimo nodded.

"Well, Cos-Ee-Mo," Stallings said. "I heard tell of this place and never been out this way. I own a few joints over in Yalobusha County and I'm looking to expand. And now that I see this place, I can see the potential. How about you, Uncle Brother? You see potential in this establishment?"

The skinny man grunted, tossing his cigarette to the floor, grinding it out under his boot.

"Hell of a business to be made here. All them use-to-be slaves living out on the old Lake County colony and working that land since the Italians left. Get some music in here, serve them folks some corn liquor. Could be hotter than the Rooster, I'm thinking."

"But I made the deal with *Signore* Palumbo for his restaurant," Cossimo said.

"Maybe I've got a better deal," he said and turned to Palumbo, whose eyes darted to the table. "What's the name? Polo something? That like Marco Polo?" The Sicilian gave a small head-shake in reply.

"Not very chatty, huh?" Stallings said and looked at Cossimo. "Maybe a better deal for you then? Hell, I don't care much which one of you greasers I make the deal with as long as we can do business."

"Larkin," Uncle Brother said sitting down at the counter. "What are we doing? Seriously?"

Stallings twisted in his chair to face his relative. "You got a problem, Uncle Brother?"

"Just don't see why we're way out here," the skinny man said. "Bothering with this place when we got plenty more than we can handle back in Yalobusha and Lafayette. Five jukes and a dozen bootleggers not enough for you? We all getting run ragged."

"Are you done with all your business advice?"

Uncle Brother met his hard gaze and leaned back against the wall, exasperation on his face. Stallings continued.

He waved his hand in the air then turned to the table. "But you want out of this business, that right, my friends?"

The Sicilian nodded. Stallings pulled a revolver from inside his coat and shot Palumbo in the stomach. The blast knocked the old man back, tipping the chair over and sending him sprawling onto the floor.

"Ok, you out," Stallings said.

"Goddamn, Larkin," Uncle Brother said, shouting. "The hell you doing?"

Cossimo leapt to his feet and caught a bullet in the middle of his forehead for his decision. He crumbled like a marionette

Serafina sat shocked, wide-eyed, and speechless.

Stallings rounded the table to stand over the gut-shot Sicilian, who lay moaning, his hands clamped on his wound, blood oozing between his fingers. The dying man worked his mouth wordlessly, blood soaked his walrus mustache and streamed in rivulets from the corners of his mouth, teeth stained red. Stallings kicked at the man's thigh, drawing his gaze. Eyes searched wildly for an answer to a question only he heard asked.

"This place obviously needs a new owner, which I believe is now me," Stallings said. "Done deal."

Stallings turned and spoke to his uncle. "Sheriff going to think this was a robbery and won't give two shits about a couple dead dagoes," he said "Yunk, you get back here this week and start setting up this joint. Come on now, let's get on back to the Rooster."

Yunk held the door open. Uncle Brother pushed off the counter.

"What about her?" he asked, tilting his head at Serafina. Stallings stopped in the doorway.

"Bring her with us," he said as he put his hat on and smiled at Serafina. "She's going to look mighty fine tending bar at the Rooster."

"Larkin, you cannot be serious," Uncle Brother said.

He looked to Yunk for support but got a shrug in return. The skinny man shook his head in disgust.

Stallings waved his gun at Serafina.

"Come on, girl," he said. "Don't make that big man come get you."

Serafina eyed all three men but did not move. Stallings looked at Yunk and jerked his thumb towards the woman. Yunk crossed the room to her and turned with an outstretched arm towards the door. She saw him blush and drop his eyes when she gave him a hard stare. When she didn't move, he went to grab her arm. She jerked away and, stooping to pick up her bag, pushed past him. The big man trailed her out the door.

# 20

Sal and Corky sat in high-backed wooden rockers on the porch of the Water Valley boarding house, watching the early morning activity of the Mississippi town's main street. The rain, light but steady, fell from low-slung clouds that ceilinged the town, propped on the steeples of the dozen churches lording over the busy thoroughfare. Cars and trucks passed in both directions, the hiss and slosh of tires plowing the water-logged street mixing with the muffled clop of horse-drawn wagons and the occasional rider on horseback.

They were three long days drive out of Sagamore. Both men were road-weary, and Corky was glad when Sal decided to stop in this small town to rest for a few days.

Sipping a coffee, Corky took in the long, straight whole of Main Street lined with shops, a two-story general store halfway down opposite an unwelcoming hotel. Further down the block was a grocery cafe, then more shops and, just beyond, a dentist office, the window painted over with an image of a large white molar. On the next corner was a car dealership housed in a large brick building with wide, tall windows that ran the entire length of both sides. Behind the windows sat an array of new automobiles and several trucks. Beyond the dealership was a train station, the dome of the roundhouse rising above a thick, hovering cloud of smoke that belched from engines moving into the switching yard.

He was filled with wonder at finding himself in a world so far beyond Sagamore. They arrived here late in the afternoon the day before. At the first hotel, they were told no rooms were available. When Sal calmly asked about the many keys hanging on the pigeon-holed board behind the desk, the man, without looking up from his newspaper, replied, "Those rooms are reserved for travelers arriving on the later trains." His eyes remained on the page when he added there was a boarding house on the north end of town that he was certain would be more to their liking.

"Run by your people," the man said and looked up over the top of his reading glasses without expression.

Corky stepped towards the desk and before he could say anything, Sal quieted him with a glance and a tilt of his head towards the door. They left and when he asked Sal to explain why they'd been told to stay elsewhere, the answer was short.

"Things are different down here," Sal said.

The pair drove along the main street to the edge of the businesses and found the two-story boarding house fronted by a large wraparound porch, run by their "people," an Italian couple who welcomed them without hesitation.

When Corky inquired as to how long they would be staying, Sal said he wasn't sure.

"A day or two to rest," Sal said. "We can relax here." But when Sal appeared on the porch earlier and sat in the rocker next to him, Corky saw the ebony handles of his revolvers in the shoulder holsters under his suit coat.

A man came up the sidewalk, wearing a long raincoat and wide-brimmed hat pulled down low, hiding his face. He stopped at the bottom of the wooden steps and looked up at the two on the porch, revealing a black face and wide smile filled with gleaming white teeth. Rain ran off the brim of his hat but if the weather troubled him at all, the old man showed no sign. He raised his hand in greeting.

"Morning, sirs" he said, his drawl thick. "A bit wet this morning but looks likes you got a cozy spot."

Sal nodded and raised his coffee cup. "You're welcome to get out of the weather and join us."

The man looked down the block towards the business section of Main Street.

"That's kindly of you. I might can stop for a short minute," he said and came up the steps onto the porch. He removed his hat and shook the water from it, holding the brim in his hand. He took a handkerchief from his coat pocket and ran it first across his face, then his bald head.

"Name's Sugar Barnett," he said. "Y'all need a little brown likka to warm the bones, take the chill off, if you understand my meaning."

Corky looked to Sal who cocked his head, giving the man a raised eyebrow.

"Yes sir. Part my job to be at the station every train with passengers. Greet the menfolk and let them know if they need anything while they stay in Water Valley, Sugar Barnett the one can help."

"With whiskey?"

"Yes sir," Sugar said. "If you want some."

"Seems a might bold, doing business like that, out on Main Street," Sal said and pointed across the road. "I've noticed more than a few churches."

"Ain't nobody gettin' in the way of Mr. Stallings' business around here," Sugar said, his eyes narrowed. "If they know what's best for themselves."

Sal studied the man's face then looked down the street. He set his cup on the porch floor and stood, arched his back in a stretch.

"Well, my friend," he said and clasped the man's shoulder. "This is just what we need."

Sugar smiled and turned towards the street where a mule was slowly making its way down the block in the rain-filled street. The animal was oblivious to the passing traffic. Strapped like saddle bags across the animal's back were two wooden boxes, one hanging on each side. When the mule reached the boarding house steps, it came to a stop, and lowered its head once as if nodding in greeting to the men on the porch. The old man pulled his collar up, stepped off the porch into the rain and went down to his mule. He returned to the porch, a mason jar of honey brown liquid in each hand.

He gave a jar each to Sal and Corky, who took his, gave it a shake and raised it to eye level to study the contents. He unscrewed the top, brought it first to his nose for a deep smell, then took a sip. He raised an eyebrow and gave Sal a wry smile that silently said it was good, but not as good as his own.

Reaching into his pocket, Sal asked. "*Quanta costa?* How much do we owe you?"

The old man shook his head.

"Mr. Tony will put it on your tab," he said. "Keeps things easy."

Sal nodded. "And if I'd like another jar?" he asked.

"Let Mr. Tony know. Or if you're wanting some and don't mind a bit of a drive, you go on out to the Blue Rooster. That's one of Boss Stallings' juke joints out of town a little way. Get you some more of this. Got a little kitchen, doing fried catfish on Friday nights. Tonight being Saturday, they got some music. Folks be dancin' all night." Sugar put his hands on his hips and shimmied. "Let you know, it's mostly colored folks, although Mr. Stallings got no problem with Eye-talians coming out there. Just no white folk at the Rooster."

He went down the steps, turned and touching the brim of his hat, said, "You just ask Mr. Tony how to get out there. He knows."

Sugar walked down the Main Street, arms swinging, as his mule followed.

Sal then turned to Corky.

"Get some breakfast. Mrs. Tony will make you whatever you want."

"You're not eating?"

"I ate earlier, while you were still sleeping."

"Where are you going now?"

Sal tilted his head towards the street. "Out."

Corky walked into the dining room. The owner pulled out a chair for him at one of the small tables. Mr. Tony's wife, a small and smiling woman, fussed over Corky, telling him all that she could make for his breakfast, a list than ran from pancakes to eggs and grits, steak, *salsiccia*, country ham and frittata. He nodded to the woman and said *si grazie* a few times. As she left his table for the kitchen, Sal came out of the office and his overcoat draped on his shoulders in the caped manner he always wore it. He crossed the little lobby, adjusting his fedora without looking or speaking to Corky, and went outside. Through the front window of the dining room that faced the street, Corky could see the top of Sal's hat as he passed, walking towards the business section of Main Street.

Corky ate. And ate. The hunger that he'd ignored, buried in the adrenaline-fueled fever dream of the past few days, dissipated with each bite. He broke a third biscuit, steam rising from the impossibly fluffy inside, and mopped at the remaining bits of the half dozen plates piled in front of him. Sausage gravy on one, the deep yellow yolk of the fried eggs that came with the pork chop on another. He pressed the biscuit into the last bite of the frittata and shoved it into his mouth, closing his eyes, allowing the mix of savory flavors sit on his tongue before chewing and washing it down with the thick hot chocolate. The woman came out of the kitchen, her face beaming with pride at the sight of the many dishes the boy had emptied, to ask if he wanted more, almost begging him to eat something else.

Corky leaned back and rubbed his stomach and shook his head.

"I can't," he said. "But it was so good. *Molto buono.*"

The woman's hands fluttered, waving off the appreciation as unnecessary, and she began clearing the table.

Corky stood, brushing the crumbs from his shirt and pants as he left the dining room to take the stairs to his room and crawl into bed. When he woke several hours later, the grey light of the rain-filled sky, unchanged from earlier, painted the window and he was unsure if he'd slept minutes or days. He rolled in the bed, rose propped on his elbows and found Sal sitting in the stuffed chair in the corner of the room, head tilted back, eyes open, gazing to the ceiling, as if lost in studying images to be found in the dark lines etched in the cracked plaster. Sal rubbed his face with both hands, then slapped them on his thighs. He looked at Corky and smiled, stood, and moved to the door. He pointed to the second bed in the room.

"Meet me downstairs when you've dressed." He left the room, closing the door gently.

Corky sat up and saw, laid out on the opposite bed, a suit jacket with matching trousers. He crossed the room and touched the garment as if to make certain it was real. He rubbed the collar of the jacket between his fingers and thumb - light wool, soft and smooth, the color an inky black so deep he half expected his fingers to disappear into the luxurious material. A vest of the same black was on the hanger underneath the jacket and a pair of suspenders, black with alternating grey and wine-red stripes, was attached to the trousers.

Next to the suit was a folded shirt. He picked it up and gently traced the thin silver-grey lines of the striping that ran through the fine white cotton. There was also a one-piece, short-sleeved undergarment made of a material softer than anything he'd ever felt, which he guessed might be silk. Alongside the shirt were two pair of dark grey socks and, on the floor, a pair of black leather boots, polished to a high gloss that shined even in the dull light of the room.

Corky dressed in the new clothes, marveling as he slid into each piece, first at the rich feel of the cloth against his skin, unlike anything he'd experienced and, secondly, the near perfect fit of everything, even the boots wrapping his feet as if they'd been custom made. He stood in front of the armoire mirror, smoothing the vest front, then tugged on the collar of the jacket to settle it on his shoulders. He looked at his reflection, starting at his boots, slowly soaking in the image as his eyes moved upward until he gazed on his own face, unrecognized for an instant, dressed in the clothes of a movie star. Or a gangster.

Dressed like Sal.

Corky brushed at the jacket sleeves, tugged on his vest, straightening himself in the mirror. He pointed a finger at his own reflection and left the room, descending the stairs to an uncertain future but certain of one thing.

He was never going back to Sagamore.

# 22

The big man, Yunk, told her they were going to a cabin Stallings owned on a lake north of a town called Water Valley. Little more than a shotgun shack, but well-built and weather tight, the small house was surrounded by acres upon acres of old pine and oak. The place was not far from Water Valley but isolated, Yunk said, as Stallings owned most of the land that bordered the eastern half of the lake and there were no other homes or cabins for miles.

Serafina waited by the door where Yunk insisted she stay while he crossed into the dark room to light two lanterns. One, the big man hung from a low beam above the small table, the other he held aloft as he moved about the cabin, holding an axe handle in the other hand. He shined the light into corners, along the walls, stopping to stamp his huge boot on the floorboards from time to time. He would stand still, an ear cocked, listening and at hearing only silence, continued his inspection. He went into the small bedroom and did the same, Serafina heard the scraping of furniture on the wood floorboards and several dull thumps of what she took to be the axe handle on bedding. After hanging the lantern in the center of the room, Yunk emerged with a shy smile on his face and waved Serafina to come in out of the night. He read the puzzled look on her face.

"Just checking for critters," he said. "Been awhile since folks stayed in this place and never know what's done crawled in and decided to call it home."

Serafina shook her head and gave him a shrug.

"Critters?" Yunk said, scratched at his beard. "Animals. Like…" he held up his hands like paws and gave her a bucktoothed impression of a squirrel or rat chomping on air. Then made a wiggling motion with his hand and arm. "Maybe snake. You know snake?"

Serafina's eyes grew wide then gave Yunk a scowl before she stepped backwards though the doorway onto the porch. She shook her head.

"No, no, it's fine. Really. I checked ever-wheres." He moved towards her and swept his arm around the room. "Ain't nothing here at all. I swear," he said, as he crossed his heart and raised a palm.

Yunk took the girl gently by the arm and led her into the cabin to the table where he pulled a chair out for her.

"Hold on," he said and went to grab a small towel from the rack above the sink. He beat the chair with the cloth and wiped the table off quickly. Then, like a waiter in a fancy restaurant, held the back of the chair and, his gap-toothed smile beaming, gave Serafina a bow and opened an arm towards the chair.

She smoothed her long skirt along the back of her thighs and sat while the big man slid the chair underneath her.

He slapped his hands together and rubbed his upper arms. "Need a fire started first thing. There's wood piled right out there on the end of the porch." Yunk went out and returned with an armload of splintered wood. He bent to the stone fireplace and had a roaring fire going in a matter of minutes. She got up and moved to the fireplace. Yunk hustled to the table and brought her chair, placing it in front of the fire.

"Imma git the rest from the truck, you git warmed up." And he rubbed his arms again and pointed to the fire.

Serafina nodded and sat gazing into the flames as she heard him clomp out onto the porch and down the steps. She was having a difficult time connecting the man involved in the murders at the grocery and her kidnapping with the gentle, shy bear who tended her now, away from his boss, Stallings. The truck door slammed, and the clomping came up the steps and across the porch into the cabin. She looked away from the hypnotic blaze and saw Yunk set a large box on the table.

"Got some groceries. You got to eat," he said and began to pull bundles and jars from the box. He placed them on the small shelves on the wall near the sink – a few cans of beans, a carton of eggs, a loaf a bread, some butter, a bag of coffee beans. He leaned past her and pulled out a butcher-wrapped bundle, undid the string and folded back the paper.

"I forgot, you don't speak English do ya, ma'am?"

Serafina smiled, arched an eyebrow at him. "I do, Mr. Yunk," she said.

"I ain't heard you say a damn thing since we took you," he said, then paused. "I mean, since this morning and all."

"There has not been much to say."

He stood holding a jar of tomatoes in each hand and looked down at the floor. She got the impression he might feel guilty or ashamed of what they'd done, something Stallings had not shown at all. That man seemed proud of the killings and pleased at taking Serafina as a prize of some sort in the deal.

"No, ma'am, I guess not," Yunk said and turned to place the jars on the shelf. He spoke without turning to her. "Mr. Stallings, sometimes he don't think about what he's going to do. He just does it. He wants me to come git you tomorrow and take you out to the Rooster. I guess you going to be working out there at his juke joint."

She shook her head.

"Juke joint is like a bar." He gestured raising a glass to his mouth. "Nightclub? They got music." He strummed an imaginary guitar, then played an equally invisible piano. "Dancing too." He held his arms up, holding a ghost partner and swayed back and forth a few times.

Serafina covered her mouth and giggled.

"Well, I guess that's a good thing," Yunk said. "Making a pretty lady laugh."

Serafina smiled and nodded.

"I better head on back before Mr. Stallings begins to wonder what happened to me," he said and picked up his Stetson hat from the chair. He studied the felt, brushed at the brim, then looked up at the young woman again, as if there was something he wanted or needed to say, but he shook his head in a silently contrary conclusion. He looked around the room. "It's safe out here, don't you worry. You rest. Keep that fire going best you can so they'll be some hot coals to start that stove up in the morning. Coffee grinder's there on the shelf." He went to the door and stepped out onto the porch. Serafina followed and stood in the doorway.

"*Grazi*, Mr. Yunk," she said.

"You don't need to be calling me Mr. Yunk, Miss Serafina. Yunk is just fine. Try not to be scared way out here," he said and he walked out into the dark.

But she knew there was no chance of that.

# 23

Sal was seated in the little sitting room. He absent-mindedly stirred a cup of espresso with a small spoon while reading a newspaper that was folded on the table. He looked up when Corky appeared in the doorway and, setting the spoon onto the saucer, turned in his chair to face Corky. He waved the boy over to the table and, looking him up and down, gave a satisfied nod. Corky looked at the floor, his cheeks flushing at the approval.

Sal came out of the chair and stood in front of Corky, who noticed the man was also dressed head to toe in new clothing. Sal brushed at the shoulders of the boy's jacket, then buttoned the top button of the collarless shirt.

"I like it with no collar, no tie," he said. "But keep the shirt buttoned, ok? It's more, *che si dice?* Sharp."

Corky's eyes sparkled with pride.

"Ok," Sal said, opening his arm towards the lobby and front entrance. "Let's go, *avante.*"

"Thank you, Sal," Corky said. "I never imagined I would have such a fine suit."

Sal dropped his hand on Corky's shoulder and, with his other, made the gesture of locking his own lips.

"The pleasure is all mine." He turned Corky towards the door and nudged him forward.

Outside, night had fallen with the rain slowing to a drizzling mist. The streets were ribboned with the shimmering reflection of the streetlights that lined Main Street. The twin rows of dark store fronts were broken on one side by the glowing windows of the hotel and, further down on the opposite side, the train station.

"Saturday night in Water Valley," Sal said. "Not quite New Orleans yet. But let's see what the good folks at this place the Blue Rooster call entertainment."

"The place Mr. Sugar told us about? I guess a juke joint is a nightclub?"

"Yes, like a nightclub," Sal said. He reached inside his jacket pocket and held up a piece of paper. "Mr. Tony was kind enough to give us directions." He tossed the paper onto Corky's lap. He put the car in gear and pulled from the curb, heading in the opposite direction from the hotel and station.

"I'm just a little curious," Sal said, as the streetlamps ended and the night closed in, the road glistening in the car's headlamps.

"About?" Corky asked.

"*Il capo.*"

Corky shrugged.

"This Stallings," Sal said. "The Boss."


The rain stopped as they drove north into the hill country. The wind had come up and clouds skittered across the three-quarter moon, the light coming and going like the sweeping beam of a lighthouse, the road fading in and out of view, the world plunging into a darkness so complete that at times it seemed impervious to the car's flickering headlamps. A wrong turn led them down a rutted track that dead-ended at a cattle gate. Sal cursed under his breath as he reversed the car out until he found a spot wide enough to turn around. They stopped once along the county road and Corky lit a match to study Mr. Tony's handwritten directions. The rear window yellowed with the lights of an approaching vehicle. It came to stop a few yards behind them, close enough to flood the inside of the car with light. Sal reached up to move the rearview mirror, adjusting it to divert the blinding light, his eyes shifting to the mirror outside his door. Corky looked over his shoulder and squinted into the brightness as the lights slowly swung out to the left, the vehicle moving to pass at a crawl. He saw Sal slide his right hand inside his coat and bring a revolver out which he laid against his chest, pointed towards the driver's side window. The lights passed to reveal it was a small truck and as it drew alongside, Corky leaned forward to see past Sal. Looking back from the inside of the cab were the unsmiling dark faces of three Negroes, two young men with a girl in between. Sal looked over his left shoulder and saw another two men pressed against the side of the truck bed, little more than a pair of white eyes in the dark. The truck inched past, the two in the back turning to sit with their backs against the cab, both raising a hand to shield their eyes from the headlights glare. There was a grinding of metal as the driver forced the truck into a lower gear when suddenly, as it still rolled forward, the passenger door swung open, and a young man stepped out onto the road to stand in the circle of headlights beam. The trucks taillights flared red, the brakes shrieking, as it jerked to a stop. The two men in the truck bed sat up but made no further move.

The young Negro standing in the road wore a dark red suit with thin white stripes, the jacket hanging open to reveal pleated trousers belted high on his waist and a white shirt with a wide tie. A fedora of the same color as the suit was tilted back on his head, the brim turned up in the front. He stood for moment, buttoning his jacket and then made a show of shooting his sleeves. He adjusted the knot of his tie and rolled his neck as he came towards the car, in a slow rolling stride. The girl appeared at the open door of the truck, her voice a loud demand as she called out to the man.

"Get yo black ass back in this goddamn truck," she said.

Otha raised a hand and continued his jaunty bounce forward. "Ain't nothing but a couple lost crackers," he shouted back over his shoulder.

"Watch that mouth, fool. Ain't no white man lost enough out here can't shoot your black ass." This from the driver, who was out of the truck, standing with his door swung wide. "Come on, Otha, let's git now."

Otha waved him off, then tapped his hand along Sal's fender as he passed. He tucked his other hand into the outside pocket of his jacket. Corky heard a loud click as Sal pulled the hammer back on the revolver he had slid from his shoulder holster. He tilted his head down, hiding his face beneath the wide brim of his hat. The Negro reached Sal's door, laid his arm on the roof above the window and bent down, his black face appearing a foot from Sal's own. He was young, his age betrayed by the wispy attempt at a mustache that the boy stroked as he tried to get an angle to see Sal's face. He then bent down further to look across at Corky, who figured the boy was not much older than he was. The Negro glanced into the rear seat checking to see if there was anyone else in the car. He straightened and looked at the truck. The girl was leaning out of the cab, the driver remained near his open door, one foot on the running board. The two in the bed had moved and were crouched at the tailgate.

"Don't want no trouble, O," said one of the boys in the back of the truck said. "Leave 'em be and let's get on down the road."

Otha scoffed and brought his face back down to the window. Sal took off his fedora and laid it on the seat, then turned to the boy. "We're not lost, my friend."

Otha cocked his head, his features scrunched in concentration as he studied Sal's face.

"You ain't no regular white folks by the looks of you," the boy said.

"We're Italians," Corky said, leaning into Sal, pushing his face towards the window.

Sal placed his hand on Corky's forearm and shook his head. Otha laughed.

"Folks around here don't see no difference," Otha said. "Got some other dark-skinned motherfuckers 'round here. Come from over in Jesus-land, Leb-O-Neese or some such. Whatever. Ain't white. Around here, colored is colored. Chineemens, they don't consider at all … rather have a pig living in the house than them heathen celestials, from what I can tell."

"Oooooothaaa," the girl called in a whine. He shot her a scowl and came back to the window shaking his head.

"We're looking for a place called the Blue Rooster," Corky said. "Supposed to be around here."

"Serious? That where you tryin' to git to?" Otha said and turned back to the truck. "Goddamn," he said. "Got us a couple lost tourists looking for The Rooster. What you think? We bring these colored boys along with us? Get they some Saturday jukin'. I know Boss Stallings don't mind. Colored money all the same to him." Four white smiles and laughs as much at Otha's routine as in relief, came from the truck. "All right then," Otha said and slapped the fender. "Rooster ain't far so all lost Italian coloreds follow the real coloreds." He leaned back and high-step strutted back to the truck.

"They really coming with us?" the girl asked him, looking back past his shoulder. "Cuz them boys is fine lookin'," she added with a wave towards the car. Otha frowned and gave her shove inside.

"Let's git to gittin'," he said and hopped onto the running board. He held on to the open door as the truck started moving and shouted, "We gone pitch us a wang dang doodle. Have us a ball." He leaned back and crowed like a rooster before sliding inside the truck. His red-sleeved arm appeared out of the window, waving Sal on.

Sal dropped the car into gear and followed, the two boys in the truck bed waving and smiling.

"That really what they think of us down here? That we're half nig … Negroes?" Corky said.

Sal tapped a finger on the steering wheel. "It is not just down here," he said. "But yes, many do."

"Like the man at the hotel? He had empty rooms, right? He wasn't going to let us stay there because we're Italian?"

Sal looked over at the boy and nodded.

"But we're not Negroes," Corky said.

"No, we're not," Sal said. "But to them, we are not white. Not as white as they are."

A minute passed in silence.

"Italians were the first people to come here after the Civil War," Sal said. "After the slaves were freed. Sicilians mostly, but paesani from the *Mezzogiorno*, too. They came to New Orleans and up into the Delta to work the plantations. Cotton, rice. Doing Negro work."

Corky looked down at the back of his hand, rubbed at the skin. There were no Negroes in his school. Other Italians, Polish kids, some Germans and the Swedes, like his friend Sonny. Most everyone with fathers who worked the mines. Men who came out of the mines coated in black dust and impossible to tell one from the other. Sonny's uncles and the German twins who went to his school, they were farmers. He thought about how his skin turned a deep brown in the summer. And how Sonny's fair skin turned nothing but bright red, his blonde hair becoming snow white by mid-summer. He never thought about there being a difference between them. Or his other schoolmates. They called each other wops, pollocks, humps, guineas, dagos, krauts. They told jokes about each other's backgrounds, but they all laughed equally, it seemed to him. There was no malice or hatred. The mines made them equals.

They followed the truck for another few miles until coming to a turnoff marked by a trio of lanterns hanging on a post. Moving slowly down the road tunneled by pines, they came upon people walking in the same direction, clustered in twos or threes, sometimes more, a few loners, all well dressed, men and women, all black faces with wide bright smiles, waving and calling out, moving to the side of the road to allow the vehicles to pass. A set of headlights appeared behind them, and the truck came up behind another truck, the bed carrying a half dozen passengers. Otha opened his door and stood on the running board, and shouted to a pair of young men who ran to the truck and jumped onto the back.

He banged a hand on the roof of the cab and let out his rooster crow as others joined in, the woods echoing with a half dozen others crowing in reply.

More people appeared, more cars and soon the road was choked with people in groups large and small moving towards the juke. Lights were strung in trees along the roadside and, off to the right, more flickered through the pines. There was a cut in the woods and the truck turned into the opening. People and another car came from the opposite direction, lanterns lining that road stretching into the dark.

They all moved with the crowd down a narrow road that emptied into a large clearing rung by more lights. In the center of the brightly lit circle was the Blue Rooster. A long low clapboard affair with a tin roof and fronted by a covered porch running the length of the building. Large lanterns hung along the porch roof. There was one large picture window to the side of the front door, painted black three-quarters of the way up, the juke's name in bright blue script across the blacked-out portion. Two dozen trucks and cars were parked at the edge of a gravel covered parking lot. People seemed to come from all direction, some from the road opposite, some appearing out of the woods.

Otha's truck disgorged its passengers, who brushed and straightened themselves, checking each other's appearances before moving towards the porch. Otha stopped, turned and motioned for the two Italians still sitting in their car to follow. Corky looked to Sal who shook his head and raised a forefinger signaling he wanted to wait a minute. Corky stuck his arm out the window and waved Otha to go on.

"See you inside," he shouted. Otha shrugged then trotted across the gravel-covered lot to catch his friends, playfully smacking the girl's bottom.

Near the far end of the porch, a few men were gathered around a fire pit passing a jar between them. They smoked cigarettes and elbowed each other as a couple of young women passed, arm in arm. One of the men said something, and the girls scuttled towards the door but leaned into each other giggling, one glancing back and smiling. There was some playful shoving between the men as the one who'd spoken broke from the group to follow the girls inside. A car pulled into the lot and parked at the far end of the line of vehicles. Two couples got out, looped arms and walked as a linked foursome across the lot, the men gallantly holding their dates hands as they stepped up onto the porch. One man held the door, giving the others a bow and sweeping his arm towards the entry, ushering them inside.

Sal tapped the steering wheel and pointed to the passenger door. The two got out of the car. Sal took his suit jacket off, handing it to Corky. He slipped the holsters off his shoulders and placed the revolvers under his overcoat on the back seat. He put his suit jacket back on and smoothed his lapels. "Ok, *avante! Musica, maestro,*" he said and pushed Corky in the direction of the juke joint.

Serafina stepped from the small kitchen at the rear of the Rooster's large single room. Smoke clouded the low ceiling in a layer of grey. The air was thick with the humidity of weather and the musky funk rising from the mass of close-packed bodies. Men and women sat grouped around a dozen tables and stood two-deep behind others seated at the bar that ran the length of the room on the left. Voices shrill and low mixed with laughs and squeals as jokes and teasing and boasts were born in the alcohol-fueled groups of workmates, friends, neighbors, enemies and competitors male and female in the courtships of a Saturday night.

She moved behind the bar and joined the Negro bartender serving the crowd. She enjoyed her time working at the Rooster. She lost herself in the work, treating it like a performance, savoring the time surrounded by the crowd, the noise, the music and the sounds of people having fun. Time away from the lonely hours sequestered in the cabin on the lake. Time away from being alone with Stallings.

Serafina greeted the men seated with a broad smile, reaching over the bar to touch hands, brushing off comments with a coquettish tilt of her head and sideways glance. She waved to women at tables, easy and familiar, stopping to sway her hips along with the raucous beat then strut a few steps as men whistled and fell against each other as she passed. She stopped, leaning to hear a request for drinks and went about pouring shots and beer chasers, pushing them across the bar, taking money and making change.

Turning back to the bar from pulling a couple of beers, she noticed the large Negro bouncer pass, heading to the back of the room where Yunk sat on a bar stool post of his own. She rarely saw the bouncer leave his post at the front door, other than to break up a fight. She scanned the room and found no commotion or threatening situation brewing. She glanced at the front door to see the unexpected sight of two well-dressed men she immediately recognized as Italians. The youngest of the two was staring straight at her, his eyes wide and his mouth open. Serafina smiled and shook her head. The reaction was one she was more than familiar with especially in younger men and boys, who got tongue-tied and seemed intimidated by her looks. The older of the pair merely glanced at her, expressionless, then looked past her.

Serafina turned and watched the Negro bouncer as he spoke into the big man's ear, and both looked back to the front door. Yunk nodded, got up from his stool and went to the kitchen door. He motioned someone over and Stallings appeared. The big man bent and as he spoke, Stallings looked to the front door with an expressionless face. After a minute's study, he nodded his head. Yunk gave a similar nod to the Negro bouncer who moved back through the room, the crowd parting. When he reached the front door, the bouncer leaned the axe handle against the stool and wagged his finger at Corky and Sal.

"Open yous coats wide," he said.

Corky followed Sal's lead and opened his jacket, raising his arms wide. The bouncer tapped at the jacket pockets, then ran his hands down their sides and around to the back of their waists. He crouched and patted their trousers down to their ankles and around the tops of their boots. He stood and pointed at their hats, and both lifted them off their heads. Satisfied, the bouncer stepped back and sat on his perch. He picked up his axe handle and poked it towards the rear of the room.

"Mr. Stallings says you have a nice time," he said. Corky looked to see the tall, white man he assumed was Stallings standing in the kitchen doorway, studying his fingernails.

"And me?" The bouncer said. "I'm saying you best behave yourselves. Got a big enough handful with this room full of folks getting they Saturday night on."

Sal gave the man a smile and tugged on his lapels, then each sleeve in turn, adjusting his jacket. His fingers touched the stiletto sheathed to his right forearm, a spot the bouncer had not bothered to check.

"We won't be any trouble," Corky said, bouncing on his feet, looking over the crowded room, his gaze returning to the woman behind the bar. The bouncer followed Corky's eye and tapped the axe handle on the floor.

"Miss Serafina may be one of you," he said. "But don't be gettin' no ideas 'bout her. She belong to Boss Stallings, you hear me? Now go on."

He jerked his thumb to the room and Sal pulled Corky through the crowd. At the bar, they sidled between two old men on stools hunched over their drinks. The men reared back, scowling at the intrusion but went blank at not seeing a black face. They swayed drunkenly and tilted to make room for the well-dressed newcomers.

"*Grazie*," Sal said, touching a finger to the brim of his fedora. The drunks cocked their heads, eyebrows lifting in consternation at the unfamiliar word. They kept their leans, avoiding contact, and went back to communing with their drinks.

Corky watched the woman work the crowded bar, pointing to the next in line, smiling as she moved her way up the bar towards the corner where Sal and Corky stood. She wiped the bar in front of Sal and, with a smile, lifted her chin to ask what he wanted.

"*Due birra,*" Sal said, raising two fingers. "*E due whiskeys, si prega.*"

Serafina eyes lit up at the sound of this handsome man speaking in Italian.

Serafina smiled at Sal then tilted her head at Corky. She arched an eyebrow in question. Sal glanced to the boy and back to Serafina, giving her the same chin and eyebrow.

"You're beautiful," Corky said, his face reddened. Sal looked over at Corky, whose eyes were fixed on the rounded curves of the woman's ample breasts. Corky felt a sharp jab to his ribs and broke his staring to meet Serafina's gaze. She rolled her eyes with a smile. His ears burned with embarrassment, and he turned to watch the crowd.

"It's ok," Sal said. "*Il ragazzo e piu vecchio di quanto sembri, bella.*"

The blue eyes rolled again but her smile disappeared as she looked over her shoulder to see Yunk on the stool watching her with a frown. She immediately started wiping the bar again then walked away to get the drinks Sal ordered.

The man on Sal's left turned, reared back, and looked him up and down with drunken eyes.

"What kinda tongue that you speakin'?" He asked and squinted, studying first Sal then Corky's face. "None you is white, is you?"

Corky looked at the man's creased black face and rheumy eyes, at his long spider-like fingers wrapped gently around the jelly jar in front of him on the bar.

"We are Italian," Corky said.

"Now don't that beat all?" the man said, his eyebrows lifting. "I done knows you weren't no white men, standing here in this place." He straightened up, lifting the jar, and waved it at the room, splashing what had remained of his drink onto the bar. "Nothin' but coloreds in here," he said to the room, his voice loud. He leaned forward to look past Sal at his friend, who scowled when he saw the bouncer glaring in their direction.

The second man shook his head. "Man, shut yo damn mouth," he said. "Actin' a fool. Don't need no attention from either one 'em big boys standin' guard. Black or white."

The first old man huffed and took to staring into his empty glass.

Serafina returned with two bottles and two small jelly jars in her hands, a brown bottle tucked under her arm. She gave Corky a wide smile, and he dropped his gaze and blushed. She set the beer bottles on the bar along with the jars, which she filled with the clear shine from the brown bottle.

"Two five tee," she said, her eyes on the bar.

"*Scuzi?*" Sal said.

"Two five tee" she repeated a bit louder, the impatience clear in her tone.

Sal arched an eyebrow and grinned, lowering his head slightly and leaning towards her. "*Vuoi due cinquanta, faccia divina?*" Serafina rolled her eyes, then looked away, shaking her head but Sal saw the flush rise on her cheeks. She turned back, a smirk on her face.

"*Si, due cinquanta,*" she said. "Two five tee."

Sal held up his palms in surrender, then pulled a fold of bills from his pocket, peeled off three singles and laid them on the bar. Serafina scooped them up and reached into the pocket of her apron, fishing for coins. Sal shook his head and wagged his finger no. She smiled and turned to serve other customers. Corky watched as Serafina moved away, transfixed by the movement of her curves under the thin dress. Sal gave him another elbow to the ribs and a smile. He passed a beer and whiskey off to Corky, then directed his attention with a tilt of the head. Corky turned to see Otha at a table, waving them over. His other hand was resting on the back of an empty chair at a small table next to where he and his friends sat. The table was being cleared of plates and jars by a young Negro. Otha waved and pointed to the empty table. Corky and Sal made their way across the room. When they reached the table, Otha pulled the girl at his table to her feet.

"This my girl, Lena," Otha said. He pointed to the Italians in turn. "That's Sal and that young blood is Corky." The girl smiled and held out her hand. Sal took it, gave her a slight bow.

"*Piacere mio, bella,*" he said. Lena's eyes brightened and she nodded her head in return. "Ooh, Otha," she said. "I don't know what he said but I like it." She turned her attention to Corky, who gave her a slight wave. He was taken by the young girl's beauty. Different than any woman he'd seen. Lena was slight but her thin dress did little to hide the ample curves underneath. She wore her hair short and marcelled in slick curls that framed around face, skin dark, smooth and flawless. Corky thought she looked like the movie star, Josephine Baker, and his heart banged in his chest.

Otha jerked his head towards the corner of the juke where a young man was lifting a guitar out of a battered case.

"That guitar player is my cousin, Robert," he said with pride in his voice. "He's the finest guitar player there is. Believe me, Robert Johnson's goin' raise a ruckus in this joint. Light the Rooster up, you wait. Folks be dancing all night."

Corky watched Otha's cousin move a chair to the corner and sit. He was thin, dressed in a tailored pinstriped suit, a fedora cocked back on his head, cigarette dangling from his mouth. He strummed the guitar. A few chords rang out, then Robert proceeded to tune his instrument. The notes were soft, barely audible. Corky wondered how one person could make enough sound to get a room full of people dancing, let alone raise a ruckus, whatever that meant.

People stood, drained their bottles of beer, their jars of whiskey, moved away from their tables and gathered on the small open area in front of where Robert sat. Some swayed in anticipation of the music, some clapped while others hooted and shouted Robert's name.

"Play that git box, Robert." "Shake it on down, son." A woman cried out, "Oh lord that boy is fine."

Lena stood in front of Otha.

"Time to dance, baby," she said and shook her hips. As Otha was dragged out of his chair and towards the dance floor, he turned to Sal and Corky and let out a rooster crow. Robert looked at his audience, smiled and waved his left hand in the air.

"All right you," he said. His voice loud and clear. "I want to see some hip shakin' from you tonight."

The crowd cheered. Corky angled to find a clear view of Robert and watched as the guitar player bent down, hunkered over his instrument. His head bobbed in time to the tapping of his foot. With his right hand, he thumped the beat on the guitar's wooden top. Corky amazed at the how loud it was. The crowd started to bounce in rhythm as Robert began to play a repetitive few notes on the bottom, lower strings. A flurry of high notes rang out on top of the riff, sounding all the world like two guitarists were playing. Corky craned his neck, raised up on his toes to try to see how Robert was making all that sound.

The floor quaked with the foot-stomping beat of the music coming from Robert's guitar while a dozen partners moved in a shoulder-shimmying, hip-shaking dance. The Rooster was vibrating, the air felt electrified. Corky watched the dancers, their bodies sliding and bumping together, the women turning to their partners, round buttocks bouncing with a life of their own underneath beaded dresses. Robert lifted his head, tilted back and began to sing along with his playing.

"Every time I'm walking, all down the street. Some pretty mommas start breaking down on me. Stop breaking down."

Shouts of encouragement and screams of joy came from the crowd. Lena danced in front of Otha, her eyes closed, her lithe body undulating with feline grace. She turned away from him, glanced back over her shoulder with half-lidded eyes. A smile came across her lips as she took the cloth of the thin dress in her fingers and slowly raised the hem, inching it upwards from her knees to stop a scant tantalizing inch from revealing herself. When she saw the look on Otha's face, a mix of surprise and lust, she dropped the hem and twirled away. The guitar player's song giving voice to Otha's thoughts.

"Baby, please, stop breaking down."

Corky looked to Sal who sat smiling, his head nodding to the beat. The boy beamed back and swayed his hips in imitation of the dancer. Sal raised his beer.

"Stuff I got bust your brains out baby. Make you lose your mind."

Sal slid around the table to sit with his back to the corner, positioned to see the entire room. Corky remained standing, beer in one hand, whiskey in the other, losing himself in the music, the shouts of joy from the dancers, the stomping feet and pounding rhythms shaking the dance floor, rising through his feet into his heart. Into his soul. Here in this most foreign of places, how familiar it all seemed. The unleashed joy and passion. No different than the family gatherings in Sagamore celebrating holidays, birthdays, marriages, and funerals. Music, food, drink all wrapped up in a release, a temporary escape from the pain, misery of hard labor and no way out.

Sal raised his bottle and reached across the table and tapped it against the one in Corky's hand. They saluted each other and drank. Corky sat and shouted above the music.

"This is amazing" he said. "That guitar player is incredible, making this place dance all by himself." His legs bounced as his eyes darted around the room, then back to smile at Sal as he took another long swig of the beer.

Sal pointed to the jar of shine and Corky grinned, and they raised their jars to each other. Sal sipped but Corky threw his back, emptying the jar. He swallowed and coughed, his face turning red, eyes watering, his entire body convulsed. He turned to Sal.

"What is that stuff?" he asked.

"Not like yours?" Sal said.

"Hell no," Corky said, wiping his eyes with the back of his hand. "Tastes like gasoline."

"Might be," Sal said. "Definitely not what we had from Mr. Sugar this morning."

Corky puffed a few hard breaths to cool the fire in his mouth and the burning in the middle of his chest, then drained half his beer.

"I could teach these folks how to make whiskey," he said, then pushed the empty jar away. "Because that's not what that crap is."

Sal sniffed at his jar, took another sip, and winced. He set it down and nudged it to the center of the table. The music stopped, Otha's cousin the guitar player stood and shouted above the crowd that he was "taking a pause for the cause. Be right back in a few minutes." He hunkered over his guitar, tuning his instrument while his gaze swept the room. The crowd milled away from the dance floor, men stepping to the bar, women going to the tables, while groups of both went outside for fresh air or to find the outhouses.

Otha wiggled through the crowd and pulled his chair from the next table to sit with Corky and Sal. "You enjoying yourselves?" he asked.

"This place is great," Corky said. "But what the hell is this stuff they selling as whiskey?"

Otha eyed Corky then looked at Sal, pointed to the jar and arched an eyebrow. Sal smiled and nodded. Otha picked it up and threw the contents back in one gulp. He wiped his lips with his long fingers. "Ain't all that bad."

Corky's head humming from the alcohol, but he sobered when he saw Stallings coming their way. The man stopped at the table where Otha's friends were gathered and brushed up close to Lena, whispering into her ear. Her eyes widened, her mouth tightened, and she stiffened. Corky couldn't see but guessed from the girl's reactions that Stallings had his hand on her ass, or possibly a more intimate place. She turned her head towards Stallings and gave him a scowl and shrugged away. The man brushed past her and continued his way towards the table. Corky saw the shift in Sal's eyes and how his face hardened as he watched Stallings. Otha caught the two looking past him and turned to look over his shoulder. At the sight of Stalling coming their way, his head jerked back to the table.

"Shit," he said, just above a whisper. He grabbed Corky's arm and stood, pulling the boy up out of his seat. "Come on, let's get some air, take a piss or something."

Stallings came up behind Otha and clapped a hand on his shoulder. He looked only at Sal as he spoke. "Don't leave on my account, boy."

"No sir, Mr. Stallings," Otha said, his voice soft without a hint of his usual wise-acre tone. "Just taking this one outside so we can, y'know, get rid of some of this beer we all been drinking."

Stallings nodded and smiled, still directly at Sal. Otha started to step away, but Stallings gripped his shoulder tighter and half turned him around.

"Boy, that's one fine-looking girl you brought in here with you tonight. That your woman?"

Otha's jaw pulsed. "We friends."

"Friends is all?" Stallings asked. "Well, you bring her around any time, hear me?"

Otha's entire body pulsed. Corky saw his hands balling into fists at his side. He glanced at Sal, who gave him a barely perceptible head shake warning against any action.

Otha nodded his head. "She like to dance so I bring her back, yes sir, no problem with that at all."

"Good boy," Stallings said and released his grip. "You go do what you need to do. Just having a word with this one here." The man watched Sal's face for a reaction to the insult but saw no change in Sal's expression. Otha stepped away and tugged at Corky's arm to follow but the boy didn't move from the table. Stallings ignored them, his gaze locked on Sal.

"You staying at Fratesi's in Water Valley, I hear," Stallings said. "I'm just wondering what two slicked up, obvious out-of-towners are doing in this part of Mississippi and coming out here to The Rooster, of all places."

"We are just passing through," Sal said.

"Passing through, that right?" Stallings said. "How about telling me from where to where."

Sal let the question hang in the air. Stallings' visage darkened. "You sitting in my joint,' he said. "Now I asked you a question."

"New Orleans," Corky said, almost a shout. Sal shot him a look that was not missed by Stallings, who smiled.

"Nawlins," Stallings said. "Now that is one helluva town. Man can have himself too much fun down there. A bit too many of your kind there now for me. They let them run businesses and taking work from the white folk in Louisiana. Don't know why they let that happen. But they did manage to lynch a bunch of wops awhile back. Strung up almost dozen, if recall correctly, for killing a chief of police, I believe it was. Animals. Didn't seem to do much good though. Place is thick with your people so you two will fit right in down there with those nice clothes."

"Animals?" Corky said, heat rising on his face. "Those men were innocent. They were dragged from the jail by a lynch mob and hung in front of the damn courthouse."

Otha grabbed his arm and pulled, but Corky stood his ground. Stallings turned to Corky, raised a finger, and wagged it in the boy's face. Corky stepped back and edged beside Sal, who sat expressionless. Stallings shook his head and closed his eyes, as if counting to dampen his rage. Sal slid his right arm off the table. Corky felt a slight tap on his leg and glanced down to see Sal had let the stiletto he carried in his sleeve drop into his hand. Corky's pulse raced.

Stallings eyes popped open, and he turned back to Sal, grinning. "You know why Italian men have mustaches?"

Sal arched an eyebrow but said nothing.

"So, they can look like their mommas," he said and cackled, eyes on Sal, who smiled but his eyes held menace. "Well, you enjoy yourselves tonight," the club owner said, suddenly putting on a broader Southern accent. "Try some of the fried chicken. Nothin' like it nowhere. Got us a real country cook back there knows how to do it good, ain't that right, Otha?" He waited for a reply without shifting his eyes from Sal.

"You right, Mr. Stallings," Otha said. "Real good."

"Be a shame not to get yourself some," Stallings said. "Since you just passin' through like you say. Going to Nawlins and not likely at all to be back this way again, having done all the sight-seeing there is to be done around here."

"Perhaps we will," Sal said. He left it for Stallings to decipher whether he meant trying the chicken or returning. Stallings pointed to the empty jars.

"Looks like you could use another round," the owner said. "Got plenty more where that came from." He held Sal's stare for a minute longer, then turned to walk back through the crowd. Sal brought his arm up to rest on the table, his hand empty. The trio watched as Stallings edged past Otha's table, where the girl had slid behind her friends to avoid the owner's touch. The man gave her a cool smile and a wink as he passed.

"That motherfucker," Otha said, in a hoarse whisper and turned to Corky. "Come on, fool. Let's get you outside and hope some fresh air pumps some sense into that fucked-up head of yours. Gone get all our asses whopped or worse stepping to that man." He turned to Sal. "All yous crazy or stupid or what?" Otha shook his head and yanked Corky away from the table. As they went towards the door, Corky saw Serafina watching, her gaze shifting from him to Sal to Stallings. The owner stopped to say something to the big man on the stool. Both men looked towards the corner table before Stallings disappeared into the kitchen. Corky glanced back at Sal, who sat sipping from his beer. As he followed Otha through the front door, he marveled at Sal looking no more worried than he had been sitting in the rocker on the porch that morning, watching the world go by.

# 25

Yunk stepped out of the doorway to make room as Serafina slid past him. She smiled at the big man, but the warmth fled her face at seeing Stallings in the small room off the kitchen he used as an office. Seated behind a wooden desk, he was writing in a notebook, his lips moving as his pencil jiggled across the page. Without a word, she went to a low cupboard, swung the doors open to reveal neat rows of tall bottles. She knelt and began to pull the ones she needed for the bar. Yunk stood leaning against the wall just inside the kitchen door, the butt end of the shotgun nestled on his hip, barrel pointed at the ceiling. His head swiveled from watching his boss to looking out through the kitchen to keep an eye on the Rooster crowd.

"Saw you had a word with them Italians," Yunk said, directing his words towards his boss. "What's their story?"

"Said they are passin' through," Stallings said without looking up. "Just lookin' for a little distraction and staying at that Italian's place. Said Fratesi sent them out here."

Yunk grunted.

"What's that, Yunk? You don't believe what that boy told me? Think they got something else in mind, showing' up in Yalobusha, dressed like city slickers and all? Railroad's bringing all kinds through here now. You got Fratesi with his hotel up the colored end of town and his brother opening that bakery on Main Street. There's Fratesis all over the Delta now. Breeding like rabbits, these greaseballs. Everywhere, like cockroaches. Can't seem to keep 'em out."

"Some ain't so bad, Larkin," Yunk said, watching Serafina, who looked up and gave the big man a warm smile.

"Says who?" Stallings said. He looked up at Yunk but was addressing Serafina. "Got a couple, how you say it? Pie-zah-nee out there tonight. Sharp dressers too. Know them boys, darlin' girl?"

Serafina clanked a couple bottles together, ignoring the question.

"Said they just passing' through, ain't that right, Yunk?"

"Yessir, I believe that's what you said. Passin' through."

"On the way to Nawlins," Stallings said.

The girl stopped what she was doing but didn't turn around.

"That got your attention, didn't it?" Stallings dropped his pencil and leaned back stretching his arms over his head. "Don't you worry, one these days I'll get us down to Crescent City for some fun."

Serafina said nothing and went about lining the bottles on top of the cupboard. Stallings shook his head, looked at Yunk who shrugged in return. The Rooster owner picked up the pencil and poked it towards the bottles.

"They are really drinking it up out there tonight, ain't they?"

She nodded her head. "*Si signore'.*"

Stallings shook his head and spoke to Yunk, his eyes on the girl.

"Why'd do I always get the feeling," Stallings said, "she understands and talks better American than that?"

Yunk and Serafina's eyes met briefly, but she gave the two men a disarming smile, shrugged and shook her head like she didn't understand what Stallings had said. She set the bottles with the others on the top of the cupboard. Without comment or looking at Stallings, she pushed away from the cupboard and went to the rear of the kitchen. She opened the door that led to the back porch and a path to the Rooster's outhouses. She stepped through when Stallings barked.

"The hell you going?"

Serafina turned and gave the man a look of exasperation, waiting for the reason to register.

"Oh," Stallings said, "Go do your business. Leave that door open. It's getting damn close in here." He picked up the pencil and went back to his accounting.

Seraphina went out, leaving the door wide. She sat in a chair against the outside wall, kicked off her shoes and massaged her left foot. The routine of long hours was wearing and by this time each night she began to long to fill the tub in the cabin with steaming hot water and sink herself in to the chin. Leaning her head back against the wall, she reached into the pocket of her dress to touch the straight razor she always carried. The time wasn't right yet, she knew. She needed money and a way out of Mississippi. A whisper came to her lips.

*Presto. Ti uccidero'.*

Soon. I will kill you.


Corky followed Otha past the parked cars until they reached the edge of the clearing. The pair stood facing the woods, back to the Rooster, unbuttoned their trousers and drained their beer-filled bladders. Corky leaned one hand on a tree.

"You need to watch your mouth around that man," Otha said, above the splashing of the streams on the already waterlogged ground. "He's one dangerous white man."

"Makes him so dangerous?"

"You seen his eyes when he look at you? Otha asked. "There's some evil in them eyes, son. When he give you that hard stare, ain't like he's threatening you with death. That man is death. Take what he want, when he want it. Don't matter none if it means killing you, me, or any damn body to get it. Like that fine lookin' Italian girl he got in there?"

"The one with the blue eyes?" Corky asked.

"All you noticed was her eyes, huh?" Otha laughed, tucking himself back in his pants and buttoning them. Corky did the same. They remained facing the woods and Otha kept talking.

"You see that scar she got?" Otha asked. "One right down her jaw."

Corky shook his head.

"Too busy noticing other things 'bout her," Otha said. "Rumor is Stallings gave her that. Don't know if that's true but not impossible with that man. Word is he killed two of yous over in the Delta. In some joint around Rosedale and brought that girl back with him."

"Yous meaning Italians? He killed two Italians?"

"That's what they say. Took over the place and turned it into a juke joint."

"And he kidnapped that girl?"

"If that's what you call it," Otha said. "When someone just shoots the men she with and make her yours. Put her to work behind the bar and doing whatever else he doing with her."

"What do you mean? What else? Like she's …"

"What else you think he gone to be doing with a fine-looking woman like that he keeps out in some cabin all by herself?"

Corky turned around and looked at The Rooster. He didn't like what he was hearing and, although it was difficult to guess, thought Sal would probably like it even less.

"Where's this cabin?" Corky asked.

"Out by the big lake west of here," Otha said. "Sardis, they call it." He pointed towards the cut in the woods and the road that led to the Rooster. "You go out and turn right. Follow that road about five miles. There's a big sign pointing to the lake. Take that left and the road loops around the entire lake. Cabin's out on that road somewhere."

"And he just gets away with it?" Corky asked. "Kidnapping her? Murdering people?"

Otha snorted. "What you think? You need to get it through that thick dago skull that around here, killing anything but a white man, shootin' one of us or," Otha said and pushed Corky to get him to look at his face, "one of you folks. They won't consider it murder. You remember that. Just smile and give that man plenty of room so he just walk on by."

The sky split, lightning turned the parking lot and clearing into day for a second, thunder boomed, and a slow splattering of fat drops like the soft crackling of hot oil began. Otha jerked his head towards the Rooster and they both ran, shoulders hunched, across the lot and onto the porch. The rain came harder, others came running from out of the dark, shook themselves off and went inside. Corky and Otha moved to a corner of the porch, the nickel-sized drops drumming the tin roof and slapping the gravel and surface of gathering puddles.

"This place ever do anything but rain?" Corky asked.

"Most rain I ever seen, and they say more is coming," Otha said. "Places up north are flooded. Streets in Memphis underwater. Some places in Missouri."

"How you know that?"

Otha scowled. "The news-pay-per," he said, exaggerating the syllables like he was talking to a three-year-old.

"I didn't mean," Corky said and stopped.

"You didn't what? Think I can't read or something?"

"I don't know what I meant," Corky said. "Sorry, I didn't mean or think you couldn't read."

Otha shook his head. "I read newspapers every day," he said. "Morning one from Memphis and the later one from Jackson. So, I know there's more to the world than what goes on in the damn Delta and Yalobusha County."

Corky fell silent, embarrassed, searching for a way to change the subject. He felt relieved of his weight when the guitar player quick stepped up onto the porch and joined them. Otha's face lit up and he clapped his hands.

"Look what come in out the rain," he said. "This one here thinks he made of sugar and might melt if he get a little wet."

"Hey cousin," Robert said and wrapped his arms around Otha. "Thought I might see your ass out here tonight." He stepped back, looked Otha up and down and whistled. "Damn, that is one fine looking suit you got on."

"Looking pretty natty your own self," Otha said. He made a show of brushing the shoulders and straightening the lapels of his cousin's dark pinstriped suit.

Robert cocked his head towards Corky. "Who we got here, cuz?" he said. "Another sharp dressed man."

"This my friend, Corky," Otha said. "He travelin' through on his way to Nawlins. Came out to get some juke joint on him."

"You got white friends, now?" Robert said, eyeing Corky's face. "Wait now, you ain't quite white neither. You got colored blood, Mr. Corky?"

"He's Italian," Otha said. "Which makes him half colored at least."

"Ain't no half measure nothin' in Mississippi," the guitar player said. "Oh, you just colored to folks around here." He brought his hand up to tip his hat. "Welcome to The Sipp."

Corky's eyes widened at the long, slender fingers that spidered the brim of guitarist's fedora. He glanced down at his own hands, which he had been told were large for someone his size. The guitarist's fingers appeared twice the length of his own.

"You play great," Corky said. "I've never heard anything like it."

"And you won't ever again, lessen it's me you hearin'," Robert said, a wide grin on his face. "Ain't no brag. Just fact. One these days soon, I'm get myself a record deal and record my own songs. Robert Johnson be on every jukebox and radio in the South."

"I sure do believe it," Otha said. "You play that box like the Devil himself taught you."

"Now what if I told you," Robert said. "That I did in fact, meet up with old Legba at the crossroads. Make him a little promise, then give him my guitar, let him tune it up and show me a thing or two?"

Both Otha and Corky began to laugh at the idea of Robert selling his soul to the devil to learn how to play so well but cut it short when seeing the serious look on the guitarist's face.

A big man lumbered up onto the porch. He wore overalls with a stained t-shirt underneath, sweat poured from his brow.

"Hey guitar man," he said and pointed a fat finger at Robert. The man stood a good head taller than Robert and outweighed him by seventy-five pounds at least. The guitar player's face was a blank. "Boy, I seen the way you lookin' at my wife, given her them winks and smilin' at her. You stay away from her, ya hear me." The man raised a balled up ham hock of a fist and shook it in Robert's face. "I'll knock you out, son. Hit you so hard, put you out so long when your skinny ass wakes up that fancy suit be outta style."

Robert pulled on his cigarette, the glow glinted off his dark eyes. "Man, you got that pretty gal in there shakin' her hips and that fine booty all around. How a man not supposed to admire God's own handiwork in all its glory right in front his eyes? Can't help but get to thinkin' about that sweet thing." Robert smiled, took another drag.

"Listen, guitar man." Big man said. "Best get them thoughts out your mind and your tiny pecker in those pants. I swear, I catch you near her, I'll cut that pecker off and feed it to my chickens. Ain't no threat. That's a promise."

Robert tilted his head back and blew smoke towards the porch roof. "Big man," he said. "You got nothin' to worry about. You get no trouble from me. So you go on back inside, have some more that good 'shine and I be in there playing good songs for you to dance with your woman."

The big man snorted, puffed his chest, pulling on the strap of his worn denim overalls. He turned and, like a big rooster, cock-walked into the juke.

Robert flicked his cigarette in the man's direction and stood looking at the

Rooster's front door. "That dumb ass farmer is going to be face down in the mud drunk in short order and I'm going to show his pretty wife how a guitar player can make her sing in ways she never knew," he said as much a threat as a promise.

"You going to get yourself killed one of these days, cousin," Otha said. "You going to mess with the wrong girl and some man going to come get even."

Robert's gaze came back and landed on Otha. "Devil going to come get his due in his own sweet time. Now I seen you inside getting an earful from the boss man," he said.

"Weren't nothin'," Otha said.

"Ain't never nothin' when you get that man up in your face," the guitar player said.

"What I tell you," Otha said, looking at Corky.

"That man done killed more than his share," the guitar player said. "Don't make no difference if folks know he the one done it or not." Robert paused to fish a crumbled pack of cigarettes from his suit jacket. He got one lit and continued, smoke rolling from his mouth as he spoke. "Hell, he killed a damn deputy over in Lafayette County. Nothing but a kid, new on the job, didn't know no better and the fool tried to pull Stallings over for speeding through Oxford town square. When his culprit told him to fuck off and started to drive away, story goes the deputy tried to stop him by jumping on the running board of the truck and laid his hand on the man's shoulder. Stallings put two bullets in that law man's face, then stopped, reversed over the body, then forward to run him over again and drove on home."

"That can't be true," Corky said. "He killed a deputy? And got away with it? What about the sheriff?"

The guitarist's high-pitched cackle keened off the tin roof. "Hey cousin," he said to Otha. "You tell me what turnip truck this tourist fell off of so I can stay the hell away from it?" He looked at Corky. "Where you think you are? That man owns this entire hill country." He waved his cigarette in the air. "Sheriff did nothing more than ship that dumb ass deputy's body home to Helena, telling the grieving parents it was a hit and run, with no witnesses or clues as to the killer."

When he saw the look of puzzlement on Corky's face, Robert shook his head in disgusted disbelief at the boy's naïveté. "Even if they did arrest him and somehow, some way managed to get his ass into a courtroom? Finding twelve men willing to sit in a jury box facing that man is not going to happen in Lafayette, Yalobusha or the next three surrounding counties. Ain't no way in hell anyone's doing that if they want to live."

Corky was silent, trying to comprehend the behind-the-curtains view of how things worked, the view he had been exposed to both in Sagamore and now here in Mississippi. The rules as he had been taught were not the rules at all. And following those rules did not lead to any kind of reward or fairness.

The noise of the crowd inside swelled as their patience wore thin waiting for the music to start up. Robert dropped his cigarette and ground it out under a twisting boot.

"You keep in mind what I said about Stallings, y'hear me?" he said. "No reason to be messing with no granddaddy cotton-mouth like that." He made the gesture of playing his instrument. "Time to work some magic on some of them fine ladies inside." With a wink, he went inside.

Corky looked past Otha, out the parking lot, to the tree line and the tumbling, emptying black clouds above. He wanted to be home, in the kitchen, watching his father bathe. Missing the silence. Suddenly yearning for the old man's presence and the comfort of the quiet between them.

"I'll tell you some more truth," Otha said. He went quiet as a knot of people pushed past, shaking off the rain and waiting until they were inside to speak. "Stallings?"

"Yeah," Corky said then heard Otha say words that were in his own head.

"That man needs to die."

# 26

Serafina leaned back against the wall next to the door. The Rooster closed in an hour at 1 a.m. No doubt the place could stay open until dawn, but Stallings told her there were two reasons for the closing time. It was partially to appease the town's church leaders so there were more in attendance and fewer drunks at Sunday morning services - a small concession that he used for leverage to keep his business running without interference. More importantly, he had learned over the years that the heavy drinking – and flow of money – happened in the earlier evening and peaked in the hour after midnight. The extra hours weren't worth the trouble and bloodshed. Nothing good happened after that hour in the morning, he said.

The other jukes and the shiners shut down an hour earlier so that the money could be delivered to the Rooster shortly after it closed. Stallings had an iron-clad rule that all drops had to be done before 2 a.m. He tolerated no excuses for missing the deadline, he had explained one night that he lingered longer at the cabin, more loquacious than usual. Any man who arrived at the Rooster past the deadline would find the juke closed tight and the parking lot empty until the headlights of Yunk's truck would come on, suddenly appearing out of the dark, sitting behind the offender, blocking the way out and any hope of escaping the punishment for being late.

"They get a beating and a warning," Stallings said. "They keep the job, don't be late a second time because there will be no second warning and you'd wish that a beating was all you got."

Serafina hadn't witnessed a single late arrival for a drop in the many Saturdays since she'd been brought to the Rooster.

Yunk would always stay until all the drops were made. Once the juke managers and still runners had come and gone, while Stallings counted the money, the big man made his rounds, checking the parking lot, the privies and locking all but the front door. By the time he returned to the office, Stallings would be finished with his bookkeeping and the money stashed in a large leather satchel which he and he alone laid hands on. The owner waved off any attempt by the big man to walk him to his car. Stallings would pull his jacket back to show the revolver tucked in his waistband. "Ain't nobody stupid enough to try, Yunk." He left it to Yunk to lock up and, with the leather satchel in one hand and his other guiding Serafina, put both in the car and drove to the cabin on the lake at close to 4 in the morning.

She knew there was another reason for the deadline. Stallings needed some time for "windin' it down," as he put it, before calling it a night and going home to his wife for a few hours of sleep before rising to shower, dress and appear at church. The infamous bad man, Larkin Stallings, playing the role of family man for all the town to see early Sunday morning. He did this every week without fail.

This was the routine Serafina was counting on as she worked out her plan. A plan she would tell the handsome Italian inside the Rooster. A plan that would make them rich and Stallings dead. Serafina returned, crossed the small room and began to gather the bottles of liquor in her arms. Stallings eyed the woman, smiled, and without shifting his gaze, spoke.

"Thought you get lost or fell in or something," he said. "Don't think I'd be jumping in there to save you." He turned to Yunk. The big man joined in the laughter but was cut short by the hard stare he got from Serafina.

Shouting came from the barroom, the sound of glass breaking and the howling of the suddenly wounded joined by a few high-pitched screams.

"Goddamn," Stallings said. "Can't we have one night without these crazy motherfuckers tryin' to kill each other?" He jumped up and strode from behind the desk and through the door with Yunk at his heels. The big man glanced back at Serafina and, before going out the door said, "Just wait here."

She set the bottles down on the desk and, moved around to the back, opening drawers until she found a piece of paper. She took the pencil and bent to write furiously. More shouting and crashing, Stalling's voice above the rest, demanding an end to the fighting. She glanced up to check the door and went back to writing. Finishing, she dropped the pencil and scanned the paper. She added a few more scribbles, then, satisfied, she folded it several times and stuck it in the pocket of her apron. She had just moved back around and gathered up the bottles again when the bartender appeared in the doorway, his hands filled with bloody bar rags.

"Why these fools always got to be cutting each other? Breaking bottles and swingin' straight razors on one of there own? Like they ain't got enough trouble in their miserable lives without tryin' to kill each other over a damn woman or a drink." He shook his head and moved back into the kitchen and tossed the rags in a tall bucket in the corner. He called back to Serafina.

"You come out now, Miss Fina," the bartender said. "Boss Stallings and Mr. Yunk done took 'em outside."

Serafina went out of the kitchen to behind the bar. The music was going again, the dance floor packed, filling the hole that the fight caused as if it never happened. She set the bottles behind the bar, nudging the bartender, and pointing where she placed them before taking one in each hand and rather than working the bar, began moving through the room, table by table, offering to fill empty jars or top off others. She checked the back door for Stallings' return, but it remained closed, and she side-stepped a couple tables, ignoring the waves and shouts for her to stop and pour, and went straight to the back corner where Sal sat alone. She came to the table and glanced over her shoulder to the back door, then positioned herself so she blocked the table from that direction with her body. Sal smiled at her but rested his hand on top of the empty jars and shook his head.

"No, *grazie, bella,*" he said.

Serafina felt her cheeks flush. She tilted her head and smacked his hand away, quickly filling both jars, then reached into her apron pocket as if she was searching for change. She laid her palm flat on the table and slid her hand towards Sal, telling him with his eyes to take what was underneath. He covered her hand with his and held it tight against the table. She looked up and met his eyes and the smile underneath. She tried to pull her hand back, but he pressed down to keep it where it was, caught under his own. A shout for her to bring the whiskey bottle came from a nearby table. Again, she tried to retrieve her hand, but he held on, a teasing grin on his face now, daring her to keep trying. She shook her head and gave him a pout, playing along until she saw Sal's eyes dart past her. His smile fled and he released her hand. She turned and saw Stallings come through the back door and was talking with Yunk as his eyes scanned the room. Serafina jerked her hand back, and turned from Sal's table, stepping quickly to the next table. She called for the men to raise their empty jars to fill and gesturing for them to get their money out by rubbing her thumb and fingers together.

Corky and Otha arrived at the table, both suit jackets dappled with dark spots from the rain. They flopped into chairs and without asking, reached for the jars. Otha's friends were gathered about the other table, faces serious, all eyes looking straight at him. The girl's eyes pleading. Corky glanced at the kitchen opening to where Stallings was leaning, a wry smile on his face, staring back at him. Otha tensed when he saw Stallings push off the wall and make his way towards the table. Otha turned, nodded to Sal, and squeezed Corky's upper arm then stood.

"Didn't say how long you staying around," Otha said. "Come on back next Saturday." He tipped his hat to Sal. He turned to Corky. "And this one? He needs to open that head up. Read some newspapers or something."

They both laughed. Corky watched as Otha walked to his friends. All four leaned into together, talking low. Otha said something that set his friends into motion, standing up, gathering coats, raising bottles and jars, draining what remained. But before they started to move away from the table, Stallings appeared.

"Can't be leaving so soon. We haven't had a dance yet." He grabbed the girl's arm and started pulling her towards the dance floor. She tried to free herself from his grip but couldn't. She turned, her eyes wide, and called for Otha. Without thinking, Otha stepped towards Stallings and said, "She don't want to dance."

Stallings stopped and turned, "What you say to me, boy?"

Rage overtook his fear and Otha spit out the words again.

"I said, she do not want to dance. We just leaving."

Stallings face darkened. In one swift motion, he pulled a pistol from his belt and back handed it across Otha's face, splitting his cheek and knocking the hat off his head. Otha staggered back and the juke owner moved in closer and brought the gun down on his head, dropping him to his knees. Corky jumped to his feet but Sal grabbed his arm, pulled him back down into his chair. Stallings pushed the girl towards the group of friends who stood edging away from the table. He bent down and grabbed Otha, jerking his head back.

"You wasn't one of my favorite colored boys," Stallings said, "you'd be dead. So get your skinny black ass out of here. Take your friends with you." He pulled Otha to his feet by the collar and pushed him into the group. He kicked the red fedora to land at Otha's feet. One of his friends bent and picked the hat up. Otha was dazed, blood streaming from his cheek and forehead, held up between two of his friends.

"You go cool off for a couple days before you think 'bout coming back, y'hear me, boy? Now git." Stallings waved his hand towards the door. Otha shook off his friends and straightened his jacket, brushing off the lapels. He took a handkerchief from his pocket and, lifting his hat, wiped the blood from his face, staring at Stallings the entire time. He folded and returned the bloodied cloth to his pocket. He gave Stallings a nod and brushed past Corky as he ushered his friends out the door. Corky watched them all leave, watched Otha's fedora move above the blacked-out portion of front window as they crossed the long porch before disappearing.

Stallings shouted above the murmuring of the room.

"All you listen up," he said, then called to the big man. "Yunk, that's it. Close it down." The big man snatched the bell's rope, yelling above the clanging,

"That's it for the night.," Yunk said. "Rooster's closed. You git on out. Don't have to go home but you can't stay here now so clear on out. Move!"

The big man and the Negro bouncer began herding customers towards the door, Yunk carrying his shotgun and the Negro using his axe handle to prod people from their seats and push them along. Sal stood and motioned Corky to do the same and they moved out with the crowd. Drunks stumbled, grumbling and shouting, but moving just the same. The room was cleared in a matter of minutes, but the two men continued their work, pushing people off the porch out into the rain, coaxed to move faster by Yunk letting both barrels of the shotgun roar, firing two shots skyward. Men and women scrambled across the parking lot, coats raised over their heads, shouting above the starting of engines and grinding gears, begging for rides, being pulled into the open beds of trucks and squeezing into already crowded back seats.

Sal moved the car with the other vehicles that jockeyed for position, horns blowing and passengers shouting, falling into a line that streamed out of the parking lot, along the drive through the tunnel of trees lit by bouncing head-lamps, and out on to the county road back to Water Valley.

She watched the spider in the corner of the ceiling above the bed. The creature hung by an invisible thread, spinning, the shadows of its multiple moving legs and rotund sectioned body, cast by the low light of lantern. Another shadow eclipsed the spider's, and she turned her head on the pillow to see a moth fluttering above the lantern, bobbing and rising, veering towards the glow, then careening away from the heat, returning to bounce off the glass, forever drawn to the light within the chimney of the hurricane lamp. Her gaze rose to the corner and she wondered if the spider knew, was aware of the moth's presence, its existence. Did it see the moth dancing below or sense the motion of a nearby prey and began weaving in anticipation of the kill? Or did it work in confidant expectation, operating on nothing more than the instinctual drive of a predator that sooner or later something would fall into its trap? The spider worked on, unconcerned or oblivious not only to her musings, but her at all. She thought about the broom leaning in the corner of the kitchen and resolving the issue by bringing an end to the spider.

Serafina observed all of this over the shoulder of the man lying on top of her, thrusting into her with, for her, not a quickening enough pace. But she had learned that, if nowhere else in her life, at these moments it was she who was in control and men who in the daylight thought themselves wolves were reduced to begging puppies, wanting nothing more than the pleasure of nuzzling and suckling at their mother's breasts and reaching their mindless, flooding ecstasy.

She felt Stalling's urgency rise and moved her hips in response, hugging him close, dragging then digging her fingernails into the skin of his back. She began to whisper in his ear, in her native language of Italian, words he took as encouragement, praise and, in his ego blindness, pleasure at his skill and prowess. For was she not crying out, calling to Jesus Christ himself as he reached his climax, signaled with a now familiar triplet of grunts. He rolled off her and lay back with an exaggerated exhale and self-satisfied look on his face. He threw the covers off himself, reached for his shirt hanging on the chair near the bedside and pulled a pack of cigarettes from the pocket. He shook one into his lips and lit it on the lantern. Stallings looked back at the girl through the cloud of blue smoke he streamed from his nostrils.

She rose on one elbow and faced him, the sheets falling from her breasts. His gaze locked on her chest, and he lost himself in the swollen curves of her olive-skinned body. Stallings whistled low through the cigarette clamped in his mouth and winked.

"Darlin' girl," the man said. "You sure know how to use what God gave you." He stood and scratched his buttocks with both hands before reaching for his trousers. He dressed, pulled on his jacket, and crooked a finger at the girl. "Come on, get up and see me to the door," he said. "Give me a proper good-night kiss."

She flashed him an actress's smile and, wrapping the quilt round herself, rose from the bed.

"You don't need that," Stallings said and pulled the blanket away, leaving her naked.

He gripped her upper arm and walked her from the bedroom through the cabin's main room and to the door. He threw it open and maneuvered the naked girl into the doorframe, exposed in the light of the lantern hanging from the porch ceiling. Stallings waved towards the black sedan parked in the rutted drive. Leaning against the front fender was the big man, the one called Yunk, who had brought Serafina out to the cabin that first night. When the big man turned to look back towards her, she met his gaze with a smile but made no effort to hide her body. She saw Yunk lower his eyes in embarrassment.

"Yunk," Stallings shouted. "You can get that car started up. We're done here." He turned to the girl, his voice low. "Now why don't you give me a bit of that Eyetalyun talk you do in the bed," he said. "Let me hear how you liked it so much you're telling Jesus all about it."

Her lips parted and she ran her tongue slowly across them and let a sigh escape. She rose on her toes, leaning in to bring her mouth to his ear, her bare breasts pressing into his chest. In a hot whisper, she said, "*La morte sta per voi, amante. Io ti ucciderò. Presto.*" Her tongue flicked across his ear. He shuddered. "*Presto.*" She pulled away and looked up into his eyes and smiled at his melting. She rose again repeating slowly, stretching the syllables, a melody flowing with her words. "*Io….ti…ooo…chee…dero. Presto … presto.*" And then she bit his ear.

He jerked away, glaring at her. She wiggled her hips. Her coquettish play softened the man.

"Presto?" he said, rubbing his ear. "That's what you say when I'm getting there. In bed. What's that mean?"

"Soon." Serafina said.

"Yeah, guess that makes sense. And the rest? What's that all mean?"

She shook her head again. "You will learn, *presto*," she said.

"You sure like to tease me," he said. "I like that … but just a bit." He grinned and smacked the girl's ass. He put his Stetson on and walked off the porch, down the steps to the truck, and moved around to the passenger side. "Behave out here now," he said as he looked around at the thick woods surrounding the cabin. "I'll be back again real presto." He got into the truck, and motioned for his man to drive.

Serafina backed slowly into the cabin and stopped, her eyes locked on the big man who just waved her back and waited until she closed the cabin door. She heard the truck start and the sound fade leaving her alone.

Inside the cabin, Serafina went to the bedroom, wrapped herself in a wool robe and began what had now become her ritual following Stallings' visits. She would not sleep in the sheets he had lain in. She stripped the bed and re-made it, then gathered the dirty linens and dropped them in a large wicker basket next to the back door. In the morning, she would boil them clean in a galvanized washtub in the back yard.

Her eye caught the broom leaning against the wall. She gripped it in two hands, returned to the bedroom and swatted the spider from the corner web. When it hit the floor, she brought the handle end down, crushing the arachnid flat. She swept what remained into a corner, leaned the broom against the wall and slipped between the fresh sheets.

She brought the thick quilt to her chin and closed her eyes.

She fell asleep to the wind carrying a whispered lullaby through the trees. The words she had whispered in Stallings' ear. How beautiful the promise had sounded in her mother tongue.

*Ti uccidero… Presto… presto … presto.*

# 28

Sundays were her own and she relished the day away from the juke and Stallings and the watchful eyes of his men. She usually slept late, rising close to midday to make a large espresso with warm milk. Then, wrapped in a wool blanket, she sat in the wooden swing chair on the covered porch, dipping a biscotti in her coffee and watching the lake. She had been in America close to four months and seen nothing but rain. But from the porch, warmed by the coffee and blanket, she sat comforted by the endless gray of the leaden clouds that filled the skies above the lake. The sun hidden, the light often remained the same throughout the day, making it impossible to the tell the hour, morning from afternoon, a perpetual dusk leaving her suspended in time. She had seen the storms bring skies dark as night, the black cloud banks rising above the tree line, like a giant wave that rumbled and crashed, carrying lightning surges that split the dark wall, illuminating the world in stroboscopic flashes of negative images. The trees, the surface of the lake, the sky all turning a searing white, then back to black. The porch was covered with a long, low roof that protected her well and she remained in her swing seat through it all. Even when the winds shifted, sending the rain sideways under the eaves, she sat, allowing the cold, stinging drops to lash her face, leaving her shivering yet exhilarated, as if she'd gone for a swim in icy waters.

The cabin was built at the top of a rise that sloped to the lake. There were two ancient oaks, limbs mottled with gray-green moss, the trunks now rising out of the water as the lake had swollen beyond the shoreline. A dirt lane broke off the road leading to the cabin.

On this Sunday, she woke earlier than usual and sat on the porch as dawn broke. The rain had stopped, and the sky lightened in the east as the sun crested the tree line. She drank her coffee and watched the undulating spill of a dozen shades of pink and gold dance on the lake. Four months in America and no freer than she'd been in Italy. She was angered and cursed God a hundred ways at the turn of events that swept her from New Orleans, where she planned on a better life. Her glimpse of the rain-shrouded city with its crowded streets and well-dressed people was more punishment than hope.

She had no money and no means of escape. Yet.

The wind picked up, the light dimming as a swirling mass of clouds took over the sky as if the world had reversed its turning and the sunrise was retreating into night. Rain came in a showering mist that ruffled the lake. Serafina watched the storm unfolding until she finished her coffee and, licking biscotti crumbs from her fingers, rose from the swing. She leaned out over the wooden railing, cocooned in her blanket, and let the rain bead her face. Her gaze was fixed on the muddy road that cut from the pines on the far edge of the lake to skirt the swollen banks and run to the cabin.

He will come today. He will bring the young one with him. She will convince them of her plan.

She closed her eyes and conjured the image of herself far from this accursed place, this dismal swamp they called Mississippi.

*Presto,* she whispered to the wind. *Presto.*

The skies cleared by the time they left Water Valley. Corky directed Sal, doing his best to decipher the crude map drawing and near-nonsensical mix of Italian and English directions the woman had slipped to Sal at the Rooster. His frustration was tempered by the image of the woman's face that floated in his mind.

"You ever see blue eyes like hers?" he asked Sal as they drove through the rolling hills.

Sal gave him a quizzical smile. "Who has blues eyes?" he asked, as Corky's cheeks reddened. "*Si, Eugenio, Lei è una ragazza molto bella.*"

Corky smiled and looked out his window. He had never seen a girl as beautiful as Serafina. Anger rose in his chest when he thought about the scar. Although to him the imperfection made her more beautiful and interesting, the idea that Stallings was the one who inflicted that wound enraged him.

"*Ma attenzione, eh?*" Sal said, his eyes on the road. He raised his finger. "*Quelli belli sono i più pericolosi.*"

"Dangerous?" Corky scowled. "Why? How are the beautiful ones that way?"

Sal reached over and tapped Corky's chest above his heart. "This is just a toy for a beautiful woman. *Capisce'?*"

"Serafina's not like that." Corky said, his voice tight.

"Maybe it's too late for you already, eh?" Sal said. He grabbed Corky's leg and squeezed. "Is it true? Have you fallen in love?" Corky brushed his hand away.

After a couple of misguided turns, Corky managed to get them to the road that skirted the lake and led to the cabin. When they arrived, Corky saw Serafina sitting on the porch, and he waved as the car came to stop. She returned his wave but remained wrapped in her blanket, sipping her coffee as the two visitors stepped out of the sleek Nash. Corky pulled a box from the rear seat and stood in the drive, smiling, until Sal pushed him towards the porch.

There were no words of greeting, none of the three spoke. They remained on the porch smiling at each other until Serafina rose and walked inside, leaving the door open. Corky looked at Sal who gave him a slight bow, sweeping his arm towards the open doorway.

Inside, Corky set the box on the table and began unloading what Sal had bought. Along with the bread, there was a foot-long stick of hard salami, a ball of provolone cheese, a jar of olives and another of roasted peppers. He lifted two dark bottles with corks jammed into the opening and slid them across the table. Sal uncorked one of the bottles and sniffed at the opening. He smiled and shrugged, then tilted the bottle, a pouring gesture by way of asking if the others were ready for a glass of wine. Serafina brought three small mason jars from a shelf above the sink. Sal filled each, passing them to Serafina and Corky, then raised his own. "*Cent anni*," he said. The others repeated the toast in unison. They drank, Sal arched an eyebrow at the taste but nodded his approval.

"*E' buono, eh?*" he said. "Mr. Tony makes good wine in that basement of his. To *Signore Fratesi*." He lifted the jar again. Corky and Serafina joining in the toast to the winemaker. Corky took the butcher wrapped bundles of pork neck bones and sausages and two jars of canned tomatoes and busied himself at the cutting board preparing the ingredients for the sauce he learned to make watching his grandmother. He lit the burner on the stove and, while the meats browned, diced the onion, celery and carrots, smashing the garlic cloves with the side of the knife, the way his grandmother had taught him to make the peeling easier. Soon the cabin filled with the smells of searing meats and the fragrant blend of the trinity cooking in olive oil and garlic. When the vegetables were softened, he added the tomatoes. He was stirring the pot when he felt Serafina at his side. She pressed against him as she leaned in to inspect his cooking. His entire body tightened then relaxed. Without thinking, he leaned into her, and she bumped her hip against his and, turning to catch his eye, gave him a smile. Corky lost himself in her blue eyes, then felt the flush of embarrassment rise and shook himself away. He returned his focus to stirring the sauce and managed to ask without stammering.

"Could you bring me the wine, please?"

Serafina bumped his hip again and went to the table. She returned with the open bottle of wine and watched Corky pour a cup or so into the pot. He stirred, then added another glug.

As he tended the stove, Sal and Serafina worked together, cutting the salami and provolone, rolling the paper-thin slices of prosciutto. They placed the olives and roasted red peppers in small dishes and gathered it all on a short board Serafina brought from the woodpile and wiped clean.

After Corky added the meats to the pot and set it to simmer, Sal lifted the board, and tilted his head towards the porch. Serafina followed, turning to Corky and pointing her chin at the wine bottle. The boy smiled and, wine bottle in hand, moved to the porch.

Serafina took her place on the swing, Sal sat on the porch railing next to the steps, his back against the upright, half turned to give him a view of the lake and the woman on the swing. Corky ducked back inside, pulled a chair from the table and brought it onto the porch. He sat on the other side of the porch steps, facing the lake but with a sideways glance watched Sal and Serafina.

They ate in silence, using their fingers to pick at the antipasti, enjoying the company and being outside despite the chill. The quiet was broken only by the occasional soft moan following a bite of food and by the sounds of the country – a hawk's cry, a heron's beating wings as it lifted from the lake's edge, the splash of a fish. A bald eagle circled, gliding in the drafts above the lake, then settled into the uppermost branch of one of the oaks, still except for the slow swivel of the white head as the bird surveyed the water and woods below.

Sal leaned over to refill Serafina's jar with wine, then raised the bottle towards Corky. The boy crossed the porch and held his jar as Sal filled it.

"I'm going to check the *sugo*," he said. "And start the pasta water." He lifted his wine to the others, took a sip and walked inside. While he was working the handle of pump at the sink, filling a second pot to boil the pasta, Corky glanced over his shoulder to the open doorway. He could see Sal still sitting on the railing, turned to face Serafina. He stopped pumping and could hear Sal talking, then the woman's laugh. He felt a sharp stab of jealousy in his chest in the spot Sal poked while warning him of the fragile toy that resided there. He gave the sauce a quick stir, and seeing the water come to a boil, tossed the long strands of pasta into the pot. As he began to fill a platter with the sausage and meats from the simmering sugo, he called towards the porch.

"*Vieni a mangiare.*"

The pair returned to the kitchen, Sal carrying the tray and the wine bottle. Serafina came to the stove and dipped a piece of bread into the pot. Corky waited for her reaction. Closing her eyes, she took a bite and moaned. Corky stared at her face and his knees trembled. She popped her eyes wide and nodded. "*Molto buono,*" she said and kissed his cheek. She dipped the bread in again and popped it in her mouth. She pinched his cheek and Corky, slack jawed and pining, watched her walk to the table, transfixed by the sway of her hips. Sal broke into his view and gave Corky a playful slap on the pinched cheek.

"Too late for you." Sal said in a low voice. He raised his finger to the corner of his eye, then a slight wag in Corky's face. "*Cosi pericoloso,* eh?" He clapped his hand onto Corky's shoulder. Sal took the platter of meat and the three gathered at the table. They ate, and talked and emptied the first and second bottles of wine, wiped their plates clean of the rich sauce with chunks of bread. After they cleared the table and, as a trio, washed and dried the dishes and pots, Sal opened a third bottle and they went back out to the porch.

The clouds returned and the setting sun slipped behind a thickening rise of thunderheads on the horizon. A wind came from the west, chop rising on the water, the early evening air wrapped in a damp chill. The three sat, quietly as the evening grew dark. Corky, more than slightly drunk, slumped in the wooden rocker, eyes heavy-lidded and close to falling asleep when he heard Serafina's speak in a soft voice.

"I'm going to kill him," she said. "You know that, right?"

Corky's eyes snapped open. He looked to Sal, searching to read the man's face in the shadows. Serafina shifted around to sit facing the two men. In the faint light, it was still possible to see her flashing eyes leaving no doubt as to the seriousness of her intent.

"I'm going to kill him," she said again. "And take his money."

"What are you talking about?" Corky said, sputtering. He sat up fully awake, if not entirely sober. "You can't just kill Stallings." Corky looked at Sal. "Tell her, Sal. She can't just take his money and murder him."

Serafina cut him off. "Yes, I can." she said. "And I will."

Corky's eyes darted back and forth from Serafina to Sal and back again.

"No, you can't," he said, his voice cracking, less a statement than a plea.

"Why? Because I'm a woman?" She said, a smile on her lips. "His men bring the bags of money from the bootleggers' stills and his other jukes after they've closed on Saturday nights to the Blue Rooster for Stallings to gather and count. And one Saturday night soon, I will kill him and take his money."

"Wait. Bags?" Corky said, "Plural?" He couldn't help the excitement creeping into his voice.

"*Si.*"

"How many bags?" Corky asked. "How much money are you talking about?"

Serafina smiled. "*Molto* bags. So many. All the money made at his juke joints and from the men who sell his whiskey in the surrounding counties." Her voice turned to a low growl, edged in anger. "And whatever they make from selling his women."

Corky's face was a question.

"Oh yes," Serafina said. "Stallings has many women working for him. So, I am going to kill him and take his money. I'm not concerned about the order in which that occurs, but it is going to happen. Then I will go to New Orleans."

Corky leaned forward in his chair. "How much?" he repeated, tapping Serafina's knee.

"Now you want to kill him, no?" She said. "Now that you know how much money there is. Or because he makes money from selling women?"

Corky said nothing.

"I don't know exactly how much, *bello*," Serafina said. "But I have no doubt it is enough. When he counts it in his office, his desk is covered in stacks of bills. Sometimes the big man, Yunk, stays and when the counting is done, he walks Stallings to his car. But usually he sends him home, counts the money, and goes home."

"Alone?" Corky asked. "With all that money on him? Isn't he?"

"Afraid?" She shook her head. "Oh, *bello mio*, no. Larking Stallings is the one who is feared. No one would try to rob him."

"Or kill him?" Corky asked.

"These people think he is a man who cannot be killed. Or they are all so afraid they haven't tried."

"Yet." Sal broke his silence, his eyes on the sky.

Now Corky was silent. He stared at the woman's face, a beauty that had stolen his heart at the first sight of her behind the bar at the Blue Rooster. *Faccia divina.* The face of an angel, he thought. Now he saw the face of a killer. When Sal said she was dangerous, this was not what Corky thought he meant. She reached out, laying her fingers on his wrist. The boy felt the heat of her touch and looked down, trying to imagine her small hands wrapped around an instrument of death. A gun. A knife. A club. He looked back to the face he adored to hear her husky whisper.

"Will you help me, *bello*?" She asked. "Kill *lo bastardo*. Take his money and leave this place?"

Corky's mouth fell open, his mind racing to comprehend what he was being asked.

"Help you?" he said in a whisper. "Kill Stallings?"

"*Si*, help me kill him and we'll all be rich." She tipped her head towards Sal. "He will help. *Tu fratello*, Salvatore, I'm sure."

Corky's head whipped to Sal. "What? You're going to help her kill Stallings?"

In silence, Sal rose and stood at the top of the porch steps. He sipped his wine and watched as the eagle rose from its high perch, spiraling above the lake. The bird slowed, tucked its outstretched wings to its sides, and dropped in a blurring dive to skim the surface. The wings unfolded to slow its racing flight, the feet stretched and, with barely a splash, dipped into the water. The bird rose on pumping wings, a plump bass gripped in its talons and flashing silver as the eagle disappeared into the ribbon of darkening sky above the tree line at the lake's western edge. Lightning flashed behind the black clouds and, in the distance, the sky below them smeared with the rain. Facing the lake, Sal spoke.

"Where will you go, *bella*?" he asked Serafina. "What will you do with all this money?"

Without hesitation, Serafina answered.

"I will go to New Orleans," she said. "I will open a clothing store and sell beautiful Italian clothes to the rich men and women of that city."

Sal turned and looked at Corky but spoke to Serafina.

"*Si*," he said. "I will help you."

# 29

Corky walked to the car without a word. He looked back to see Sal hug Serafina and approach the car. Sal got in behind the wheel and they drove away in silence. The rain moved across the lake and fell hard. Thunder punctuated the rhythmic battering of fat drops on the car. It wasn't until they reached the main road back to Water Valley that Corky spoke.

"We can't just kill the man," he said. "Can we?"

Sal said nothing, his eyes fixed on the road. Corky sighed and sat back. Murder. This is what we're plotting, he thought. Killing a man for money. For Serafina, it was something more. Revenge. For all Stallings' transgressions. This he could understand, seeing the life she was forced to live. Captured. Caged. But there could be more. Something he recognized. Felt in her presence. Saw in her eyes. Something he knew and felt himself but kept buried. Retribution for all the hurt and pain she'd endured in her life. For being abandoned, for all the abuse by all the men who took advantage of her. The decisions life and circumstance had forced upon her, a life of few options beyond using her beauty and body to survive. Stallings represented it all and she had decided that he would be the one to pay. The money wasn't enough - it would take his death to balance the scales for her and, maybe for the first time in her life, tip them in her favor so that she could at last live the life she deserved. Was owed for all she had endured.

He closed his eyes and laid his head back against the top of the seat, letting it bounce with the car's jolts. But why do I need to be part of her reckoning, he thought? Murder? Wasn't it enough to be accused of one already, enough to have to deal with the one I *didn't* commit? Wasn't that what had started all this? Maybe I should just leave the two of them to their plan. Forget about New Orleans and go back to Sagamore. Explain to Sheriff Johnson what had really happened.

As he rolled the story through his mind, it all sounded absurd. Who would believe him? Corky and his grandmother were the only ones in Sagamore who had seen Sal other than Markle, who was dead. And Lisitano, dead along with his monkey. Cranio, too. Sal was the murderer. There was no one to tell this story to who could help, even if they did believe it. Sal didn't exist in Western Pennsylvania until after Corky became a suspect in Markle's murder.

"Sal, please, another murder?" Corky said. "What if we get caught? I mean, Jesus. They want to hang me for one I didn't do and you're in trouble for the ones you did do. Now you want me to be part of killing someone? Let's just leave. Tonight. Tomorrow morning. Go to New Orleans like we planned. Leave this Nash and take the steamboat you told me about with the great food, the music. And all the women you said we could find there. Please, Sal. Let's go. Now. We won't have to kill anyone."

"He is a bad man, *si*?" Sal said. "And this woman, Serafina? She will not just leave. Not without hurting him as he has hurt her."

"She's not dead. She can leave any time she wants."

"With what, *Eugenio*?" Sal asked. "What does she have? How does she live? On her back? Is this what you want for her? "

"Christ, no, that's not what I want for her," Corky said. "Let's all go, then. We can leave. Together, if that's what you want."

"She will not just leave. She will kill this man or die trying."

Corky sank back and groaned. "Can't we just rob him? Take the money and leave? The whole thing is crazy with all those hill country *stronzos* around him. But yeah, we get the money. Somehow. Steal it and then we leave, right? We go to New Orleans, get your uncle to fix things back in Sagamore so they stop looking for me and I don't need to worry about getting hung up by the neck for something I didn't do, right? And she goes wherever she wants to go, but we stick to our plan."

"And you think this man," Sal said, "this big boss Larkin Stallings will be fine with being robbed? By her? By us? Because there will be no doubt in his mind who stole his money. The three of us disappearing right afterwards. What, he'll say? *Que sera sera*, and go about his business?"

Corky sighed and shook his head.

Sal continued. "No, he will not, this you know. He will chase us, hunt us down wherever we go. He has his people all through the Hill country. He could not do the type of business he does without them. This is his land. Not mine or my uncle's. I would not be surprised at all, with the people he has in his pocket – lawmen, government people – that he will learn about the game warden soon and it won't be just Stallings looking for you down here."

The thought shook the boy who had felt confident they were within reach of the haven of New Orleans and the end of the game warden problem. He turned away from Sal to the dark country beyond the window.

"And what if Serafina does go her own way?" Sal said. "Who is to say she gets away? What happens to her if Stallings catches her? What then? No, we must kill him. It is the only way."

"Why?" Corky said through clenched teeth, his voice rising to a shout. "Why take the risk? Why save her? We don't even know her, Sal. Who is she to us?"

"Because I see how you look at her." He reached over and tapped his fingers on Corky's chest. "I know what's in here."

Corky slapped the hand away, whirled to Sal, his face twisted in anger. "It doesn't mean I'd kill for her. I can't do that. I won't."

A smile came to Sal's lips. "Oh, *fratello mio*." He clucked his tongue and shook his head. "How can you be so sure?"

Corky slumped into the seat, dropping his head against the window. He was stunned by Sal's words but wondered himself if he could kill Stallings for Serafina. If he had to. Maybe it was never going to be, the fantasy Sal spun of going to New Orleans and life being just fine because of the uncle who would make everything right. Wave whatever magic wand he had to fix things back in Sagamore for Corky and smooth the tension between the Calabrese and Napolitano organizations over Sal's killing Lisitano. Setting both free from being chased to certain deaths.

And now what? Robbery? Murder? That was never in his dream of New Orleans. Clearly, Sal was thinking otherwise now. He said once he was face to face with his uncle, he would be able to explain to his patron his actions. He was confident, Sal told him, that his uncle could make it right with the bosses of both families in Pennsylvania and he would go on working for his uncle and doing what he had been trained to do.

Which Corky now understood meant killing people.

But with this new plan to help Serafina, Sal seemed to be hedging his bets on that outcome. That he was no longer sure his uncle would back his play and there would be a price to pay. Which, according to the family's code, killing without first getting permission – could cost Sal his own life. Maybe he saw robbing and killing Stallings as an opportunity to take money to his uncle as tribute, to help his cause and chance of surviving.

Maybe now, Sal was planning on never going to New Orleans. He'd take the money and go elsewhere. West to San Francisco or back to Italy.

With Serafina.

The boy couldn't help but wonder where that left him.

# 30

Saturday night came. Sal and Corky ate dinner, packed their bags, and waited until the church bell rang a single time before making their way out of the rooming house for the last time. They got into the car, but Sal did not start the engine. The older man sat as if deep in thought for a few minutes before turning and reaching into the back seat. He brought his satchel forward and set it on the seat next to Corky. He motioned for the boy to open it. Corky studied Sal's face but just got a head tilt towards the bag. He opened it and pulled out a cloth wrapped bundle. He laid it in his lap, surprised at the weight, then glanced at Sal who motioned for him to open the bundle. Corky unwrapped the cloth and found two Colt .38 Special revolvers nested in a leather shoulder holsters. He looked to Sal, eyes wide and back down at the guns.

"These are beautiful," Corky said. "Thank you." He slid one of the guns from the holster, weighing it in his hand. The boy held the revolver up to catch the light from the streetlamp overhead. The metal was polished to a high shine and covered in fine engravings. He ran a finger over the black ebony inlays of the handle, cross hatched and edged in carved designs. Corky broke the revolver open and spun the cylinder, checking the chambers and finding them empty. He snapped the gun closed and raised it to the windshield. His finger slid onto the trigger, and he squinted, sighting down the barrel.

"I trust you know how to use them?" Sal asked.

Corky smiled, and pulled the trigger, the hammer click loud inside the car.

"I do not want you in The Rooster," Sal said. He put his hand on Corky's shoulder. "*Capisci?*"

"Why?" Corky asked.

"*Eugenio*, think, eh?" Sal brought a forefinger to his temple. "Someone needs to be outside. Watching. I will take care of all that needs to be done inside."

They arrived about a half hour before the 2 a.m. closing time. Sal backed the car down a dirt track off the road leading to the juke. They sat in the dark, waiting, Sal with his head laid back against the seat, his fedora lowered over his eyes.

Corky in the front passenger seat, his knee bouncing. His finger tapped the handle of one of the new Colts resting in the shoulder holster he wore. He looked at Sal, marveling at the man's calm. In some moments, he found it believable, beyond doubt, that this evening would be as easy as Sal described. Listening to him as they sat at the little table in their room, a map spread open between them as Sal laid out the plan. Hearing the simple words he used. Walk in, kill the man, take the money and ride into the night, rich and free. At other times, like now, he was gripped by a breath-robbing fear.

The clanging of the closing bell was followed by a collective moan that rose out of The Rooster. Sal sat up, shifted his hat back and rubbed his hands across his face. He reached over and laid a hand on Corky's bouncing knee. The raucous, drunken crowd poured out into the night, the shouts and laughter mixing with sounds of engines cranking to life. The two remained in the Nash as cars and trucks streamed by, filled with passengers waving and shouting at each other. Others on foot, walking arm in arm, some staggering and held by friends. Causing consternation and angry shouts of reprisals, two trucks came from the opposite direction, honking their horns and relying on several gunshots to clear the way as they moved against the tide of the exodus from The Rooster.

"Those are coming to make their drops," Sal said. "Serafina says there are ten of them. Four from Stalling's other juke joints and six from his bootleggers. We need to count and when they've all been made, I'll go in."

Corky nodded. Within twenty minutes, The Rooster crowd had vanished, leaving the parking lot empty. By 2:30 a.m., according to Sal's pocket watch, six more drops had been made, the vehicles pulling up to The Rooster's front door. The pair watched as, each time, Yunk came down the steps to take a bag from the passenger and then walk back inside as the car drove away. Another ten minutes passed before another sedan drove by and completed the drop routine.

"One left," Corky said. Sal nodded, opened his door and motioned Corky out of the car. He straightened his coat, adjusting his shoulder holster and settled the *lupara* at his side. "You ready?" he asked Corky, who nodded and opened his coat, exposing the Colts strapped underneath. Sal pointed toward The Rooster and the two walked to the edge of the parking lot.

"You stand over there," Sal said, pointing to an overhang of low branches amongst the trees. "You can see the front porch and anyone coming down the road. There's one drop left but they're cutting it close, and I don't want Stallings to decide to leave before they get here, or they don't show at all."

"What happens if they get here while you're inside?"

Sal reached out and flipped back one side of Corky's coat. "These aren't for fancy target shooting, are they?"

"What if there's more than one of them? Some of those trucks had two men making the drop."

"You have a gun for each of them then," Sal said. Corky's head bounced his unsteady agreement.

"I'm going around back," Sal said. "Serafina will meet me there." He reached out, gave the boy's face a gentle slap. Corky watched as Sal walked the edge of the parking lot, making his way in the dark to disappear around the back of The Rooster. His leg still bouncing, Corky tucked his right hand inside his coat, his finger tapping the handle of the revolver. *This will be easy*, Corky kept telling himself. *Walk in, kill him, take the money, and drive away.*

Rich and free.

# 31

Stallings sat in the back room behind the kitchen. The drop money was laid out in stacks wrapped in rubber bands of a hundred dollars each, covering his desk. He began a second tally, tapping each stack, counting aloud as he went. Yunk whistled low when the man reached the end and called out the number.

"Not bad at all. Don't get too excited, be a sight less after I take care of our so-called friends in Jackson." He lifted a stack and held it out to Yunk. "Happy birthday."

"Ain't my birthday, you know that."

"Well. Late on the last one or early for the next, you take it just the same, hear? You been takin' care of things around here just fine so get yourself an ass-pocket full of lettuce 'fore I change my mind."

Yunk took the cash, stuffing the bills into his shirt pocket. After buttoning the flap, he patted it and said to Stallings. "I want my money up front where I can keep an eye on it."

"Knew you was the smart one in the bunch," Stallings said. "Now send that bitch in here. Might as well use my time wisely while I'm waiting for those peckerwood Lawler brothers." He began making notes in a small ledger. "Sardis ain't but thirty minutes down the road and those two cannot get their shit together to be here on time."

Yunk winced at hearing the word Stallings used for Serafina. To him, she was anything but a bitch. "They still got a bit of time to get here before the deadline," he said.

"Them two been late once already this month," Stallings said. "I knew a beating wasn't going to be enough to get through those hillbilly skulls of theirs. Thicker than a damn pig's and nowhere near as smart. Should have saved us all the aggravation and put them down the first time. Now get that woman like I asked."

Yunk slid off his stool and went out of the office through the kitchen to the bar. He found Serafina wiping down the bar and motioned for her to follow him to the back. "Boss wants to see you." She slapped the rag down on the bar and pushed past the big man without a word. Yunk shook his head and as he walked to the front door, muttered an unheard apology, "I'm sorry, Miss Fina." He broke the shotgun and checked the load, snapped it together and went out to stand on the porch. When Serafina entered the office, Stallings, without looking up from his accounting, jerked his thumb towards the storeroom. Serafina's face hardened.

"I have to use *il bagno*," she said.

"What's that? A banjo?" Stallings asked.

"*Il bagno*, Larkin," Serafina said. "You know this word. How you say in English? The privy? I need to use the privy before we …" She hesitated.

"Fuck? That the word you're looking for, in English, I mean?" His gaze still on his ledger.

She gave no reply. He waved her off, then pointed to the back door. "Well, get on with it. You know where it is." He stood, opened the top door of his desk, took the revolver out of his waistband, and placed it on the desk. He slipped his suspenders off his shoulders, letting them hang at his side. "And be quick about it. I ain't got but a few minutes for fun," he said, shooing her towards the door.

Serafina went out the back door and crossed the small porch. Sal stepped out of the shadows, the *lupara* gripped in both hands.

"It's him and the big one," she said in a whisper. "He put his gun away because he's waiting for me to …" She stopped, then leaned forward, her eyes wide. "There's more money than you can imagine."

Sal glanced over her shoulder to the door. "I will follow you in," he said. "Then step aside, *capisce'*?"

Serafina shook her head. She reached inside Sal's overcoat and pulled a pistol from the shoulder holster. "No, Salvatore. *Capisce'*?"

Sal met her gaze, nodded, and pushed his chin towards the door.


The rain came in a fine mist and a sound of sizzling, like bacon in a pan, rose from the trees. Corky lifted the collar of his overcoat against the wet as he watched for signs of Sal and Serafina. He pulled his overcoat back and rested his hand on the pistol holstered under his left arm. Another few minutes passed with no sounds from The Rooster. No other vehicles came down the road. If Serafina was correct about the number of drops, one more was still to happen. His leg began to bounce as he gripped the revolver's handle. Sal did not tell him what to do if things went wrong. He lost all sense of time, struggling to get a sense of how long it was since Sal went inside. He waited, his temples pulsing, with his hand resting on the gun as his finger tapped the holster. With a deep breath, he pushed away from the tree. He straightened his shoulders and rolled his head, loosening the tension in his neck. He wiped his hand across his eyes and pulled the pistol from the holster. The gun remained tucked underneath his coat as Corky made his way towards The Rooster.

He eased onto the back porch. The back door was open, and he heard shouts and arguing from inside. He slipped into the back-office room, his gun pointing the way. Moving slowly through the empty room, he slid along the wall to the doorway into The Rooster's main room. His heart sank at the scene. Sal was on his hands and knees in the middle of the room. His head down, hair hanging in his face. Stallings stood over him, a revolver pointed at Sal's head. Serafina was behind Stallings, at Yunk's side, his left hand wrapped on her upper arm, his sawed-off shotgun in his right.

"You believe this shit, Yunk?" Stallings said. "These two wop greaseballs think they can steal from me? Larkin fucking Stallings?" He reached down and grabbed Sal by hair, jerked his head back to look in his face. "Surprised you, didn't I, boy? Wasn't where you thought I'd be. Or where this dumb bitch told you. Just walked by that storeroom door, the two of you. Always thought you dagoes was dumb as bricks but, damn, thinkin' you could come in here and, what, steal my money? Kill me?" He let go of Sal's hair with a shove.

Corky pressed himself against the wall, his heart slammed against his rib cage. He managed to look out again, bringing his pistol up to his chest. He had a clear shot at Stallings, but with Serafina visible behind him, he held off, not wanting to risk hitting the woman.

"Got to kill you, now, don't I?" Stallings said. He brought his leg back and kicked Sal in the side, knocking him to the ground. The juke owner turned to Serafina. "I haven't forgot about you. No, we're going to have some real fun before I put you down like the bad bitch you turned out to be." He stepped to put his face close to Serafina's and ran his finger along her scar. He turned her face to the unscarred side. "Think we'll start by adding another one of these on this side. Oh yes, we're going to have a real good time."

Serafina turned her gaze to Yunk, fixing the big man with pleading eyes. Yunk coughed, clearing his throat and said in a calm voice. "Don't."

Stallings snapped his head to stare at Yunk. "The fuck you say?" Stallings said, glaring at his employee.

"You heard me, Larkin." Yunk's face a stone mask.

"Oh, we on a first name basis, now, Carl?"

Yunk said nothing.

"You lost what little mind you was born with?" Stallings said, pulling Serafina to his side and facing Yunk. Corky cursed under his breath, realizing the big man wasn't a threat and his only target was Stallings, who was now shielded by the woman.

"Ain't no need to do this," Yunk said. "You been gettin' what you want from her ever since she got stole from over in Rosedale. You got the money. Let her go. Let them both go."

"You are serious? Let them go?" Stalling's eyes narrowed as his voice tightened. "They were going to rob me. They come here to kill me, you big dumb fuck. Kill you, too, and anyone else got in their way, be my guess. The fuck I should let them go?"

Yunk looked at Serafina. "She wasn't going to kill nobody," he said. "They come for the money. That's all."

"What makes you so sure about that? You think this bitch ain't got it in her to kill? You in for a surprise, son. And that one?" He pointed at Sal. "What you think, he's some kind of choir boy traveling salesman?"

"Don't know. Don't care," Yunk said. "All I know is that money is sitting right there in that satchel so ain't no real reason other than meanness to kill that girl." He tilted his head at Sal who remained on his hands and knees. "He didn't hurt you none. They fucked up. Send them on their way. Let the girl get on with her life, away from this place. Do the right thing, Larkin. Reach in that bag of yours, give her one 'em stacks and send her on her way."

Stalling's visage darkened. "Goddamn, boy," he said. "My ears gone and left my head because I can't be hearing what you just said. Let her go? Both, now. Give her my money. The money she tried to steal from me." Stalling's eyes widened in disbelief. "Then just open that door and wave her goodbye, all sweet-like? 'You have a nice trip. Thanks for stopping by. Don't forget to write.'" He spat on the floor.

"Just send them on the way on," Yunk said. "To wherever they going and be done with all this. It's too much."

"Goddamn, another one chewing my ass about this business being too much, "Stallings said. "You and Uncle Brother been jawing like a couple old women behind my back? Too much? Too much what? Money? The hell's wrong with all yous? Ain't never enough money far as I can tell. Let me explain this so even a brain-dead peckerwood such as yourself can understand it. Ain't no one going to come here and try to take my money without paying a very fucking dear price." Stallings swung his revolver onto Sal, only to hear Yunk cocking the twin hammers of his sawed off. The juke owner turned to find the barrels pointing in his direction.

"You gone insane, boy?" he said. "Putting that gun on me?"

"I told you to let them go," Yunk said. "And I meant it. Not letting you hurt her no more." He nodded at Serafina. "Miss Fina, reach into that bag and take one 'em stacks of money. Hell, take two. Then you get your friend here and be on your way." Holding his gun on Stallings, he glanced at Sal. "You get up and get gone. Don't ever be coming back here."

"Stay put, dago," Stallings said, leveling his revolver at Sal, who was up on one knee meeting his gaze. "Yunk, you take that blunderbuss offa me and you think this through. Ain't nobody going nowheres. They got to pay, and you know it."

Yunk's gun remained on Stallings. Corky prayed for Stallings to move away from Serafina.

Stallings shook his head in exasperation. "Yunk, I swear if you don't stop this shit."

His threat was cut off as headlights swept the window and the sound of a vehicle coming to stop out front. "Well, now, looks like the cavalry done arrived just in time. That best be those Lawler hillbillies with my money, because I've had enough of all this nonsense," Stallings said and, keeping his gun on Sal, walked towards the window.

The sound of steps on the wooden floor of the front porch brought a single silhouette to the middle window. Corky caught a glimpse of a red fedora in the porch light above the painted section of the window. When he saw Stallings move away from Serafina, slipped into the room and took aim at Stallings.

"About time you showed up with my money, Mickey," Stallings said. "You just going to stand there or what?" Stallings shouted. He stood at the window and raised his pistol to tap on the glass. "Got us a situation here, you can help me out on."

The window exploded in a shower of glass, light and the throaty roar of a shotgun came with it. The blast caught Stallings in mid-sentence, knocking him backwards, lifted him off his feet, and tore his stomach open, spraying the air with thick ribbons of blood and chunks of clothing, flesh and bone. He was thrown back, his body skidding to a halt at Serafina's feet. Stallings moaned, his hands clutching at his exposed insides.

Otha Hunter stood in the opening of the broken glass, the shotgun in his hands belching smoke from the barrel. He calmly pulled a shell from the pocket of his suit jacket, reloaded, and stepped through the now open window. He looked at Corky.

"I told you," Otha said. "That man needed to die. Now what the hell you doing here?"

In the chaos, Sal pushed up off the floor, grabbed Stallings' revolver and pointed it at Yunk, who held Serafina's arm.

"Sal, no," Serafina said. "Don't. You heard him. He was trying to help."

Sal thumbed the hammer back on the pistol.

"Mister, I got no truck with you," Yunk said. "I was only wanting to get Miss Serafina out of that man's world. You take that money bag and be on you's way. I'll take care of this mess here. No one going to miss him."

All eyes looked to Stallings writhing on the floor, his moans like a cow's lowing as blood pooled on the floor.

"You can put that gun off me," Yunk said, laying his shotgun on the floor. He kicked it towards Sal.

Sal nodded and waved Serafina towards the leather bag on the floor. "Get the money, *bella*," he said. "*Andiamo*." The woman shook her head and knelt beside Stallings. She grabbed his face and turned to look into the man's eyes.

"Are you having a real good time?" she asked. A smile came to her face as she pulled the straight razor from her pocket. The blade came out with a flick of her wrist, and she held it in front of Stalling's face. Serafina waited until she saw fear register in the man's eyes.

"*Buono*," she said. "Now, was this what you had in mind for me?" She pressed the razor into the flesh of Stallings face and drew the blade down his jawline to his chin. Blood, dark red, streamed from the cut.

"Serafina," Corky said, shock in his voice. "What are you doing?"

"*Basta*," Serafina said, and held her hand out towards Corky to silence him. Through a low, gurgled groan Stallings spoke.

"Fuck you," he said. "You half-nigger bitch."

Serafina's eyes blazed. In one swift motion, she raised the razor above her head and, swinging it down, slashed Stalling's throat.

"I told you, *pezzo di merda*," she said to the dying man. "*Ti uccidero*. I will kill you." She rose when the light went out of the man's eyes. Serafina wiped the bloodied razor on the sleeve of Stalling's shirt, then crossed the room to pick up the satchel.

"Now we can go," she said to Sal.

Yunk called out to Otha. "I know you had good reason to do what you did," he said. "I don't know nothin' bout what happened here tonight. Far as folks know Boss sent me home, said he'd take care of things with the drop. Truth is, he got some people in these parts will be lookin' for the money more than who killed him. Just the same, Otha, I say you should get on out of the Hill Country, too, case someone gets wind of you being out here with trouble in mind."

"He's right," Corky said. "You need to come with us. Sal, he can help us find our way."

Sal looked at Otha, weighing the risks of traveling together through the south to New Orleans. He nodded approval.

"You drove up here," Yunk said to Otha. "Whose car is that?"

Otha smiled. "Not quite sure who the nice folks I borrowed it from are exactly, but they stays out towards Oxford."

"Well, I'll get it out of here," Yunk said. "Leave it someplace near there."

Serafina smiled at Sal, patting the bulging satchel she hugged to her chest.

"*Avante, avante*," Sal said and swept his arm towards the door. The quartet walked out of The Rooster and stood on the porch. Through the broken window they watched Yunk as he reached behind the bar and grabbed two bottles of the moonshine. He tore a couple strips off a bar rag and stuffed the ends into the bottles. Stepping out on to the porch, he lit the rag ends and threw the first bottle through the door to shatter on the floor near Stallings' body, sending flaming liquid across the dead man, igniting his clothes. The second bottle, he sent crashing into the row of bottles lining the wall behind the bar. It erupted in a fireball that torched the wooden beams of the ceiling and sent a waterfall of flames pouring onto the floor.

They backed off the porch and out into the parking lot. They stood watching as The Rooster turned into a furnace and flames rose from the other windows to lick the outside walls. More bottles exploded, the sound erupting in the crackling and popping of wood punctuating the twang of the piano wires snapping as the upright burned. The rain sizzled against the tin roof, clouds of steam mixing with the black smoke rising into the night.

Yunk looked at the four, tipped his hat and started to walk towards Otha's car. Serafina wrapped her arms around the big man and hugged him close.

"*Grazie*, Yunk," she said, reaching up on her tip toes to kiss his cheek. Yunk smiled and touched his cheek. Without a word, he got in the car and drove to the road, turning in the direction of Oxford.

"I'll get the car," Sal said, trotted to far end of the parking lot, moved to the driver's side and got inside. Otha hustled along with him and opened the front passenger door to sit beside Sal. The engine roared to life just as a black Model T raced came into the lot headed for The Rooster. Back lit by the blaze, Corky and Serafina were caught in the headlights. The car slid to a muddied stop and a young man leapt from the passenger side. Corky heard him shout above the roar of the fire and car engines.

"What the fuck you done?" the young man asked. He stepped toward Serafina and pointed at her. "You that bitch works here, right? You got Boss Stallings' bag?" He reached into his coat and came up with a pistol in his hand. Without hesitation, Corky moved in front of Serafina, drew one of his revolvers and shot the man three times in the chest. A look of surprise spread on the young man's face as he crumpled like a marionette.

The driver came out of the car and Corky swung the gun and fired at him, sending the driver back into the car. Sal pulled the Nash up, Otha swung the rear door open. Corky pushed Serafina into the back and leapt in. Sal gunned the sedan past the Model T and out of the lot.

# 32

Uncle Brother came out of the back door of his farmhouse, his hat low, collar pulled up against a misting rain, and crossed the yard to his barn. His mood was surly, being awakened out of a sound sleep, which at his age was a rarity. Between keeping a farm running and being partners in his nephew's jukes and bootlegging, he didn't have time for dumbasses like Billy Lawler showing up at his door in the middle of the night. Or any time, for that matter. His oldest boy had knocked on his bedroom door, saying Lawler had appeared, his car all shot up, crying about his brother being dead and The Rooster burning to the ground. Brother was about to cuff his son for waking him up over something that could have waited until morning but restrained himself. Why the boy couldn't figure for himself that if The Rooster had burnt wasn't nothing could be done about it now. Same with that dumber-than-rocks younger Lawler being dead. Dead is dead, don't matter what hour of the day or night.

Then his son told him that Lawler was saying that Larkin was dead, too, burnt up in the fire. He slapped the boy and asked him if he didn't think the last bit of news was the most important and he maybe should have mentioned that first off. His son rubbed the side of his face, glared at his father but said nothing when his father told him to let him get dressed and waved him out.

The Lawler's truck was parked in front of the barn doors. Brother noted the shot-out windows and bullet holes as he passed and went into the barn. A lantern hung from a low beam. In the circle of pale light stood his two sons, hair the color of the straw layering the floor, disheveled and bleary-eyed from sleep. Billy Lawler was slumped on a wooden stool, elbows on his knees, face buried in his hands. Brother could hear the muffled sobs as soon as he stepped into the barn. He laid a hand on the boy's shoulder. Billy looked up, tears streaming his face which was flecked with cuts, pieces of shattered window glass glinting in his skin and hair. When he saw no compassion in the old man's eyes, he broke into crying again.

"They killed Mickey," he said, his head falling back into his hands.

Brother looked to his sons, who both shrugged. He gave the distraught boy's shoulders a stiff pat.

"Who killed your brother?"

Billy jerked upright, his fists balled as he punched his thighs.

"One of them damn Eyetalyun that was out at The Rooster," the boy said. "They had that colored boy with them who said he was the one killed Boss."

Brother stiffened, his face hard. He grabbed a fistful of Billy's hair, yanked his head back, bent down and put his face in Billy's, his eyes narrowed. Billy's face blanched, his eyes bugging in fear.

"The fuck you talkin' about?" Brother asked. "Who killed my nephew?"

"That colored boy from down in Tula, Otha." Billy said. "Told me he sent Mr. Larkin to hell where he belonged."

Brother let go of Lawler's hair, then rose, and brought a backhand across the boy's face that knocked him off the stool. "Pick him up," he barked at his sons and pointed at the stool. The boys picked Billy up and dropped him back onto the stool. He sat rubbing the side of his face, crying softly.

"Now you tell me what happened," Brother snarled, "From the beginning."

Billy sniffled loudly, hawked spit into the straw.

"Mickey and me was coming to make the drop. We was running late and when we got there, whole damn Rooster was burning. We come into the parking lot and we see these fuckin' wops standing there."

"Italians? How you know that's what they were?"

"You know what them greasers look like," Billy said, looking from brother to his sons. "They got that colored skin, and these two were all dressed fancy. Suits and all. And they had that woman with them, the one works out at The Rooster. She's one of them, too. Right?"

Brother's eyes narrowed. "You talking about Serafina?" he asked. "She was with these other two?"

Lawler snuffled a yes, then broke down sobbing again.

"Get to it," Brother said.

Billy choked on his crying, sighed and rushed through the rest of the story.

"That it?" the old man asked.

"Yes sir, near as I can recollect."

"Where is Yunk?"

Billy rubbed his face. "I didn't see him, but he wouldn't have left Boss to die in there, alone, you know that."

Brother nodded. "Anything else?"

Lawler hesitated, his head dropped, he spoke to the floor. "They had the drop money."

"What you say?" Brother hissed, looming over the seated boy.

**140**

"The woman carried the leather bag" Lawler said. "The one Boss always puts the money in. Everybody knows that bag and knows better than to even think about touching it."

Brother spat and wiped a hand across his mouth. "You saying they got all the money?"

"Mickey jumped out of the car and was going to get the bag, take it from that woman. That's when that greaseball, the young one, shot him. Didn't say nothin' just pulled out a big old Colt and shot him dead." He broke into sobs again and stared at the floor.

"Hey, answer me," Brother said. "All of it? They got all of it?"

"No, not all," Billy jumped to his feet, and pointed to a canvas bag that sat at the feet of Brother's oldest son. "That's the drop from our still."

Brother tilted his head at the boy, then crossed to his sons and picked up the bag. He opened and rummaged inside, then handed it to his oldest.

"Well, that's something, ain't it," Brother said.

Billy gave him a weak smile. Brother began to pace, ranting. "I told him when he pulled that stunt in Rosedale, his dick would be the end of him. Told him if he can't keep it in his pants for his own wife, to at least stick to his own kind." He sighed, a disgusted look on his face. "Wasn't enough, all these jukes and stills making money for us, he had to go messin' with the Italians. All this damn trouble over a woman."

"We going back out there, right?" Billy asked. He looked to the boys. "We got to go after them, right? Get that money back and make that ni …"

"The fuck we going to do that for?" Brother said. "You said yourself the place was all burnt up. Not like we going to get there in time to put the damn thing out. And Larkin and his big fat friend in there, getting barbequed like a couple of whole hogs? That's what you said, right?"

Lawler nodded.

"Well, the fuck I want to go out there for now then. They dead and gone, son. And those Italian folks? Hell, probably halfway to New Orleans or up in Memphis drinking in the damn Peabody Hotel."

"What about Otha?" Lawler asked. "I know where his people stay."

Brother shook his head. "I am just too damn old for this shit," he said. "All I wanted, all I told that nephew of mine, was just have a little business on the side. Make some extra scratch so life's a bit easier and everyone can enjoy themselves. He listen to me? Hell, no. Had to open one juke after another. Made more trouble for all of us than it's worth. I am done."

"That's crazy, Pa," Brother's oldest son said. "We just going to give up all that money we can be gettin' if we take over all Uncle Stallings' business?"

"Yes, boy, we doing exactly that," Brother said. "We got money rollin' in but cost us a fortune to keep it running without the law up our damn asses all the time and Larkin doing stupid shit like shooting that deputy and on and on. A goddamn headache. I'm too old for this. Just want to sit on that porch and watch you boys here take care of my cows and them hogs. That too much to ask? Let the place burn down to the ground and we'll bury what's left of those two and be done with it all. Someone wants those other jukes, I'm fine with it. Larkin's family will be relieved far as I can tell. All the shit he heaped on them? I'm damn well surprised his wife didn't put a knife in his chest while he was sleeping or at least cut his damn pecker off. Those Italians done them and all us a favor seems to me."

His son started to speak but Brother held up his hand to silence him. "This ain't no discussion, boy," Brother said. "I need me some coffee." He walked towards the door but stopped and glanced over his shoulder at Billy. "What was that thing you said? Back at the beginning of your story?"

"Which part?" Billy asked.

"Right there at the beginning," Brother said. "When you were bringing the drop money to The Rooster." He rubbed his chin in thought.

"I said we was bringing the drop money," Lawler said. "And we was running late and we saw the fire and …"

"That was it," Brother said. "You were running late." He stepped towards Billy, brought his Colt out and shot the boy in the head before he was able to speak another word.

"Ain't no second warning." Brother said, looking down at the body. He holstered his pistol and waved at his sons. "I am done with this nonsense once for all. That shitheel talking about going after Otha's family, causin' more trouble. Feed that dumbass to the hogs and let's hope it don't make them as stupid as he was. And get that car out there dropped into the lake." He took the canvas bag from his oldest boy and started for the door.

"Pa," the boy said. "You want us to make the coffee first?"

"Goddamn boy, what I just tell you to do?" He shook his head. "I'll make my own damn coffee." He went out, slamming the door, muttering curses as he went back across the yard to the house.

The two brothers watched the old man go into the house.

"He really gonna quit the business and leave all that money behind?" The younger boy asked. His older brother spat in the dirt.

"I tell you what, lil' brother," he said. "I am not going to sit around here to take care of a bunch of cows and hogs for that man's pleasure. All that money to be made?"

"What you going to do?" the younger one said.

"Wasn't like that juke was some swanky high-end joint," he said. "Don't think it'll be too tough for us to find a place, get a bar built up in it, call it 'The Blue Rooster' and get into business ourselves."

# 33

Corky sat in the back seat, his left knee bouncing, the gun still clutched in his right hand. He had to do it, he told himself over and over again. There was no choice. He stared into the black outside the window, refusing to close his eyes in order keep the images from returning. The sound of the three shots. The look on the young man's face. Corky felt Serafina move to his side and her hand dropping on to his knee, to stop the bouncing. She then lay her head on his lap and within minutes, Corky could hear the soft breathing as she fell asleep. He helped with the heist for her. He stroked her hair. His heart pounded in his chest.

He killed for her.

They arrived in Greenwood at 3:30am and found Lusco's, the restaurant Sal was told was a safe place to stop. Serafina sat up, yawned, and straightened her hair.

"This is a place that stays open late," Sal said. "More like a speakeasy. I was told we can get some food. Wait here." He got out of the car and went down a narrow walkway to a side entrance near the back of the house. Light spilled onto his face when the door opened, and he stepped inside. A few minutes passed and Sal came back to the car. He opened the rear door, held his hand out to Serafina.

"We can go in," he said.

The trio got out of the car. Serafina stood, holding herself and shivered against the damp. Corky took his topcoat off and held it open for her. She turned and he draped the coat on her shoulders. Serafina turned back to face him, and the boy adjusted it, buttoning the top button as if doing the clasp on a cape. She smiled and gave him a small curtsy. Sal motioned for Corky to hand him the satchel, then leaned into the front seat for the *lupara* that had been resting across his lap. He broke the gun open, checking the load and slipped it into the satchel along with the heist money. Serafina placed her hand on the bag's handle and locked eyes with Sal. She tugged on the long leather handle, trying to take it from his grip. He held tight but she dropped her hand on his and without much resistance pried it away. She looped the handle into the crook of her arm, pulled the bag to her side and it disappeared beneath the overcoat. She smiled at Sal, who nodded his approval.

The four walked to the rear door. Sal knocked again and when it opened, he motioned them in. They stepped into a small kitchen where two Negroes worked. The cook shifting pans on the stove. The other, a waiter, organizing plates. Sal was welcomed by the owner, Al Lusco, a tall, thin Italian man. He wore a white dress shirt and tie tucked into a buttoned vest. His hair was slicked straight back. He smiled as Sal introduced Serafina, then Corky. The smile vanished when he saw Otha. He looked to Sal, shook his head. Leaning close to Sal, he said in a quiet voice.

"Salvatore, *scuzi*, I cannot have this … in the main room. The other customers, they …"

Sal raised his hand. "*Signore* Lusco," he said. "This is my friend. We've come a long way, as you know, and we'd like to eat. Our friend in New Orleans said we would be welcomed."

"*Si*, and you are welcome," Lusco said. "There is a booth set for you." He held a hand towards the speakeasy's main room. "But please understand. My business is not open to …" He turned and looked at Otha.

Corky glared at the owner. "Otha's with us," he said. The cook and waiter stopped working and turned to watch.

"We eat,' Corky pointed to the group. "He eats."

Sal smiled at the owner and nodded his agreement.

"No, no," Otha said. He held his palms up. "Not a problem, really. I understand, Mr. Lusco. Don't want to cause any trouble. I know how Greenwood folks is." He turned and seeing a small table in the corner of the kitchen, pointed to it.

"How about I just sit in here," Otha said. "You go inside and eat. Be fine in here, talking to these gents and getting something to eat my own self."

"*Perfetto*," Lusco said, nodding, relieved. He held out his arm and directed the others through the curtained doorway into the main room.

There were a half-dozen tables in the middle of the room and a row of five booths along the wall. Dark red curtains hung at each booth which could be closed for privacy. All were open and empty. A couple sat at a table near the front door, eating from large bowls of spaghetti and meatballs. Corky elbowed Sal and lifted his chin towards the table and smiled. Two men were hunched close at the small bar, drinking. They both turned and cast bleary-eyed glances as the group came into the room. Both men straightened at the sight of Serafina and raised their glasses at her. She rolled her eyes but smiled. Lusco stood by the middle booth.

"We're about to close," he said. "But please sit, we'll have the cook prepare something. They are very, very good. I'm sure you'll be happy with whatever they make for you." He clapped his hands together. "Now, *vino por tutti?*"

"*Grazie*," Sal said with a nod and the owner went back through the curtains to the kitchen.

Sal moved to the side of the booth that would leave him facing the door. He waved Serafina into the booth on his side. She shook her head and tapped a forefinger to her cheek below her eye, then pointed at Sal. Corky caught the wink he gave the woman and felt his chest tighten. Sal made a motion to ask if she wanted to remove the overcoat. Another head shake as she patted her side where the satchel hung. She slid into the booth on the opposite side. Sal sat and Corky hesitated, unsure of which side to sit on. Serafina slid over and patted the bench seat.

"You sit next to me, *cara mio*," she said.

A jolt sang in Corky's ears at the term of endearment. A rush of warmth filling his chest. He blushed and sat beside her.

"I'm starving," he said. "Smells so good in that kitchen and those meatballs?" He glanced back over his shoulder at the couple eating then turned back kissing his fingertips. "*Bellissima*."

Serafina leaned into him, her voice low. "Killing is hungry work, eh *ragazzo*?"

Corky blanched. He looked at her face, saw her eyes glistening in excitement. Another singing in his ears. This one carrying a chill that shuddered his legs. What had happened only a few hours earlier seemed impossible. As if it were all a dream or a story from a book his brother read to him at night.

Lusco returned and placed four small glasses on the table, opened the bottle of wine, and filled each glass. He took one for himself, raised it and nodded to the trio.

"*Cent'anni*," he said. The trio of guests raised their glasses and echoed the toast.

The owner excused himself and went to the couple at the table who had finished their meals. Corky stood, glass in hand.

"I'm going to go watch the cook," he said. "And I'm going to eat with Otha." He didn't wait for an argument and left for the kitchen. When he walked through the curtains, he saw both men at the stove. The cook turned and nodded. Otha was standing at the back of the kitchen, watching as the pair worked. Corky went and stood beside him.

"This here's Luther and Langston," Otha said. "And I know yous think we all look alike but they's actual twins." Two heads turned in unison and gave Corky identical smiles.

"Hey," came their unison greeting before they both went back to work. Corky shook his head in amazement then leaned in between the pair to eye their labor.

"What's that you're making for us?" he asked.

"Chicken-fried steak," Luther said, as he gently flipped the four breaded steaks frying in the large cast iron pan.

"And mashed taters and gravy." Langston finished, lifting the lid on the pot.

"You don't be forgettin' them collards," Otha said and got two scowls in response.

"Get you some collards, son," Langston said.

"Pot likker, too," added Luther.

"And cornbread," Langston said. They looked at each other and nodded.

"What?" Langston asked. "You think just 'cause we can cook that Italian food, we forgot how to cook down home?"

"Best check yourself, Mr. Otha Hunter from Batesville," Luther said. "Hate for this here steak of yous to jump out the pan, hit that floor." The brothers snapped their heads to look at Otha, bug-eyed, then broke into cackled laughter.

"What's pot likker?" Corky asked.

The laughter stopped. Both heads and pair of bugged eyes landed on Corky.

"The hell?" they said at the same time.

"Come here," Otha said. "Let me show you." He went to the stove and reached to the large pot simmering on the stove. Before he touched the lid, Langston rapped his hand with the wooden spoon. The twins each raised a forefinger and wagged it at Otha.

"That's chef business, son," Luther said. Otha raised his hand and stepped back from the stove.

"This is pot likker," Langston said, dipping a ladle into the pot and letting a stream of dark green liquid fall back into the braising collards." He dipped again and set a small piece of cornbread into the likker on the ladle. He held it out to Corky.

"Taste that, Mr. Where You Been All Your Life?" Luther said and the twins did their cackling laugh again.

Corky took the sopping cornbread and stuffed it into his mouth. His eyes grew wide at the rich savory broth and sweet cornbread.

"Oh, that is really good," he said and licked his lips, then his fingers. The twins looked at each other with a mutual nod of congratulations.

The curtains opened and Lusco stood in the doorway. The twins went quiet and turned to their tasks on the stove. The owner slid the curtains open wide. Corky could see the couple had left and the two men at the bar were standing, putting coats on to leave. They were moving to the front door when the taller of the two turned and came towards the kitchen. The other went outside, the wind gusting into the room through the open door. The tall man came to the kitchen doorway.

"The bathroom?" he asked. "Long drive ahead of me." Lusco pointed towards a hallway. "All the way down the hall. Door on the right. And please," he said and raised a finger to his lips, cautioning quiet. "The one on the left is my children's bedroom." The man nodded and went down the hallway.

Lusco came to the stove and watched as Langston, knowing without being told the steaks were nearing perfection, began to plate the mashed potatoes. He then held the plates as Luther placed a steak on each, spooning hot gravy on top of the potatoes. Lusco picked up two of the laden plates, shifted one to his forearm and was reaching for the third when Corky touched the plate.

"I'll have mine in here, Mr. Lusco," he said. The man eyed him, then glanced out to the room.

"It's fine," Lusco said. "No one's here. It's late and I'll close now. Go, take your friend. Sit at the booth."

Corky studied the man's face. Lusco nodded.

"Go," he said, handing the plates to Corky then looked at Otha. He pointed to the remaining two plates. Otha took them and Corky smiled. "Grazie," he said to Lusco, who waved them towards the dining room.

The trio turned and jockeyed for who was going first. The tall man came from the hallway. He looked at Corky, brought a finger to the brim of his fedora, then shoved his hands into the pockets of his overcoat and went through the doorway to the main room. Corky saw Serafina leaning out of the booth, looking to the kitchen, the overcoat still on her shoulders. He held up the plates and she clapped her hands. He saw her glance to Sal and nod, her eyes wide. She picked up her napkin and shook it out before laying it on her lap. The tall man walked along the row of booths towards the front door. Corky saw Serafina look up as the man approached, then drop her eyes and scowl. The front door opened, and the wind whipped the curtains of the booths. The shorter of the pair that had been at the bar stepped back into the restaurant and Lusco moved past Corky carrying the bowl of collards and plate piled with cornbread.

"I apologize, my friend, but we're closed," the owner said.

The tall man walked past the middle booth and turned to address Lusco. "He's with me," the man said, and half turned to the door before stopping. He looked back to where Sal sat, his face screwed into a "don't I know you from somewhere" contortion. The man's arm came up as he stepped towards the booth, Corky thinking he was offering to shake hands with Sal.

A burst of flame came from the man's hand, the shot sounding like the crack of a ball on a bat. Another flash and crack came before Corky saw the gun in the tall man's hand. Serafina screamed. The smaller man raised a shotgun from beneath his coat, racked and fired towards the kitchen. The shot caught Lusco in the shoulder. The man spun, collards and cornbread scattering into the air. Corky dropped his plates and dove to the floor and crawled to the wall beside the doorway. The shotgun roared again, the blast hitting the stacks of dishes on the center island of the kitchen, showering ceramic shrapnel in every direction. A unison cry of "Goddamn" came from the twins and Corky saw them both hunched down near the stove. Otha moved past the cooks in a crouch then rose and sprinted for the back door. The shotgun was racked again, and the frame exploded behind Otha as he dove through the door. Corky heard Serafina cursing in Italian. He poked his head out just far enough to see the tall man dragging her from the booth by her hair. She screamed and cursed, swinging a fist at the man, her other arm still looped through the satchel but unseen underneath the overcoat. She was pulled to her feet, the tall man forcing her towards the front door. The shotgun turned toward Corky and roared, blasting a hole in the wall above his head. He looked out again. Serafina was pushed through the front door by the tall man. The man with the shotgun walked backwards, shot again into the kitchen before turning and following the pair out into the night.

Corky leapt from behind the wall and ran to the booth. He found Sal slumped back in the corner, his mouth and dead eyes open. There was a black hole of an entry wound in his forehead. His shirt front and suit jacket were soaked in blood fed by the leaking hole in his chest above his heart. Sal's right hand rested on the ebony handle of his undrawn Smith & Wesson.

Corky's knees buckled but he braced himself against the table. The sound of gunfire came from outside. A revolver volley answered by guttural thunder of the shotgun. Corky reached across the table, lifted Sal's hand, and slid the pistol from the holster. He ran outside where Otha stood in the street, a long-barreled Colt leveled in the direction of the car racing down the block. Corky leapt off the porch and ran into the street, chasing the car. Otha came up on his side and both fired off a shot each as the car turned a corner and disappeared.

# 34

Corky and Otha returned to Lusco's. Inside the owner sat at a table near the kitchen with his wife tending to his shoulder. The shotgun blast had gotten more suit jacket than flesh. One of the twins was cleaning the middle booth while the other was scrubbing the floor. Sal's body was nowhere to be seen.

In his rage, Corky was only able to see the owner's face. He crossed the room in long strides and swung his pistol up, backing the wife away from her husband's side with it. She stumbled back, eyes wide with fear. Corky stood over the wounded owner. He pressed the end of the barrel against the man's head. Lusco winced.

"Who did this?" Corky shouted. "Who were those men?"

"I don't …" Lusco said.

Corky thumbed the hammer back. The owner winced again at the sound, closing his eyes.

"Tell me," Corky said, his voice rising.

The man opened his eyes, pleading mercy.

"I don't know these men," he said. "I don't know …"

Corky stepped back and pressed the barrel into the man's wounded shoulder. Lusco groaned in pain.

"Tell me who," Corky said. "Or I swear to God, I will shoot you."

The wife began to cry and Corky heard her praying in Italian. Corky let the gun drop to his side. Lusco's chest heaved and answered through with low sobs. "I was told that two men would come late. That I was to welcome them and feed them. That's all." Lusco looked at Corky, tears streaming his face. "Nothing about the girl." He looked past Corky at Otha. "Or that one."

Corky's pistol came up again, but Otha put a hand on the boy's forearm and shook his head. Corky relented and motioned at Lusco's wife. "Take care of him."

His rage ebbing, he turned to look at the dining room, where the two cooks were standing. He looked first to Otha, his face screwed in confusion, then to the owner. Lusco answered his question before it was asked.

"In the cold room," he said and jerked his head to the back of the kitchen.

Corky went as directed and opened the large door of the cold storage room. He saw Sal's body on the floor covered by a checkered tablecloth. Blood stains blossomed on the cloth from his chest and head wounds. He sank to his knees and lifted the cloth back for Sal's face. Whether due to shock or exhaustion, no tears came. He stared at Sal's face drained of color, a lifeless grey, a patch of dried blood surrounding the dark hole in his forehead. His jacket and shirt stained dark red, another dark hole in his chest above his heart. Corky felt Otha come up behind him.

"What we going to do now?" Otha asked. "Miss Fina gone, too."

Corky didn't answer. He covered Sal's face and stood. He motioned for his friend to follow, and he went back to the table where Lusco sat. He pulled out a chair and waited for the owner's permission to sit. The man shooed his wife away and nodded for Corky to sit. Otha stood behind Corky. The man held a finger up as the twins approached, one with a pile of bloodied rags gathered in his arms, the other carrying the mop and bucket. The two cooks stopped. "You say not a word," he said.

"About what?" Langston asked. "Got no word, do we, Luther?"

"No word." The twin said. "No one to tell if we did. That right, brother?"

"No one to tell," Langston said. "No one care about what we got to say, anyways, far as I can tell."

"What they always say about us, brother?"

"Langston and Luther be lying about the time of day."

"*Basta*," Lusco said, his thumb pointed towards the kitchen door. "Go home. Burn those rags first thing in the morning."

Heads bobbed in concert and the twins took their cleaning supplies to the kitchen, then left through the kitchen door without another word.

Lusco turned to Corky who asked, "The police going to find out about this?"

Lusco snorted. "The *polizia* here are some of our best customers," he said. "The mayor and his wife. All the politicians and plantation owners. They come here, sit in these booths behind the curtains and make their deals. Even if they do hear that this happened, do you think they care about an Italian gangster getting killed? By some of his own?"

Corky's eyes flashed, and his hands tightened into fists. "Sal wasn't."

Lusco shook his head and clucked his tongue.

"*Ragazzo*, please," he said. "I don't know exactly why this happened, but it was no accident. These two men were sent to do this. Maybe you know why."

Corky started to speak but Lusco raised his hand.

"I do not care to know," he said. "This is not my business. But as far as the police are concerned and, to be clear, for me." He tapped his chest. "What happened here, never happened. You." he pointed a finger at Corky then Otha. "And you, will go away."

"That's fine by me," Otha said. "Let's get gone, Corky." He dropped a hand on his friend's shoulder. Corky shook him off.

"What about Sal?"

Lusco shrugged. "He will go away, too."

"Go away where?" Corky asked. "Are you going to bury him here? In this town?"

The man gave him a wan smile.

"He will go away, that's all," Lusco said. "*E' necessario, capisci*?" The owner brought his thumb and fingertips together, his hand bouncing, waiting to see a sign of recognition in the boy's face as to the implication.

"No," Corky said, his face drained of expression, his eyes lidded. He leaned forward and spoke in a tight voice that he recognized not as his own, but his grandmother's. "*Tu lo capisci*, eh? He goes nowhere but to a funeral home. You know one here, right?"

Lusco shrank at the deeper menace in the boy's demeanor. A cold heart where the hot rage had been. "*Si*, I know one," Lusco said.

"Good. Get Sal there," Corky said."

"And then what?" Otha asked.

Corky glared at his friend. "I don't know but," he jerked his thumb at Lusco, "we're not going along with his plan."

Otha nodded.

They turned down Lusco's offer to let them sleep in the dining room. Neither Corky nor Otha wanted to be in the room where Sal was killed. The old man was visibly relieved to hear their decision to leave. He muttered his assurances that he would plan for Sal's body to be taken to the funeral home and that the owner, an Italian, could be trusted to be discreet.

"Just tell him to do his best job and that I'll see him in the morning."

"And who should I tell him will be taking care of the costs?" Lusco asked, his eyes on the floor.

Corky scoffed and was about to reply when Otha cut him off.

"You might think about steppin' up," Otha said. "Seeing you had a part in what happened to the man."

Corky waved his hand at his friend. "Let it go," he said then turned to Lusco. "You tell the man not to worry about it. Just fix Sal up for a proper burial."

"*Si, si*," Lusco said and ushered the pair to the back door. They went out and the lights inside were turned off, the entire place dark before they reached the car.

# 35

"Why did you bring her?"

This from the shotgun man in the front passenger seat as he glanced over his shoulder at Serafina. She was sitting on the large back seat of the two-door sedan. The tall man was driving. He had forced her into the back seat before getting behind the wheel while the shotgun man traded shots with Corky and Otha outside of Lusco's. When the car leapt forward, she looked out the rear window and saw the two running after the car, guns raised. She watched until the driver threw the car into a hard turn and the two boys vanished from view.

"The job was just the *Calabrese'*, no?" Shotgun asked.

The tall man scoffed. "They said don't do the kid," he said. "You? You shoot the fucking owner and I'm thinking, Jesus Christ, now we got to kill everyone."

"That was a mistake," Shotgun said. "I was going for all them darkies. The old man got in the way."

"Go in, wait for this Gentile to show up, we were told," Tall Man said. "I do the thing. Boom-boom. You make some noise to scare people, so they don't remember anything. No need to kill everyone. Ruin the man's business."

"He got no business if he's dead." Shotgun waved his hand in the air.

"They make money off this guy's place," Tall Man said. "What don't you get? We take out the one we're supposed to and disappear. A week, everybody's forgotten this happened and the place is packed with people drinking like usual."

"You think the owner knew?" Shotgun asked. "He get tipped this was going down?"

"Don't be stupid," Tall Man said. "They aren't going to take the risk he gets hinky and tips the guy or whatever."

"That man knows what would happen to him," Shotgun said. "If he opened his mouth."

"Right and he knows, too," Tall Man said. "That this all goes down the way it's supposed to, there's some extra for him if he don't know nothing. Which is why he doesn't get told."

Shotgun jerked a thumb towards the back seat. "So, what about her?"

Tall Man smiled. "Nobody said nothing about anyone being there but the kid," he said. "Who we were not to touch. Nothing about them others or ..." He tilted his head towards the back seat. "This one."

"Yeah?"

"I figure it'd be a real waste to kill such a beautiful piece of ass without getting some first," Tall Man said. Shotgun Man looked back at Serafina who met his leering with a blank face. She shifted on the seat and looked out the side window. Thick pine woods a black wall in the country dark night.

"We get a bit further on," Tall Man said, "we'll find us a quiet spot out one of these little side roads."

"Help break up this long ass ride back to New Orleans," Shotgun said. "I see your thinking." He turned back and spoke to Serafina. "We'll get you all good and relaxed. Worn out some, you sleep all the way there."

"Oh, she'll sleep alright," Tall Man said. "But don't think she'll be waking up in New Orleans or anywhere else for that matter. Ain't no one expecting her to turn up anywhere far as I know."

Shotgun Man looked back again. Serafina nothing more than a shadow. They rode in silence for close to half an hour. They passed no other vehicles on the road. Dawn was still an hour away and the car was enveloped in darkness. The car slowed as a turnoff appeared in the headlights.

"This ought to do just fine," Tall Man said, cranking the wheel and pulling off the main road. The tires crunched on gravel as the car crawled down the country road. A hundred yards in, another road cut in from the left. He took the turn and brought the car to a stop, cut the engine and ratcheted the hand brake. A heavy silence descended. Tall Man nudged his partner in the shoulder, motioned for him to get out. The man didn't move.

"I think you can step on outside," Tall Man said. "Have yourself a smoke."

"Why don't you go have a smoke," Shotgun said. "While I ..."

He was interrupted by the staccato eighth notes of the *lupara's* twin hammers being cocked. As Shotgun jerked towards the sound, Serafina pulled the first trigger and the man's head vanished in an explosion of blood, bone and brain. The car filled with smoke and a misting of wet. She swung the gun to the tall man, held it on him. He sat frozen, his face splattered in what was once his partner. His eyes widened as Serafina leaned forward. She wiped her cheek and came away with fingers sticky and damp. She studied it for a second then returned her gaze to the driver. She felt a calm descend, a sense of well-earned contentment in knowing the last thing the man who murdered Sal would see was her blue eyes above her smile. She pulled the trigger and the inside of the car erupted in a thunderous searing white heat again. Her ears were ringing as she reached across the lifeless body of the tall man and managed to get the door open. The body fell from the car, and she stepped over it as she got out. The satchel remained crooked in her arm. She gave a moment's thought to rifling the dead men's pockets but decided there was no point. The satchel was filled with money. The woman broke the gun open and removed the spent shells before rummaging in the satchel for replacements. She reloaded and snapped the gun shut.

A half- moon hung in a sky of moving clouds. The surrounding trees stood vigil, seeming to swell and recede as the light faded in and out. Serafina shifted the satchel to her shoulder and pulled the overcoat tight. She could not see in the moonlight whether the material was disgraced by her handiwork.

They were parked far enough off the main road and into the woods that she knew the coyotes and maybe the "painters," as Yunk had called them, would make short work of the bodies long before anyone discovered the car. Serafina felt no concern as she walked back the way they came from the main road. She reached the main road and tried to get her bearings.

Trucks appeared out of receding dark, carrying workers whose eyes latched on to the lone figure, some craning their heads to stare until well out of sight. Their faces betrayed no surprise or curiosity, just silent observers assuming what they saw was nothing more than an apparition, another of the many hoodoos and *haints* that roamed among the living of the delta. There seemed nothing alarming or un- usual in this ghost being a white woman who carried a sawed-off shotgun.

She was caught in the flare of headlights from behind, which sent her shad- ow ahead of her in a long streaking of black ink against the grey morning. The vehicle slowed in its approach, coming to a crawl alongside her. An old man in a small truck. Farmer by the bibbed overalls and battered sweat-stained straw hat and red handkerchief tied around his neck. He leaned towards the open passen- ger window and called to Serafina, "You walking a far piece from anywhere and more than halfway to nowhere out here, young ma'am. Get in and I'll least get you close to somewhere." He swung the passenger door open.

Serafina stopped and bent to look at the stranger. She studied his worn face and found kindness in his eyes. She slid into the seat, placing the satchel on her lap. The farmer pointed to the sawed-off still in her hand. "No reason to bother with that mean looking thing," he said.

After studying the man's face again, Serafina placed the gun in her bag but left it open. Her finger resting on the *lupera* handle.

The truck moved forward, the famer shifted through the gears and above the noise of the engine asked, "So where is it you are headed?"

She let the question hang in the air before she answered. "New Orleans."

The man let out a low whistle. "That's a long ways past where I'm going to be stopping, miss. I can get you as far as Rosedale."

Serafina leaned her head back against the seat, closed her eyes, without a trace of irony in her voice said, *"Perfetto."*

# 36

The two boys slept in the car parked behind a small barn of an abandoned farmhouse and managed to get an hour or so of fitful sleep before the morning sun woke them both. Otha drove them into Tula. The town was nothing more than a few buildings clustered at a crossing of two county roads. A feed store. Gas station that was also a blacksmith. Otha's uncle ran a general store that was a cafe, post office and barbershop. The center of life in Tula. Three old men sat in rockers on the porch, all Negroes, all wearing faded overalls, one with a frayed straw hat, the other two in sweat-stained fedoras. Three pair of eyes watching and commenting on the smallest aberration in the oil painting that was Tula. The sentinels ceased their rocking when Otha and Corky got out of the car and walked up to the storefront. Three heads cocked slightly as one, three pair of eyes squinting as if trying to unsee the mirage that appeared at the porch steps.

A Negro and white boy together.

"What we gots here?" The one in the straw hat said, speaking to his cohorts as if the boys were deaf.

"That one's related to Booker some ways, I believe," a fedora said, waving his hand towards the inside of the store.

"Which one?" the other fedora said. "Did not know Booker got himself some high yellow in his family. That boy ain't quite white, is he?"

Otha stepped up onto the porch.

"You know me," he said. "Getting senile sitting out here on this porch every damn day." He turned to Corky and waved him to join him on the porch. "Never mind these old fools. Been head-kicked by they mules too many times."

"Got to be Otha with that mouth," the straw hat said, shading his eyes with his hands.

"What you young mens doing here abouts?" Fedora number two asked.

"Seeing my aunt and uncle and getting breakfast like it's any of your business," Otha said. "You like a bunch of old womenfolk. Worse than that with the snoop-nosing you do out here."

The straw hat raised a long thin hand, pointed to the door.

"Show some respect of your elders and get yous asses inside," he said.

"And take that ofay one with you," The fedora said. "Before some cracker rides by and sees you together. Must be out yo minds."

Otha waved them off and held the door open for Corky, pushing him inside.

"Mornin', Uncle Booker," Otha said to the man standing behind the counter. His uncle was short, as round as he was tall, a bald head, glasses perched on his nose. He looked up from sorting cans on the countertop and a wide smile came across his face at seeing his nephew entering the store. The smile fled when he saw who was with him.

"This my friend, Corky," Otha said, dropping his hand on the boy's shoulder. He pointed to one of the small tables next to the front window. "We get some of Auntie's breakfast?"

Booker studied Corky over his glasses and shook his head. "You set over that table," he said, jutting his chin to a table towards the kitchen far away from the window.

Otha arched an eyebrow, but his uncle shook his head again. The two boys sat at the table as asked. Booker pushed away from the counter and waddled to the kitchen door.

"Dolette, yo' nephew out here wantin' some breakfast," he called to the kitchen.

"What nephew?" A women's shrill voice called back.

"Janelle's boy, Otha," Booker said. "He out here with a friend."

There was a squeal and a female version of Booker – shorter and rounder – rushed out through the doorway, wiping her hands on a dish towel. She came to the table, smiling, and shaking her head.

"Boy, let me look at you," she said, her hand on Otha's shoulder, then patting his face. "You sure gettin' grown, that's a fact." She frowned. "Why you don't come around here more often. See your Aunt Dolette and Uncle Booker?"

"I'm here now, ain't I, Auntie?" Otha said, squirming away from his aunt's hand.

The woman turned her attention to Corky, tipping her head to look over her glasses, an imitation of her husband, to give the boy a long once-over appraisal. "And who this you brung with you?"

"This my friend, Corky."

"Pleased to meet you," Corky said. He tried to stand, got halfway up out of his chair and gave the woman a bow, at which the old woman waved her dish towel at him to sit back down. She pointed to a stack of newspapers on the counter.

"Got your reading material there, nephew. I'm-a get you some eats. Some coffee, too?"

"Yes, ma'am," Corky said.

"Yes ma'am," she repeated, smiling at him. She swatted Otha with her towel.

"You hear how he speak, all polite?" she said. "Best you take a lesson from this nice young man." She waddled off to the kitchen.

Otha got up, took a newspaper off the stack and returned to the table. He sat, unfolding the newspaper with a snap, then laid it on the table and began reading.

"You make sure you fold that paper back up neat when you done, boy" Booker said.

"Don't I always?" Otha said, without looking up from his reading.

Corky watched as Otha read, his lips moving as he ran his forefinger under each line of print. His own mind was too cluttered with the events of the past twelve hours and trying to make sense of what happened to read. A tiny, clear-headed part of him knew he needed to formulate a plan of some kind, but his thoughts were paralyzed by grief and incomprehension at all he had seen. His heart ached with the loss of Sal, but it was swamped by waves of panic induced by the vision of Serafina being dragged out of the restaurant and the car disappearing in the night. He stared out the window as if expecting to see Sal and Serafina appear, smiling, alive and beckoning him to their waiting car so they could continue their way to New Orleans. Together.

Otha's aunt came to the table with two plates heaped with scrambled eggs, slices of ham alongside biscuits and gravy balanced on one arm. A pot of coffee in her other hand. She laid the plates in front of the boys and filled their mugs with hot coffee. She gave Otha a gentle slap to the back of his head then leaned in and kissed the same spot.

Corky dug into his breakfast while Otha took bites of his without shifting his eyes from the newspaper. Occasionally, Corky tried to read the upside-down print but couldn't beyond the bolder headlines. He mopped his plate with a biscuit, carefully constructing a last bite combination of egg, ham covered in gravy and then stuffed it all in his mouth.

"Where you say you from?" Otha asked, his face still on the paper.

"Pennsylvania," Corky mumbled while chewing his mouthful.

Otha looked up and rolled his eyes.

"I know Pennsylvania, fool. What town?"

Corky washed down his food with a gulp from his mug. "Sagamore."

"Yeah, that's what I thought." He turned the newspaper around, slid it across the table to Corky and tapped on a headline.

"This it, right?"

Corky read the headline below Otha's finger, his eyes widening as he read until he snatched the paper from the table.

"Them your mines that collapsed?"

Corky's eyes jumped from the article to Otha and back again. He dropped the paper back onto the table, both hands going to his head, pulling at his hair.

"Otha," he said in a whisper, not wanting to believe his own eyes, "Can you read those names for me."

Otha spun the paper around, found the article and began to read aloud. "Let me see ... ok ... 'Miners unaccounted for and believed trapped in the collapsed shaft are Guiseppi Palumbo, Alberto Tamburri, Thomasso Trunzo, Stanislaw Kovalchik and Walter Johnson, Jr. Rescue workers continue to dig ...'"

"Enough," Corky said. Otha looked at his friend who sat dazed, staring at the floor. "They your people?"

Corky nodded.

"Which?"

"Third name."

Otha scanned the article. "Thomasso Trunzo."

"My father."

"Goddamn, Corky. I'm ..."

"Last name is my best friend back there. Everyone calls him Sonny."

Corky took the newspaper back and sat, reading through the article again, staring at the names in print, as if he could will the letters to rearrange themselves and reality.

"What you going to do?" Otha asked.

Corky said nothing. He closed his eyes as Otha's question echoed in his brain, demanding an answer that he could not find. Otha didn't press his friend for an answer, deciding it best for the moment to let him take in the news. He picked up the paper, folded it in half, held it up and began reading, his face hidden. Several minutes passed, the two sitting in silence as the activity of the cafe went on around them. Corky got up from the table, went to the counter and refilled his mug from the pot. He sat back down and sipped the hot coffee, his mind awash in a flood of thoughts. There was no money now. He had no idea where Serafina was or what happened to her. Going to New Orleans was no longer possible, as the people Sal thought would help had turned on him. He knew he had to go back to Sagamore now but was well aware he'd be walking straight into a jail cell. Sal's confession of sorts, admitting that he hadn't murdered Markle as ordered, still left the question of who was to blame for the killing.

"We need to get over to that funeral home this morning," Corky said and began patting his pockets for the slip of paper Lusco had given him with the address and name of the owner. In the breast pocket of his vest, he found the prayer card his grandmother had given him the night he left Sagamore with Sal. Surprised he'd forgotten about it, he studied the image of St Michael the Archangel. He flipped the card and saw his grandmother's handwriting on the back. He would swear later that it was as if he'd landed upon the combination to a lock and he could hear the tumblers falling into place. He closed his eyes, swept by a wave of relief.

No money. No Serafina. No New Orleans.

Just Sal's body.

"What you got there?" Otha asked. Corky raised the card to show his friend. A smile came to his lips as he answered.

"A ticket home."

# 37

As a pale rose dawn edged the horizon, the coming light failed to convince Serafina that she was not caught in a blood drenched dream as she traveled through a surreal waterlogged landscape.

She came to the road sign announcing the town limits and saw the cafe grocery a hundred yards beyond. The windows were lit but no cars or trucks were parked in front. She walked the distance and stood across the road from the place. Nothing had changed. The sign still carried the name the dead Sicilian had chosen. Pickles. No indication that it had been turned into a juke joint as Stalling had intended. She crossed the road and slid the lupera into the satchel that remained crooked in her arm, hidden beneath the overcoat. Moving past the front windows, she could see the tables were empty. She felt an odd relief and, through her exhaustion and shock, buoyed suddenly, that she had been brought back to this place.

She stepped inside, the bell above the door announcing her entrance. A smile came to her lips when she recognized the voice that called out from the kitchen.

"Be with you in a minute. We ain't quite open but have a seat."

Serafina hesitated then crossed the cafe to the table by the window and stood staring at the chair she had sat in only a few months and several lifetimes ago. The memory of the day and all that occurred flooding her mind. She glanced back at the door, seeing Stallings and his men entering. Her gaze went to the floor where the Sicilian owner had lain first, then her father. Both men dead, their blood pooling the floor. She pulled the familiar chair from the table and sat, wrapped in the overcoat. The satchel rested on her lap, the top opened with her hand resting on the lupera. Her gaze shifted to the window and the same sodden landscape of her first visit beyond.

She turned at the sound of footsteps approaching the table.

"Brought you some coffee to get you st…"

The sight of her face stopped the cook, Isiah, in mid-sentence. He stood slack-jawed, a pot of coffee in one hand, a cup and glass of water gripped in the other. Serafina smiled and the man blinked several times, seemingly unsure of what his eyes were seeing. After a moment, he stammered a question.

"Ma'am…" he searched the deep blue of her eyes and found them focused on some unseen distance. "…are you alright?" He stepped closer and set all he carried on the table. No answer. He pulled a dish towel from his apron and held it out to Serafina. "It's clean. I'll get some water so you can…" He circled his face with his finger then nodded at her.

Her movements happened in slow motion, as if the air had turned to liquid. Serafina touched her face and felt the crusting that flecked her skin. She brought her hand away, stared at her fingers puzzling at the deep brown flaking on the tips. Her eyes fell to the overcoat and was puzzled further at finding the shimmering grey material held splatterings of deep crimson. She reached out and took the offered towel, giving Isiah a silent smile of gratitude. She dipped the cloth into the glass of water and cleaned her face. She studied the sullied cloth as if hoping to divine meaning in the patterns. She then wiped absentmindedly at the overcoat, frowning to see the effort brought no erasure of the stains. She folded the towel and laid it on the table.

"You want to take that coat off," Isiah said. "I'll see what I can do back in the kitchen. Maybe some hot water…"

Serafina shook her head and sipped her coffee, returning her stare to the window. The cook picked up the cloth without inspection.

"How about I fix up some breakfast? Make you a couple eggs and some of my famous biscuits. Set you straight."

Serafina sat silent but answered with a slow nod. The cook made a move away from the table but stopped. He half turned to face her but his eyes were on the floor. "You that woman came here with…the day Boss Stallings was here… and he…when he killed…"

The answer came in another nod. "Serafina."

"Pardon?"

She turned from the window and extended her hand. *"Mi chiamo Serafina."*

The cook smiled and took her hand, surprising her with his reply. *"Piacere, Serafina. Mi chiamo* Isiah."

Serafina's eyes went wide, and she giggled. The dream made more surreal by this Negro speaking her native tongue. *"Tu parle Italiano?"*

"Just a little," Isiah said. "Learned some from Mr. Cossimo." The smiles fled from both of their faces as the man's death replayed in their minds and silence fell between them.

The cook said nothing further and went to the kitchen, the sounds of his breakfast prep commenced.

Serafina finished her coffee and was halfway through her second cup when Isiah returned with the breakfast. There was a plate of twin fried eggs with hashed potatoes along with several strips of thick bacon. A second plate piled with a trio of fluffy biscuits, the rising steam declaring them freshly baked. He pulled a small jar from the pocket of his apron and twisted off the cap.

"This here honey is from my nephew's hives. Nothing sweeter on God's green earth." He smiled and stood waiting for Serafina to start. She picked up a bacon strip and poked it into the over easy center of one egg, dipping it in the oozing deep yellow yolk. Her eyes closed as she savored the bite and a soft moan rose from her.

"That's some good eats right there," Isiah said, a proud grin. "Take yous time and enjoy." He returned to the kitchen and left Serafina to her breakfast. She ate, taking her time, and watched the low hanging clouds ooze across the sky. Each bite and accompanying sip lifted the veil of her dream state. By the time she was sopping her plate clean with the last chunk of honey soaked biscuit, she was overcome with grief. Her sobbing came in waves that rose up from the depths of her chest, a stabbing pain from heart as if gripped in the razored talons of some great beast. Behind eyes squeezed tight, visions flooded her mind, of Sal, Stallings, Yunk, all bathed in the dark red of blood of violent deaths and engulfed in scorching flames. The blinding hot white explosions of the lupera in the car and the showering of more red.

She jumped at the weight of a hand on her shoulder and her hand dropped onto the *lupera's* handle, the satchel still cradled in her lap. She opened her eyes to see through the cascading blur of tears, Isiah at her side. She allowed herself to be lifted from the chair as she slipped her arm through the satchel handles, pressing it tight to her body with both arms. Isiah guided her to a room behind the kitchen, his gentle whisperings carried assurances that all she needed was to rest. There was a cot, a pillow and a folded blanket lay at the foot. When Isiah tried to lift Sal's overcoat from her shoulders, she clutched at the lapels, gathering the garment tight in her hands, but relented at his repeated promise his only purpose was to do what he could to clean it. She sat on the bed and Isiah bent to remove her muddied shoes, his soothing voice carrying his intent to clean them as well. He held out his hand to relieve her of the satchel but she only gripped it tighter and with closed eyes shook her head. She lay back, placing the satchel against the wall and, turning on her side towards the wall, curled herself around the leather bag. Isiah lay the blanket over her and gathered her shoes and overcoat. He turned to leave, and Serafina spoke, her voice a hoarse whisper.

"*Grazie*, Isiah" she said. "Thank you."

She slipped into a deep slumber wondering what world you woke to when you fell asleep in a dream.

# 38

The exhausted woman drifted in and out of sleep, awakening in the dark room, once to the sounds of clattering dishes and voices shouting indecipherable commands mixed with laughter and a murmuring of conversations floating through the dark like wind rustling leaves of trees. She woke again hearing a single voice in song accompanied by what she believed was the soft shushing of a broom across the floor accented by the scrape of a chair being moved. Serafina rose, slid the satchel underneath from the cot and, wrapped in the blanket, made her way out of the dark room. She went through the kitchen which had been scrubbed clean and neat stacks of dishes lined the long shelf. A wooden tub piled high with grime streaked towels sat near the back door. A mop stood in a pail of murky water. She moved into the front room with its tables empty. The large front windows were black with the fallen night. She found Isiah reflected in the dark mirror of the tall glass, sweeping the floor and moving chairs to clean underneath the tables, the source of the sounds she'd heard upon waking. Without looking up from his work, he sensed her presence and spoke.

"Hope you got some good rest. Done slept right through the dinner crowd," he said. "Had a full place, too. Could have used your help." He stopped his sweeping and pointed towards the kitchen. "Got some hot water on that stove. There's a wash basin in that room back there. Some towels, too, so you can freshen up a bit."

Serafina nodded.

"Go on then," Isiah said. "I'll get you some dinner going."

"*Grazie mille*, Isiah, but please, don't go to the trouble. *Sto* bene."

He waved his hand. "No trouble, Miss Serafina. Go freshen then *tu mangiare*, eh?" He said and returned to his sweeping.

A knock came as she was finishing what she knew was called *il bagno puttana*. Serafina wrapped a towel around herself went to the door.

"*Si?*"

Miss Serafina," Isiah's voice from the other side. "Thought you might need something else to wear."

She opened the door a foot and poked her head from behind the door. Isiah held out a dress.

"One of my missus'" he said. "Never could bring myself to getting rid of any of her things."

Serafina understood the meaning. "*Mi dispiace*, Isiah. I didn't know."

"Been a long time now. Glad to have someone get some use."

"*Grazie.*" She took the dress.

"Got you some dinner ready. Out on the table when you're ready."

She returned to the dining room, the cafe was dark, lit by a single lantern on the table. Isiah had turned off all but one light in the kitchen. Framed by the large front window, the sliver of a new moon floated in night sky awash in stars. Serafina took her seat and Isiah appeared with a plate of roast chicken and rice. He set a bowl of greens on the table.

"Them collards from the garden out back. You make sure you sop that pot likker up with that cornbread, now. You hear me?"

She smiled and nodded her thanks. She ate and Isiah watched from the kitchen with obvious satisfaction as his guest once again ate every last bite of what he had prepared for her. When she pushed the plate away, he came to the table, two small glasses and a jar of moonshine in his hands.

"Mind if I join you for a nip or two?" he said.

Serafina smiled and waved him into the chair opposite her. He sat, gave each glass a two finger pour and slid one across the table to her.

"This here is apple pie moonshine. My cousin, Ronnie, makes the smoothest corn liquor in the state."

Serafina giggled. "You have quite a few cousins making the best things here."

"No brag, Miss Serafina. Just the truth." He tapped his glass against hers and waited until she raised it to her lips before they both sipped.

She coughed at the liquor's burn but was surprised at the taste.

"It tastes just like apple pie," she said through another cough.

"Tole you," Isiah said. He drained his glass and fell silent as he poured a second.

Serafina sensed his nervousness as she watched him trace the glass edge. When he finally spoke, his voice was quiet.

"That day..." he stopped, looked out the window, then dropped his gaze back to his glass. "I didn't know...." He looked at Serafina's face in the reflection. "There wasn't nothing I could do. If I'd a said one word. They'd a..."

She looked to the window and her eyes sought his reflection in the black of the pane. Isiah glanced up and their eyes met in the glass. Serafina turned to face him, reached across the table and squeezed Isiah's forearm. She felt the tension in his muscles there loosen under her touch. He sagged a bit, relieved at her understanding, and gave her a shy smile.

"He said you were his partner. That this place…" she waved her hand at the room. "Was going to be one of his juke joints. But all I see is the same. Inside and out. The sign is still the same."

Isiah glanced about the cafe, his finger tapping on the edge of his glass.

"Truth is," he said. "After that day…when…" His eyes darted to the floor and he reached for his glass of shine and drained it. "The man never came back. Two weeks or so later, that one was with him? One with that mixed up name only some the skinny ass cracker could have. Sister's brother or…"

"Uncle Brother."

"The fuck kind of name is that?" he snarled, anger in his voice and a look of disgust on his face. "*Scuzi*," Isiah said, adding the apology. "Just a slip of the tongue, that language."

Serafina smiled and gave him a wink.

"That one showed up here. Said the man Stallings was busy and for me to just be patient, run the place just like I always did."

"When was this?"

"A week or so after…" he hesitated again, his discomfort at bringing up the day again showing. "Couple months back, now, I guess."

"And that was all he said?"

"Not another word. He did help himself to all money in the cash drawer. Never saw him again and good riddance." Isiah flicked his chin with his gathered fingers. "Been running this place on credit ever since and that man is going to come knocking any day and I ain't got nothing. *Niente, eh? Oogatz.*"

Serafina warmed at hearing Isiah using slang and an Italian hand gesture. But her expression darkened as she registered the cook's plight and after a minute in thought, she nodded to herself at some decision she had come to. She pushed her chair back and stood. "*Scuzi, Isiah, un minuto, per favore.*"

Isiah got halfway out of his chair and pointed towards the kitchen. "It's out the back door. There's a lantern on…"

Serafina wiggled her forefinger and shook her head. "*Grazie, ma non necessario.*" Isiah, embarrassed at his suggestion, closed his eyes and waved her away.

She returned carrying the satchel, sat and placed the bag on the empty chair next to hers. Her elbows on the table, she leaned forward and waited for the cook to meet her gaze before she spoke.

"He's dead."

Isiah straightened. "What you mean? Who's dead?"

"Stallings."

"How? Who…" Isiah stammered. Serafina answered him with a shrug. His eyes narrowed, searching Serafina's face for a liar's tell and found nothing but truth in the deep blue of her eyes.

He whistled softly. "What about that Uncle Brother?" A sneer and hope in his tone.

"He wasn't there."

"Where?"

Serafina ignored the question and turned to open the satchel. She pushed the lupera aside, stopped and looked up at Isiah. The cook's face wary and questioning. She gave him a smile and returned to the satchel, reaching inside once again. With her hands underneath the table, she shifted in her seat and straightened, her face serious.

"*Quanto costa?*"

Isiah shook his head.

"*Tu non capisco? Quanto costa?*

Another head shake accompanied by a shrug.

"How much is it?"

"How much is what?"

"What you owe. The debt for this place."

Isiah wiped his hand across his mouth and shrugged again.

"*Dimmi*, eh? Tell me. *Quanto?*"

She decided the man's pride was going to keep him from telling her the amount. And if he did, she doubted it would be more than half of the real number. She brought her hands from under the table and placed a stack of bills in front of her. Isiah's eyes widened.

"This much?" She riffled the bills with her thumb.

The man stared at the stack then up at Serafina. He reached across the table and repeated her riffling to check the denominations. He frowned but remained mute.

She tilted her head, studying him. Her lower lip pushed outward, and she bobbed her head. She reached back into the satchel and laid another stack of equal height beside the other. She tapped her fingers on both and bent to catch Isiah's gaze. "How about this much?"

His mouth dropped. "Where? How?"

She flicked her wrist at his question. She pushed the stacks toward him. "Pay your debt and use the rest to run this place."

"Miss Serafina, I can't take…"

"*Amico mio*, this is not a gift."

Isiah's brow furrowed.

"You need a partner, no? Since the other is…" Her wrist flicked again. The cook's expression shifted from surprise to disbelief and doubt. "I can cook, clean, greet the people and take the orders. Whatever is needed." Serafina extended her hand. "*Come si dice? Meta a meta. Cinquanta per ciascuno?* Fifty fifty, eh?"

Isiah's knees bounced, and his head bobbed like a rooster's unsure of whether to shake or nod, clearly stunned at the offer. He took Serafina's hand and then clasped it in both of his and shook on the deal. A wide grin came to his face, his eyes sparkling and brimming.

"Ok," he said. "Fifty fifty."

He loosened his grip and wiped his eyes. He opened the shine jar and tipped a healthy pour into their glasses. His raised his and waited for Serafina to do the same. He tapped his glass against hers. *"Grazie', bella*. Fifty fifty" he said and threw the shot back. Serafina sipped hers and they sat for a few minutes in silence until Isiah spoke, his face full of concern.

"What if," he glanced out the window and stopped. Serafina waited watching Isiah as he searched the darkness as if expecting to see someone approach out of the night. "What if he comes back?" He turned to Serafina, his face tight and serious. "I don't know what you done or what happened to them two or anyone else. And I don't want to know. But what happens if they come looking for you and what you have in that bag?"

Serafina looked out into the night beyond the window. The moon had risen out of sight leaving a thick swath of stars behind. Her thoughts drifted to Sal and Corky. Knowing what had befallen one but not sure of the other. Had the boy gone to New Orleans? Would he know the men that came after Sal, the ones that took her and were now, as she hoped, panther fodder, had been sent from someone in that city. Someone who knew Sal and betrayed him. Would he know, as she did now, that New Orleans was not safe for either of them? She studied the stars, bright and thick in a night sky bereft of clouds, finding hope that the clearing means the end of the ceaseless rains. Isiah's question repeated in her head. What if? Uncle Brother was the one who said he was done. Tired of all the troubles Stallings created at every turn. His lamenting the money was not worth the price.

Her gaze turned from the stars and swept past Isiah's questioning eyes as she took in the interior of the cafe. There was nothing to fear from the Italians Uncle Brother had warned Stallings about since this was not going to be a juke joint. A cafe posed no threat to their income from the illicit business they controlled along the river. She looked out again, towards the single road that ran through town. Rosedale was miles from Water Valley. Miles from what remained of Stalling's world. If they...whoever they might be, somehow discovered her alive and living in this small town? She would see them coming.

Serafina looked at Isiah then reached into the satchel. She brought the lupera out and laid the sawed off shotgun on the table. She smiled at his shocked face.

"Let them come."

# RETURN TO SAGAMORE

# 39

Sheriff Johnson stood beside his brother, Walt, under a canvas tent that served as the command center for the rescue effort. Both men sipped coffee from metal mugs, their eyes locked on the mine entrance, waiting for any sign of movement or word from below. Behind them were gathered families of the men trapped along with Walt's boy, Sonny, in the cave-in. Men stoic and blank-faced, women quietly sobbing, children gathered in the arms of mothers and aunts. All dark eyes fixed on the entrance, pressing forward as one when a worker emerged, then receding at the man's slow head-shake signaling no news. Workers stood near the entrance waiting for the mule-drawn carts loaded with rock and debris to emerge from the shaft, leading them away to be emptied and returned and sent back down in the shaft again.

Lightning flared and collective breaths were held, waiting the barrage of thunder to follow, the ground rolling as if liquid, prayers rising off trembling lips that the shockwaves would not cause another collapse.

Walt explained that the blast had been caused by a spark from a lamp or machine that ignited a pocket of methane gas. But it was the explosion that followed, when the methane fireball raced through the tunnel and hit a section where the air was saturated with coal dust, that had caused the collapse.

"It goes up like gunpowder," his brother had said.

Buzz had always known about the danger of methane and coal dust but was always puzzled by how the air could ignite when it was so damp you could almost drink it.

The explosion had collapsed a section of tunnel at the head of a steep slope leading down into the deepest section of the mine. The bodies of eight men and two mules had been brought out in the first hours of the rescue. Six men including his nephew were unaccounted for still. No telling if they were alive – lucky, in the word Walt had used, not to have been crushed beneath a mountain of rock and coal. Left alive and trapped in the dark or weakening light of a carbide lamp, listening for the scraping and scratching of your rescuers as they hopefully worked to clear a hole large enough to slip through. How long before you begin to regard your fellow survivors as thieves of a dwindling oxygen supply and wish their demise came before yours … one less body robbing your air? Your life?

Johnson knew the miners - if they were alive - would remain motionless, conserving their energy and also knowing any movement or attempt to dig out could cause another collapse. Any man who'd survived a cave-in would tell you they were most terrified when the sounds of rescue workers digging reached their ears, safety an arm's length away but knowing one misplaced pickaxe strike could bury them. And who knew what a misplaced strike was. You held your breath and prayed for the hand of God to guide the shovels and axes.

He had asked Walt for the list of names of the unaccounted-for miners, nodding at those he recognized, which were most. But it was the last that gut-punched him.

"Jesus, Walt," he said, turning to his brother. "Thom Trunzo?"

His brother nodded.

Johnson turned to scan the faces of the families huddled in the tent.

"Where's his brother-in-law, Benny?"

"On the rescue crew," Walt said. He gripped the upper sleeve of his coat, massaging the stump of his arm. "Been down there without a break. He'll dig with his hands if he has to." He glanced at his brother. "Any word on Corky?"

The sheriff dragged a hand across his face, tugged at his mustache.

"Nothing," he said and tossed the dregs from his cup out of the tent.

"They still on you about Markle?" Walt asked.

Johnson snorted. "Governor's man calls every day," he said. "Sometimes twice a damn day. What am I supposed to tell him? The kid you want to hang for this has disappeared and I don't think – hell, I know he didn't do it. And I'm even less inclined to look for him over the real killer, although I have no clue as to who that might be now."

Walt tossed the dregs of his coffee out of the tent.

"State police looking for Corky?" Walt asked.

"This asshole in Harrisburg says there's no cause to get them involved. Wants to keep this as low-profile as possible. Wants it all wrapped up nice and neat so that it's some Italian killed the warden and helps the whole bird-killing crazy immigrant story that they got going." Johnson shot his brother a hard look. "Why you so interested in this now? Your boy is trapped in a cave-in and you're asking me questions about a case of mine got nothing to do with any of this here."

Walt studied the inside of his empty mug but didn't answer.

"Look," Johnson said. "Markle was bent, you know that. And connected with the Black Hand up in Kittanning. Hell, they may have killed him for the gambling debt I heard he had or maybe just for getting out of hand, drawing too much attention."

Walt remained silent.

"Little brother, something on your mind other than being worried to death about Sonny down there?"

"I never gave him a choice," his brother said and spit tobacco juice into the rain. "Just shook him awake day after graduation and handed him a helmet …" His voice trailed off. He glanced at the families gathered in the tent. "I wish all these folks would get on back home and wait there. Doesn't do anybody any good, them being around this mess. And I sure as hell don't want any of them here when we start bringing more bodies up."

"You mean if, Walt," the sheriff said. "They're going to get Sonny and the rest of the men out of there. He's going to be ok."

His brother sent another stream of tobacco juice beyond the tent opening. "Been almost sixteen hours," he said. "Chances of getting anyone out alive are getting slimmer by the minute. And time's not the only problem I got."

"What else?"

"This goddamn rain is what else," Walt said. "You see how much water is running through here? You happen to see the lake on your way out here? Never seen it so high and you know as well as I do that there's all kinds of streams under these hills."

He lifted his boot and both men watched as the footprint filled with muddy water.

The sheriff looked out across the widening pools covering the mine yard.

"All this water," his brother said. "Got to go somewhere. They don't run out of air first, they might just drown down there."

"Jesus. I never even." Johnson stopped. The image of these men – his nephew – being trapped, slowly suffocating as the air ran out was horrifying enough to him, but the thought of them drowning shook him. "Walt, they'll get them. They must be close by now. Don't …"

His brother raised his hand and wagged a finger, warning that reassurances were not wanted.

Walt took the empty tin mug from the Sheriff's hand and set it with his own on the makeshift table. "There's something else," he said. "Come on out to my truck. Got something you need to see."

Johnson eyed his brother but before he could ask his question, Walt turned and walked from the tent. He followed, his brother pointed him to the passenger side and both men got in the truck. A small duffel was on the seat between them. Walt pushed it towards the sheriff.

"What's this?" Johnson asked.

Walt stared out of the rain-streaked window at the mine entrance.

"I brought some clean clothes for Sonny," he said. "He'll need them when he comes up." Johnson heard no conviction in his voice. "Open it," Walt said.

Johnson did as directed. Inside the duffel were a neatly folded shirt and pants, clean underwear and socks. He looked at his brother.

"In the bottom," he said. "Wrapped in that towel."

Johnson lifted the towel, surprised at the weight. He laid the bundle on his lap and unfolded the towel to reveal a Colt 45 revolver. The long barrel was nicked and scarred, sure signs of being used often as clubs. The pearl handle was edged in a dark reddish brown crust Johnson knew to be blood. He also knew who the guns belonged to without needing the inlaid monogram to tell him. He glanced at his brother, whose gaze remained on the windshield.

"Where'd you get this?" Johnson asked.

Walt brought his hands to the steering wheel, squeezing hard enough that Johnson saw his knuckles whiten.

"Brother, this is Markle's gun," Johnson said. "What the hell are you doing with it?"

"I know whose gun that is," he said, his voice a low monotone. "I went into Sonny's room to get some clothes. For when he comes up."

Johnson sagged, his eyes closing, wanting to unhear his brother's words, and hoping when he opened them the gun would be gone. But the gun remained. "Where was it?"

"Does it matter?" Walt said, turning to look at his brother, his eyes wet.

Johnson tugged on his mustache. His mind reeled as he tried to refute the evidence that was leading to only one conclusion.

"This makes no sense," Johnson said. "If he did what you're thinking."

"What we're both thinking, Buzz. No sense in kidding each other. You know what this looks like."

"There's got to be an explanation, Walt. I mean, if you're a mur-" he choked on the word thinking it applied to his nephew. "You don't hang on to things that can link you to a killing. You toss this gun in the goddamn lake." He rewrapped the bundle but left it on his lap contemplating what to do with them. "Shit," he muttered and looked out the side window, searching for an answer in the rain. "Why'd the hell you show me this, Walt?" he asked, without looking away from the window. "Should have buried it some place, for God's sake."

"And let Corky take the fall?" Walt said. "Let that boy hang for something he didn't do? You think I can live with that? Look at my own boy every day and think the only reason he's alive is because his best friend isn't? Can't do that, Buzz. If Sonny did this? He must face it like a man."

Johnson looked at his younger brother and wondered how it was that Walt held a more defined sense of right and wrong than he himself did. As if in losing his arm, he had gained an unshakable conviction to a moral code and a clear distinction between right and wrong.

Johnson's years as a lawman had blurred that line and he knew nothing was so black and white. He thought of Gina Ferraro, what he'd done with her, for her and all that had come from his ignoring her lesser indiscretions. He saw it as the price for a greater good. He could get rid of the evidence laying in his lap and no one beyond his brother and Sonny would know. Walt was right, though. That left an innocent Corky to take the blame.

"Look," the sheriff said. "That man's body was out there for a couple hours before we got there. Maybe Sonny was out that way hunting again, found the game warden dead, and took the gun? Didn't tell anyone? Markle carried two of these. Where's the other one?"

Walt shrugged. The two men sat without conversation, listening to the rain battering the truck. Johnson wondering if the same thought was sitting in his brother's mind as his and hoping that the noise would drown out the voice whispering, they'd all be better off if Sonny never made it out of the mine.

They were jolted by the blast of the steam whistle sounding the rescue crew's return. Sheriff Johnson looked at his brother, the man's face pale, his jaw clamped. Without turning his gaze from the windshield, Walt tilted his head towards the bundle. "Best you keep that."

Johnson sighed his agreement and stuffed the bundle back into the duffel. He laid his hand on the door handle and turned to his brother. "Come on, Walt. Let's get over there. I'm sure Sonny's walking out of that mine right now and he's just fine."

Walt yanked his door open and looked back at his younger brother.

"That's what I'm afraid of."

Johnson dropped into the chair behind his desk, exhausted after the long and emotional day at the mines. After the whistle call, he stood with Walt waiting as the rescue crew emerged. Buzz heard his brother's long sigh of relief at seeing that Sonny was one of the three miners who walked out. He watched as the two embraced and both broke down. Their sobbing turned to laughter when they pulled back and saw each other's tear and soot-streaked faces.

The bodies of the other three miners were brought out on a mule drawn cart, Thomasso Trunzo's among them. Johnson accompanied his brother and nephew to Walt's truck and, after embracing both, watched as reunited father and son drove away. The pleading look in his older brother's eyes haunted Johnson on his own ride home.

He had sat brooding in his armchair, sipping Gina's whiskey, assuring his wife that nothing was wrong now that Sonny was safe and shooing her off to bed. He spent most the night wide awake searching for a solution to his nephew's situation. In his mind's eye, he saw himself in his small fishing boat dropping the bloodstained evidence into the middle of Keystone Lake. But he knew, while his doing so kept his nephew safe, it left the Trunzo boy as the suspected killer. He knew also he would not be able to live with himself, let alone face Gina Ferraro again, if it resulted in her only grandson being hung for a crime he did not commit. But what if Sonny hadn't done it? What if he had come across Markle's body and taken the guns? Was it possible that the killer was still out there? Johnson scoffed at his own stupidity in stretching for an explanation for what his experience and instinct told him was far beyond any likelihood. It was impossible for him to accept his nephew was any more capable of the game warden's brutal murder than Gina's grandson. But if he was forced to choose between his own family and Gina's, what choice did he really have? A wave of despair rolled over him and he took a long swallow of the 'shine. The warmth of liquor bloomed in his chest but brought no inspired solution.

When the eastern sky lightened, he rose, washed up, put on a clean shirt and, gulping a half cup of coffee his wife handed to him, drove to his office. His stomach now in a sour grumbling roil that matched his mood as he shuffled papers mindlessly, scanning without registering the words that swam before his weary eyes. The previous day's Gazette lay still folded at his elbow, the headline in bold caps declaring Sagamore Explosion Traps Miners. The rescue would be old news by the time the evening edition came out. He gazed out the window and watched the rain fall in grey sheets. It had fallen for several days, steady and unchanging as if the skies had unleashed an ocean suspended in the clouds.

The creeks were swollen beyond their banks, hollows had turned into rushing rivers, flatlands of the farms now knee-deep lakes. The bone-chilling damp seeped into everything and everyone.

The sheriff rose from his chair and crossed to the corner of the room. He used a poker to open the door of the potbellied stove and added a log to the blazing fire. It took nearly laying his hands on the iron of the stove to get the feeling back in his fingers. He turned his backside to the warmth.

Thunder rumbled, rattling the window, and rolled through the floorboards. The storm that had swept into the valley brought a barrage of thunder and lightning strikes, shaking the world like the concussion of cannonade that pounded the battlefields of Cuba where Johnson had fought.

The front door of the outer office opened, the wind whipping the papers on Johnson's desk, as his deputy nephew entered. He pushed the door closed and shook the rainwater off his coat.

"It's goddamn biblical out there, Uncle Buzz," he said and walked to stand in front of the stove, rubbing his hands. "I'm serious, if these ain't the end times, I'm not sure if I want to be around to see what it's really going to be like."

The older man nodded. "No locusts yet," he said.

His nephew laughed. "'Yet' being the operative word in that sentence."

"It's early in the day, nephew," Johnson said. "One thing I have learned, don't ever think things can't get worse."

Johnson went to his desk and sat down, returned to shuffling papers. He heard Dennis going about his routine of making his poor excuse for coffee and was glad for the full cup of his own brew that remained in his mug. His nephew called from the outer office.

"You see the note I left about the phone call yesterday?" the deputy asked. "Came while you were out at the mines."

Johnson sighed. "I hope you told whatever asshole from the governor's office it was squeaking about Markle's killer that we had our hands a bit full down at the mines. Hell, you'd think they'd know that. They must get the newspaper in Harrisburg."

Dennis appeared in the doorway, coffee pot in hand.

"Wasn't the governor's office," he said. "It's on the note."

Johnson began to pat the scattered papers.

"Where'd you leave it?"

His nephew came in and leaned across the desk.

"Left it right on top," he said, fingering a stack in the center of the clutter. He fanned the small pile.

"Here," he said, lifting a torn off corner of a tablet sheet. His uncle gave him a disgusted look.

"Now how could I have missed this?" Johnson asked.

The deputy shrugged.

Johnson held the note, squinting behind his reading glasses.

"Damn, Dennis, you practicing to be a doctor with this hen's scratch? What's this say now?"

"It's a phone number ..."

"That I can see," Johnson said. "I'm talking about this squiggly bit here." He turned the scrap towards his nephew.

"Says, 'Please call Mr. Crocetti in Pittsburgh. Very important.'" He smiled.

"Dino Crocetti called here?"

"I can't say for sure if it was him but definitely an Italian talking with 'Please-ah tell-ah Shereeef-ah Johnson-ah to-ah ...'"

A hard glare from Johnson cut him off.

"I explained you were out at the mines," the deputy said. "He just said what's on the note. Call him at that number and it was very important."

The sheriff waved his nephew away. "Good coffee is very important," he said, and stared at the note, trying to divine the reason for the mobster's call. If Crocetti had wanted to know about the situation at the mines, he only needed to called the mayor's office or the mining company direct. The man certainly had enough stature and power to by-pass the county sheriff for that kind of information. He dialed the number and waited for the person who answered to get Crocetti on the line.

"Sheriff Johnson," the old man said. "Thank you for returning my phone call. I know that you're very busy."

"Certainly, Mr. Crocetti," Johnson said. "We're all relieved that some of the men ..."

Crocetti interrupted. "Yes, yes, as I am, Sheriff," he said. "Thankful some of the men were saved. This is a tragedy, and our fraternal organization will do as we have always done for the unfortunate families of those men lost. This is not the reason for my call but rather another matter I believe is of your great concern."

"Another matter? I'm not sure I follow," Johnson said.

Crocetti cut him off again and Johnson listened quietly as the old man continued then ended with a simple goodbye. He hung up without waiting for Johnson to reply. The sheriff cradled the phone and sat looking at it, puzzling over what he had heard. Dennis walked in with a steaming cup of coffee in both hands, stopping to sip from one as he held the other out to his uncle. Johnson rose to lift his coat from the back of his chair and slipped into it. He took the offered cup and blew across the hot liquid before drinking.

"Get your coat," he said. "We're taking a ride."

"Now? Out in this?"

Johnson fixed his nephew with a scowl and the young man went for his coat.

"Where we going?" Dennis called from the outer office.

The sheriff put on his Stetson and took a long gulp of coffee. He grimaced and managed to refrain from spitting it back into the cup. He shook his head and set the mug on his desk.

"We're meeting Crocetti in Saltsburg," Johnson said and walked to the front door as his nephew gathered his belongings. "In this weather, it'll take an hour, maybe a bit more."

"What's so important the boss himself comes out of the city?" Dennis said, sliding into his coat as he came to the door. "In this weather, too?"

"Well, what he told me on the phone," Johnson said. "Was that he had the man who killed Markle."

The deputy froze. "Seriously?"

"That's what he said."

The sheriff tossed his nephew a set of keys. Dennis gave him a puzzled look.

"Your truck? Shouldn't we be taking the car, if you're bringing a prisoner back?"

Johnson opened the door and tipped his head towards the exit.

"No need," he said. "The man's dead."

It was noon, the sky dusk-dark and the rain falling in a steady shower, when the two lawmen pulled off the main road just west of Saltsburg, Johnson directing his nephew onto a country lane that cut through the woods a short run and ended at a derelict building, the ceiling half collapsed, windows broken out.

Johnson motioned for his nephew. "Let's get turned around so we can see them coming up the road."

The deputy swung the truck in the small parking area and backed up, the headlights now pointing to where the road came out of the woods.

Light flickered across the windshield and two sets of headlights flashed through the trees. A long black sedan followed by a panel truck drove into the little parking lot. The vehicles circled the sheriff's truck and came to stop about ten yards past Johnson. The sedan on the left and truck on the right, engines idling. A steady puffing of grey smoke drifted from the tailpipes. Lights flared through the trees as a second sedan came up the drive and into the lot, circling and pulling up on the far side of the first sedan. Johnson could see two men in the front seat but was unable to tell if there were others in the car. A man - beefy in thick long overcoat, fedora and gloves - got out of the passenger side of the first sedan and stood near the rear door. He crooked a gloved finger and nodded towards the sheriff's truck.

The deputy turned and reached for one of the shotguns resting on the rear window rack, but Johnson dropped a hand on his nephew's knee, shook his head.

"Wait here," he said and got out of the car. As he approached the rear passenger door of the long black sedan, the man stepped towards him, placed his hands on the sheriff's chest and began to pat him down. The rear window came down and voice, quiet and commanding, spoke.

"There is no need for that. *Lo Sceriffo è un nostro amico.*"

The bodyguard dropped his hands and stepped back, a heavy-lidded stare locked on Johnson. He tilted his head towards the window.

Johnson bent down and tipped his hat. "*Ciao*, Dino," he said. "*Come stai?*"

The window came the rest of the way down.

"*Ciao*, Albin," the old man nodded at Johnson and wagged his hand. "*Mezzo e mezzo*," he said. "At my age, it's the best one can hope for, eh?"

"You'll outlive us all, I figure. All that olive oil."

Crocetti shrugged, a slight smile on his lips. "I thank you for driving all this way, in this …" He waved his hand in a circle. "A bit unusual, I realize but …" his voice trailed off.

"*Non è un problema*," Johnson said.

"*Stai parlando molto bene Italiano*," the old man said.

"Our friend Gina's a good teacher. I'm still having trouble with the accent on certain words but trying."

"*Buono, amico mio*," Crocetti said. "More of your people should make the effort. The same as we learn your language. We might get along a bit better."

"No argument from me," Johnson said and after a pause. "So, you have …"

Crocetti cut him off. "The man who killed the game warden? Yes, sheriff. This whole thing needs to be put to rest. The man caused some problems when he was alive but can solve a few now that he is *la morte*. The man responsible …," he said as his gloved hand came to the open window holding a folded set of papers. "Is … was … Salvatore Gentile." He passed the papers to Johnson. "These are his identification papers."

Johnson took the papers.

"How do you know this … Gentile … is Markle's killer? Why did he …"

The old man waved him off.

"You have your killer, Sheriff," Crocetti said. "That's all that matters now. We can all, including the governor, move on and, more importantly, get back to business. I'm sure you agree." He nodded to his man who held out his arm towards the truck. Johnson straightened and walked across the lot to the truck, Crocetti's man at his side.

Two men stepped from each side of panel truck and moved to the rear, standing at the double doors with hands in the pockets of their long overcoats. When Johnson reached the rear of the truck, the bodyguard wagged a finger at one of the men and pointed at the doors. The man swung the doors open to reveal a wood casket. Johnson could see a heavy canvas lining spilling out from between the bottom and the wooden top. Another finger wag and the man lifted the top.

Johnson turned to his truck.

"Give us some light, Dennis," he called, and headlamps came on. He turned back to the open panel truck. In the casket, a body lay on a bed of ice, wrapped in sheets. Johnson stepped back and watched as Crocetti's men lifted the casket and loaded it into the back of his truck. He walked back to Crocetti's car. The window came down halfway. Johnson leaned down to look inside again.

"I'm sure the governor will be satisfied that you've solved this situation," Crocetti said.

"And what do I tell him? This fellow just showed up dead?"

Crocetti smiled. "You're a smart man, Sheriff" he said. "You will find a way to explain it well enough, find the necessary connections. I'm quite sure."

In that moment, Johnson struggled to come up with how to connect this Gentile with Markle. Some way to place the Italian at the scene of the crime that was believable.

"You know the story. These men, like this one, Gentile. They are *animale*. They bring the old country ways here and prey on their own *paesani*. They have no honor. And they die sometimes." The old man brushed his coat sleeve with a gloved hand.

"You have everything you need, Sheriff," the old man said, "And more, I believe you'll find." Answering the question on Johnson's face he added. "The murders in Kittanning, Sheriff? The fat man and the one who worked for him. I'm certain Gentile was responsible for those killings, as well. I'm sure you can agree that many of your problems are now solved, no?"

"It would seem so."

"And we can assure our friend, Gina," Crocetti said. "That this should certainly end any thoughts that the Trunzo boy was responsible or involved in any way."

Johnson leaned down again to lock eyes with the old man. He nodded. The old man smiled and, reaching inside his coat, brought a small leather billfold. Crocetti opened it and drew out a business card which he handed to Johnson. The card was imprinted with only the old man's name on one side and blank on the other.

"Sheriff," Crocetti said. "Please bring the lovely Mrs. Johnson to enjoy an evening at one of my nightclubs as my guest. The food is excellent and the finest musicians in the country perform nightly. Come any time. There is no need for reservations. Simply show this card to the doorman and you will be treated very well, that I can promise you."

Before Johnson could respond, Crocetti tapped on the back of the front seat.

"*Avante*," he said and gave Johnson a small nod before rolling up the window. The driver dropped the car into gear and rolled away, the panel truck following.

The other sedan pulled up, stopped and the rear door opened. A young Italian man stepped out. He was short, well-dressed in a tailored suit. His hair oiled and slicked straight back. A pencil mustache graced his upper lip. Johnson noticed a diamond stick pin in his tie and the glint of a diamond cufflink when the young man extended his hand.

"Sheriff, I'm Mister Crocetti's son, Dino," he said. "*Il mio amico mi chiama Junior.*"

The pair shook hands.

"I can see the resemblance," Johnson said. "Lucky for you, you favor your mother." Junior gave him a smile but shook his head.

"I won't tell my father you said that." He stepped back from the car door and spoke. "My father has something else for you."

Another passenger slid from the back seat and when he got out, Johnson found himself looking at Corky Trunzo. He watched as the two young men hugged, then kissed each other on both cheeks. Junior turned to Johnson.

"*Ciao*, Sheriff," Junior said. "Take good care of our friend." He got back into the rear seat of the car and was driven off.

Johnson turned and pulled Corky into a hug, squeezing him tight. Relief flooded through his body. He leaned back, grabbing Corky's upper arms and said, "Let's get you home." He draped his arm around the boy's shoulders and led him towards the truck.

As they walked, Johnson wondered if there would come a time when he would tell Corky what he knew about Sonny. Or if he would be able to leave the secret lying with the guns on the bottom of the lake. He was still bothered that the man's other revolver had not been found. A crucial piece of evidence that could point to someone other than Sonny. He slid his hand into the pocket of his coat and fingered the card Crocetti gave him. A night out in Smoketown as the man's guest would be a real treat. He smiled at the power this small piece of paper held and represented, carried by the man in his little leather billfold. It was in that instant he recalled the game warden's leather billfold that contained the dead man's Special Agent badge. He realized that the piece of evidence he needed to place Gentile at the scene of Markle's murder was sitting in the top drawer of his desk.

Corky opened his eyes but knew the time without needing a clock. Six days a week, he rose at four in the morning, dressed and slipped from his bedroom on the second floor, the soft groaning of the floorboards the only betrayal of his being awake as he moved like a ghost through the house. He passed the door of the attic room where his father had always slept, then eased down the hall past what had been his mother's bedroom. In the kitchen, in a cloaking darkness broken only by the single match he struck to light the stove and the soft blue glow of the burner's flame, he made and drank his morning coffee. When he was finished, he rinsed his cup and left it to dry on the sideboard. He laced his work boots, put on his coat and hat and left the house by the back door, carrying a metal lunch pail to stand by the roadside, waiting for the headlights of his uncle's truck to appear out of the black predawn.

So began his days and the routine of his life since returning to Sagamore. To his parent's house and his father now dead. Sal gone. His plan failed, and he was left no choice. He buried his dreams of escape to the promised land of New Orleans along with his father, and the day after the funeral, went to work in the mines. Now convinced he was a fool to think he could avoid what he came to see as his true fate as a son of Sagamore. Trapped behind the veil.

Walt Johnson negotiated a deal for the company to continue leasing the house to Corky, that consideration the only compensation he would get for losing his father to the mines.

Sheriff Johnson waited until a few days after the funeral to come see him, showing up at the house in the early evening. The two sat in the kitchen, Johnson starting the conversation by apologizing for all the trouble Corky had endured. He refrained from asking Corky questions about where he'd gone and what had happened.

"It's over," Johnson said. "The governor seems satisfied. Maybe a bit too much so, being that he got his Italian killer after all." He shook his head. "But it is over now, Corky. Over for you, for your grandmother. And I can honestly say, I'm happy the way this has turned out for you. Can't say I'm feeling the same 'bout you working the mines. Figured you'd be off to college and something better for yourself."

Corky looked down, suddenly interested in the floor. Johnson stood, put on his Stetson and started for the door.

"I understand a lot has happened to you, son. Losing your father, all this other nonsense. None of it deserved. But don't give up on yourself. Mining ain't for you. We both know you got other talents that will help see you through this patch. Might want to rethink your plan. Or get one. Maybe talk to your grandmother, see if she has any ideas." He opened the door and stopped, waiting for Corky to look his way. "But you didn't hear that from me." He winked and left.

The days rolled into weeks, then months. The summer of his returning slipped into autumn and now, with each ascent at the end of his shift, it was as if he dragged the darkness of the mines above ground to devour the light of the world and the black dust that invaded his clothing, his skin, and his lungs, rose with him like a wafting smoke that choked the sun and shortened the days into winter.

His life passed encased in darkness. Christmas came and went as did the new year. Both holidays - the first without his father - were spent quietly and were no more than a brief respite from the mines.

It was somewhere in this rosaried string of days that the package arrived.

On a day like any other, he came home from work, stripped to his soot-encrusted union suit while he boiled water for this bath. Shedding the long underwear, he slid into the tub and sat in the steaming water, lost in the exhaustion of another day, soaking the ache from his muscles and weariness from his bones, scouring the grime and black dust from his skin.

More than once during his baths, he had looked at his hand, studying the black edging underneath his fingernails that remained no matter how hard he scrubbed, and saw his father's hands.

On that day, it wasn't until he had dressed and gone to front porch to check for mail that he found the slim box wrapped in brown paper and secured by twine propped against the front door. He returned with it to the kitchen and sat at the table. Addressed to him in an elegant cursive, the return read simply "General Delivery, Rosedale, Mississippi." He used a kitchen knife to cut the string and edged the blade through the brown paper wrapping – then, folding it neatly so that the addresses showed, set it on the table. Wary curiosity slowed his opening of the box. He stood, staring at the top, then lifted the brown wrapping to study the return address again. Mississippi and all that happened there came back to him in cold-sweat nightmares. And in quiet moments, like this, if he closed his eyes, he saw himself standing in the kitchen at Lusco's, watching as the stranger walked through the door, raised his hand and shot Sal. Again. And again. Serafina being dragged into the night to disappear forever.

A shuddering ran along his spine. Opening his eyes to the box on the table before him, he let out a sigh, placed his hands on the table, bracing himself. For what, he wasn't exactly sure, but nothing good had come from Mississippi.

He lifted the top off the box and set it aside. He pulled back the tissue paper and leapt back, as if a coiled rattler sat in the box. Struck by equal parts wonder and confusion, he found himself staring at Sal's overcoat. He glanced about the room half expecting to find someone - Sal or Serafina or both - watching, his ears waiting to hear their laughter at the surprise. But no one was there.

He picked the coat up and held it aloft by the shoulders, turning it back to front, his eyes sweeping, inspecting, searching. It was clean and unmarked - exactly as when worn by its always impeccably dressed owner. But it was Serafina was who was wearing it at Lusco's. He lay the coat full length out on the table, and through the tears welling in his eyes, conjured a vision of Sal, alive, smiling and laughing. Not lying in the pooling blood on the floor of Lusco's. He ran his hands down the black cloth, believing for a half-second that his touch could deliver the man to this place, to materialize inside the coat, to stand in this kitchen. His hand came across a hard lump. He flipped open the coat and began patting the lining until he found the carefully hidden pocket and pulled an envelope from the opening. It was sealed and inscribed with his name. Grabbing the knife, he slid the blade through the paper and its contents spilled onto the table. There were five strapped bundles of $100 bills with the number 10,000 imprinted on the band.

Fifty thousand dollars.

Without taking his eyes off the bundled cash, he groped for the chair, found and set it upright, then dropped down into it, and sat slump shouldered at the table. He felt gut punched, stunned, and unable to catch his breath. He picked up a bundle and riffled it. All hundred-dollar bills. He checked all five bundles. All hundreds. Fifty thousand dollars. His share of the Rooster heist money. He stacked the bundles. They stood two inches tall. That much money should be taller, was the only thought his whirling brain could muster. He fanned the stack, then tucking his fingers under the outermost bundles, flipped the fan over and back like a magician handling a deck of cards.

Fifty thousand dollars.

He flipped the bundles again, then gathered and squared them in a single stack. Picking up the envelope, he looked inside hoping for a note, but found instead a folded clipping from a newspaper called The Clarksdale Press Register. Corky remembered being told Clarksdale was a town in the Delta. On the page, below the headline declaring the opening of a new clothing store just outside of Rosedale, was a photo of a store front, the two large windows scripted with the words "Fine Clothing for Men & Women" and "Italian Fashions." A smiling woman in a white dress stood with her hand raised, pointing to sign above the doorway which read, "Serafina's."

He brought the clipping to within a few inches of his nose. There was no doubt, it was her. Alive. In Rosedale. The very place she had told him her father brought her to be bartered away to a husband she didn't know. The place Stallings killed her father and the café owner and claimed her as his own property. Corky burst into laughter and then slumped into the chair. Tears followed, coming with deep sobs at all that happened came back. All that was planned and all that came undone. He had not shed a single tear over any of it or grieved the losses. His father. Sal. Or Serafina who, until this moment, he was certain was dead. As dead as his dream of New Orleans and never returning to Sagamore. And the dream of escaping the mines, dead along with the rest.

When he was cried out, Corky wiped his sleeve across his face. He stared at the stack of money on the table, mystified and amazed in equal measure and, after a time, a smile eased onto his lips. He stood and draped Sal's coat across his shoulders.

"Ok, sheriff," he said aloud as he stuffed the money and newspaper clipping into the pockets. "I have a plan."

In the spring, one year after his return from the south, Corky bought the lone hotel in Sagamore, a large, twenty-room, three-story building that sat on a hill overlooking the town. There was a covered porch that ran along all four sides. Inside was a large parlor and sitting room with a wood bar, a large dining room and a spacious, well-equipped kitchen. He hired Sonny away from the mines to work as the general manager and the two friends oversaw the renovations that began after the purchase. They designed the kitchen and dining room large enough to operate as a restaurant as well, open to the public. After some lengthy arguments and presenting her with drawings of the new rooms, Corky convinced his grandmother that, when the renovations were done, she would move into one the large suites on the top floor. Gina acquiesced only after Corky agreed not to sell her house.

Construction crews worked through the summer, and during those months of renovation, there were letters and then phone calls south. Dreams were shared, plans discussed, and after much cajoling and convincing, arrangements made, and train tickets bought.

The leaves had begun to turn, the air carried the crisp scent of fall as Corky drove to the station in Pittsburgh to meet the train arriving from Memphis. He stood on the platform watching as passengers disembarked. From a car close to rear of the train he saw Otha, a small suitcase in his hand, step down the stairs. Otha scanned the platform, a broad smile on his face at finding Corky. He raised his hand and waved and when Corky reached his friend they greeted each other with hugs and wide smiles. There were a few stares and frowns from other passengers at seeing the Italian and colored men embracing, but most ignored the pair. Pittsburgh was a city of immigrants with a large black population, and the train platform was a throng of mixed languages and skin tones.

The pair moved out of the station and packed themselves and their bags into Corky's sedan. On the long drive to back Sagamore, he answered his friend's non-stop questions about the city of Pittsburgh, the smoke-filled sky that hovered overhead, about the steel mills and the coal mines. Once they passed beyond the steep inclines that surrounded the city, Otha waved at the rolling hills.

"Sure looks like the north Mississippi Hill Country around here," Otha said.

"Plenty of things here not all that different than down south," Corky said. "Poor people just trying to get by, working hard labor for little pay."

The questions turned to the hotel and the plans Corky had shared in letters and conversations over the past months.

They arrived at the hotel on the hill, the fresh white paint glowing in the mid-afternoon sun. Otha spilled from the car and stood a bit slack-jawed as he took in the sight.

"Pretty nice, eh?" Corky said. "Didn't lie, did I?"

"No, you did not," Otha said. "Not one bit."

Sonny appeared on the porch.

"Welcome," Sonny said with a wave as he came down the stairs. "Took you long enough. How was the train ride?"

Corky introduced Sonny who shook hands with Otha, repeating welcome, welcome, glad to meet you as he worked the visitor's arm a like pump handles.

"It's alright, Sonny," Corky said into his friend's ear. "No call to be overly nervous."

Sonny nodded, his eyes on the ground.

"Apologies," he said. "I'm just, well. I never met any."

"Coloreds?" Otha asked. "Neeeee groes? Darkies? Nig-"

Sonny shook his head. He looked to Corky.

"Otha's just kidding," Corky said. "His way of making white people feel comfortable."

"Corky says you good people," Otha said. "That's enough for me."

Sonny relaxed and smiled at Otha.

"Lessing of course you prove otherwise," Otha said. "Then all bets is off, because you sure is one white son-of-a-bitch."

"Enough," Corky said, and Otha offered his hand again to Sonny. The pair shook and Corky left them together to go inside.

He returned to the porch with a bottle of amber liquid and a stack of small glasses and joined Sonny and Otha.

"This is your plan, now?" Otha asked. "You buy a hotel and what us all to run it? You know I ain't calling you 'Boss,' right?" and laughed.

Corky shook his head, then motioned for Otha and Sonny to follow. They walked the porch around to the back of the hotel. Corky set the glasses down on the railing and filled three, handing one to each of his friends. He held his out and they touched glasses in a silent toast. Otha sipped and eyed the glass in admiration.

"That is righteous," he said and took a second taste. "Where you get this from?" Corky and Sonny exchanged a knowing smile.

"Hotel's only part of the plan," Corky said and sat in a tall-backed wooden chair, waving for the others to do the same. Otha sat. Sonny leaned back against the railing. "I couldn't tell you everything I had in mind in the letters. Some things weren't in place until a few days ago. But I don't want you working for me at the hotel."

"Then what am I doing here?" Otha asked. "You want the twins here in the kitchen. You thinking about me managing this place with your boy here." He poked his chin at Sonny.

"I am not his boy," Sonny said with a tight smile. "I'm his partner."

"Which is what I … we want you to be, Otha," Corky said. "A partner."

Otha squinted. "In a hotel?" he said. "I don't know nothing about running a place like this."

"Not much to it, really," Sonny said. "But I think Corky's got something you do know about running."

"Well?" Otha said to Corky, who waved at the large open field that sloped away from the porch. At the back of the property was a penned-in area where a dozen hogs lazed. Otha looked at Corky, studying his face.

"What the hell?" he said. "You want me to be a pig farmer?"

Corky smiled. "In a manner of speaking," he said, and nodded at Sonny, who left the porch and walked inside. His friend came back to the porch carrying a briefcase.

"Looking like a proper businessman with that thing in your hand," Corky said.

Sonny set the case on the railing and snapped it open. He reached in and pulled out a banded stack of bills and set it on the armrest of Otha's chair. The young man's eyes widened.

Corky tapped the stack. "This is yours," he said. "A share of what's left from The Rooster. After buying and fixing up this place, and what Serafina had after she bought her store in Rosedale. We both thought you deserved this and more, but that's what's left."

Otha picked up the stack and fanned it with his thumb. He let a low whistle escape.

"You sure, Corky?"

"Yes," Corky said. "You deserve it."

"What now?" Otha asked, riffling through the bills. "I take this and go back home?"

"If you want. Rather you didn't, though," Sonny said, pulling two more banded stacks from his briefcase which he placed on the arm rest. "We'd prefer you stayed here and help us keep this coming our way." Otha's eyes bounced from the stacks to Corky to Sonny and back.

"Where'd you get that?" Otha asked.

Sonny pointed to the rear of the property and the hogs. A few yards away stood an outbuilding, thick streams of grey smoke pouring from two metal chimney pipes. Open framework was attached to one end that when completed would double the size of the building.

"You know the thing about a hotel this size?" Sonny said.

Otha turned his palms upward and shrugged.

"You need to do a lot of laundry." Sonny and Corky both laughed.

"What am I missing?" Otha asked.

"When that's finished back there," Corky said. "We're moving everything that was in my *Nonna's* laundry shed from behind her house in that larger building."

"And?"

"Besides the laundry tubs and boilers," Sonny said, "there is the still where that whiskey you're liking so much was made."

Otha looked at his glass.

"You made this?" Otha asked and turned to Corky. "I thought you were full of shit talking 'bout knowing how to make 'shine."

"This one," Sonny said, pointing to Corky. "He's been making the best whiskey around here for years now." He drained his glass and held it for Corky to refill it.

"When that shed's finished and we set up again," Corky said, "we'll be able to make twice, maybe three times what I was doing at the old house."

"And you sell it and make this kind of money?" Otha said, tapping the double stack.

"I ... we ... have one customer," Corky said. "Takes everything we make except what we might keep for ourselves and a few friends. We make it, bottle it up. A truck comes, takes the load and leaves our envelope. This same customer keeps any unwanted attention away, as well."

"Not that anyone seems to care all that much," Sonny said. "Common knowledge Corky's been doing this awhile. His grandma before him. My uncle never bothered about it."

"Your uncle?" Otha asked.

"Sonny's Uncle Buzz is the sheriff," Corky said.

"Damn," Otha said. "You got this place fixed up tighter than Boss Stallings back home. Who is this customer you talking about?"

Corky and Sonny exchanged glances. Sonny shrugged.

"Same man who got me out of Mississippi," Corky said. "Mr. Crocetti is a very powerful man in Pittsburgh and has many business interests there. He's well connected and respected. One of his businesses is the most popular night-club in Smoketown."

"Where's Smoketown?" Otha asked.

"That's what everyone calls Pittsburgh," Sonny said. "You see the air in that town when we passed through? Ain't nothing to breathe but smoke."

"Thought you was calling it that because of my people living there," Otha said.

"The club is in the colored section, yes," Corky said. "But it's the place to go for everyone who's anyone and wants to have a good time and, most importantly for us, to drink good whiskey. Main thing is, besides being where our very good whiskey ends up, the best jazz musicians in the country all play there. And I'm thinking that there should be more places for the musicians to play. I want to open clubs in smaller towns between the big cities."

"You talking like juke joints?" Otha asked.

Corky smiled and raised his glass to Otha. "You getting the picture now?"

"We're thinking that you," Sonny said, tipping his glass towards Otha, "would be the perfect person to run that business."

"Why? Because I'm a smoke?" Otha said, anger rising in his voice.

"Goddamn, Otha," Sonny said and came off the railing. "This got nothing to do with you being colored. Corky says you're smart, saved his ass in Mississippi and someone we can trust. That's all. You want in on this or not?"

Otha scowled as he stood and walked a few paces down the porch. He went to the railing and stared out over the slope of the lawn. Corky gave Sonny a nod and went to stand beside Otha.

"You'll make a lot of money, my friend," Corky said. "Doing something I know you enjoy. Running a club. Classier than The Rooster. Great musicians coming through. But if you want to go back home, I respect that. I'd rather you didn't, like I said. I need someone I can trust as a partner in this and that I know I can do with you."

Otha took a drink and looked past Corky to Sonny. His eyes came back to lock on Corky's. "He going to be a problem for me?" he said.

Corky shook his head. "Sonny's never been anywhere but western Pennsylvania," he said. "But he's good people, Otha. Give him a chance to get acquainted. He worked the mines with every kind of person and the way he sees it, you come up out of the mines together, everyone is black."

Otha scoffed. "You can't seriously believe that."

"Look, I'm not saying it won't be difficult at times up here," Corky said. "Folks think they're somehow different than the white folks down south. Which is not true. Everyone sees color. I never got a taste for what it's like until I was in Mississippi and saw how people treated Sal and me. Even you called us that word."

"Half niggers," Otha said.

"Yes. Half niggers," Corky said. "Never been called that up here but it'd be a lie to say there's no prejudice against us or Sonny's people."

"Ain't the same," Otha said. "And you know that."

"Not saying it is," Corky said. "Far from perfect up here. Just thinking that there's a way of making some real money doing something you might like to be doing. Hell, try it. If it doesn't work out, you can go back home with those stacks in your pocket and losing nothing but a bit of time. We'll put you up in my grandmother's house. Nobody going to say nothing about it, knowing you are working with me and, more importantly, my *nonna* and Mr. Crocetti. And that club in Smoketown? The owner is a colored man. Mr. Crocetti is that man's partner. Not the other way around. Business knows no color but green and that's the truth."

Otha went silent, studied the tree line for a few minutes. Fall colors were already showing in the leaves, glowing in the early evening sun.

"What Miss Serafina say about all this?" he said, giving Corky a sideways glance. "She know what you got going on here?"

"I wrote her" Corky said. "Called her, too, just like I did you. She was the one asked me about it, saying she knew there had to be something else besides a hotel business. How she knew, I don't have a clue, but I didn't ask."

Otha nodded. "That one could run all these businesses, no doubt," he said.

"Always reminded me of *nonna*, truth be told," Corky said. "Not to be messed with or disrespected, that's for certain." His thoughts drifted back to night of the heist and Serafina's razor. He slid his finger into the slit pocket of his vest and touched the ring he carried there every day since returning to Sagamore. It was his mother's engagement ring, a small diamond that his father had given her on their tenth anniversary. There was no money for such an extravagance when they were married. His mother was buried wearing her wedding band, but his father kept the diamond. Corky found it in the few belongings his father kept in a small box in the top drawer of his dresser.

"We've talked," Corky said. "She says she's thinking about selling the store, happy to leave Mississippi." A grunt and a nod from Otha. Sonny refilled their glasses. The three sat and sipped in silence, watching the early evening sunlight glint off the leaves, sprinkling of reds and golds among the countless shades of green that blanketed the hills.

"When we left Sagamore, Sal told his uncle in New Orleans about The Rooster," Corky said. "And all about Stallings' business. He was certain his uncle would be interested in moving from the ports and expanding their business by taking over the Hill Country." Corky's voice trailed off. He took a long swallow of his whiskey. "When I came north, it was not Mr. Crocetti who asked me about the juke joints and what kind of business setup was down there. The old man waved it all off, saying it was a distraction from his other businesses."

"Thought you said he wanted to build all these clubs?"

"He doesn't," Corky said. "His son does. Dino Jr. is the one who deals with the club in Smoketown. Junior loves being at the center of all that glitz, the celebrities and stars that show up at the club when they're in town. All the local bigwigs. Everything his father avoids."

"Junior loves the women, no doubt," Sonny said. "Fancies himself a singer from what I heard."

"He does." Corky said. "On both counts. But there are a lot of Italians playing jazz. Eddie Lang and Joe Venuti from Philadelphia are great."

"The hell kind of Italian name is Eddie Lang?" Otha asked.

"His real name is Salvatore Massaro," Corky said. "That Eye-Tal-Yun enough for you?"

"He plays the blues, too" Sonny said. "Makes records with Bessie Smith and Lonnie Johnson."

Otha's face screwed half question, half surprise. "What the hell you know about the blues?"

"Now who's making assumptions on certain attributes?" Sonny asked, returning the look.

"Sonny's record collection stretches all around his room." Corky said. "Got everything from blues to jazz. All kinds of Italian opera. Caruso's his favorite."

"What blues people you know?" Otha asked Sonny.

There was no small amount of pride in Sonny's voice as he listed his favorites.

"Ma Rainy and Bessie Smith, of course," he said. "Guitar player named Sylvester Weaver does all instrumental blues that are amazing. I have almost everything on the Paramount and Okeh labels. Blind Lemon Jefferson. Blind Blake. I've heard about Charley Patton."

"He's from Mississippi," Otha said, pride in his voice now. "Saw him at The Rooster more than a few times. That man could flat out sing the blues. Play 'em, too."

Corky smiled, listening to the two friends from different worlds finding common ground.

"My cousin, Robert Johnson is the best bluesman there is," Otha said. "Playin' the jukes and makin' the house rock all night."

"I can vouch for that," Corky said. "He played at The Rooster the night we were there. Incredible guitar player and singer."

"Robert can play anything," Otha said. "Blues, jazz, country, too. Anything that gets folks dancing and shaking them tail feathers. He hears a song on the jukebox once and next thing you know he's playing it perfectly. Going to be famous someday. He just needs to get somebody to record him. Maybe I'll just go down and get him and some of the other great ones, bring them back up here like you said."

"That mean you're in?" Corky asked.

"This Junior know what he's doing?" Otha asked. "He wants to be a singing star or a club owner?"

"Which ever gets him laid the most," Sonny said, which brought laughs all around.

"I don't know if Junior's any good as a singer," Corky said. "But he loves the music and the musicians. And it's one place in that city open to everyone. Italians, Polish, coloreds. Anyone with class and money to spend. Junior wants all the joints the same, which is one reason he got very interested when I told him about having you as a partner. He seems to know how to run a club. Or know enough to leave it to his partner to take care of things. Which makes him a good partner for us if he's that smart. Doesn't hurt he's got his old man's permission to try another place and see if we can make a go."

"Where this man want to do his nightclub?" Otha asked. "Around here?"

"Not in Sagamore," Corky said. "He wants a few up along the river heading north towards Erie. His father has connections in Buffalo and Rochester and some in Toronto and Montreal. The old man already controls everything on the river from Pittsburgh south and has partnerships with the organization that runs everything on the Mississippi River. Junior sees a string of places where the best jazz musicians can play a circuit that goes from Canada down to New Orleans."

"A bit bigger than Boss Stallings had with his jukes," Otha laughed. "You really think this can work?"

Sonny pointed to the stacks of bills still laying on the armrest.

"That's just from one week's production going to Smoketown, he said. "No doubt there are plenty more thirsty folks up and down the river."

"What happens now that this Prohibition thing is over?" Otha said. "Won't that hurt the whiskey business side?"

"People like their 'shine and getting it without paying any taxes on it," Sonny said.

"Crocetti buys a small amount from the legal distillers," Corky said. "Just to keep appearances up but he buys most from us. No doubt he pays the right people to look the other way. So we're good to go."

"Still ain't said where you putting this first joint," Otha said. "And me."

"There's a place not far from here," Corky said. "Up the river in Kittanning. Already set up as a club but been vacant for a while now. Junior says his father worked out some sort of arrangement and this place is his. Ours, if we want now."

"Going to need a new name, that's for certain," Sonny said, shaking his head with a bemused smile on his face.

"Got one in mind?" Otha asked.

Corky closed his eyes and took a sip from his glass. After savoring the taste, his eyes opened. The sun had fallen behind the tree line and the sky was smeared in rose pinks and gold. He held the glass up against the fading light and studied the contents, as if divining the future in the amber liquid and recalling how his father lost himself in the smoke of his pipe as if doing the same. He met the gaze of his two friends.

"We will call it Sal's."

The three fell silent until Otha raised his glass. "Well, truth be told," he said. "Ain't no other name for it." He tapped his glass against Corky's, then Sonny's.

"It was a long trip, and you must be exhausted," Corky said to Otha. "Your room is the first one at the top of the stairs. There's a big tub in the bathroom. Get yourself a hot bath and a good night's sleep." He embraced Otha, who in turn shook hands with Sonny.

"Alright partners," Otha said. "Glad to be here."

He went inside, leaving Corky and Sonny alone on the porch. The friends sat sipping whiskey, looking out at the clear night sky.

"Have to hand it to you." Sonny said. "You're making this all happen. Honestly, didn't think you could. But damn, son. Here we are." He lifted his glass to his friend. Corky raised his own glass. "And brother," Sonny said. "I do hope it all works out with your Serafina. Been enough heartbreak around here."

Corky's mind drifted back to the days when he first returned to Sagamore. To the hours he spent walking the hills above the town, when he could be found late afternoons in the cemetery, sitting on a bench he had placed next to the plot where his father, mother, brother and now Sal were buried. He spoke to them, recounting his day, his thoughts, recalling the things they had said or done and more often spoke the things he wished he had been able to tell them while they were alive.

He whispered in turns to his father, mother, and his brother, Rudy. Professing how much he missed and loved them. Telling each that, even after all the years gone by, there was no knowing what would cause them to rise in his mind or whether the memory brought a smile or a pain in his heart that dropped him to his knees along with a flood of tears.

Corky told Sal of his plans and how he wished more than anything he was a part of them. That none of it would be possible without him. He cursed God aloud at the unfairness of it all but felt grateful to have the means now to realize a new dream. He let Sal know his true feelings for Serafina and his vision of a future together. His breath caught as his thoughts turned to the ocean blue depths of her eyes. He felt his heart flutter. His finger once again plumbed his vest pocket and touched the fine edge of the diamond. His hand then traveled with a mind of its own to rest on top of the breast pocket where, along with the St Michael's prayer card he always carried, was a train ticket. One way to Pittsburgh from Rosedale, Mississippi.

"Guess time will tell," Corky said. "But right now, nothing makes me happier than having you as my partner and both of us out of the mines.

Sonny stood and turned to face his friend. "I don't know how you managed to convince my father I could quit the mines"

"I believe it was your uncle who had the conversation with him," Corky said. "I don't know exactly what was said but seems your father agreed that getting out of the mines for this business was the best thing for you."

"Maybe he threatened him with jail time," Sonny said and laughed. "I need to have a talk with Uncle Buzz and thank him." The friends clinked glasses.

"I'm glad you are part of this," Corky said. "Wouldn't want it any other way." He stood and embraced his friend. "I mean that. We're family. Brothers. Always have been." They parted and Corky kissed his friend on the cheek.

Sonny began to speak but stopped, as if struggling to find the words he wanted to say. What he wanted to tell Corky ever since he returned to Sagamore. He spoke one word. "Family" and brought his hand to his heart. They parted and, as he turned to go, Sonny opened his briefcase and brought out a wooden box.

"Something for you," he said. "I think you should have this."

Corky's face was a question, but he took the gift and set it on his chair. Sonny left the porch, got in his truck and with a wave drove down the long driveway.

After watching the taillights of his friend's truck fade into the night, Corky picked up the gift. He opened the box and lifted the pearl handled revolver with the silver inlaid monogram in his hand.

# JACK SONNI
## 1954-2023

Jack Sonni's first love was music. He was best known as the "other guitarist" in Dire Straits, playing with the band during the height of their fame, through the iconic "Brothers in Arms" tour of 1985-86, in front of millions of fans across the globe. He also performed with them at the historic Live Aid from Wembley Stadium. Jack later founded his own band, Jack Sonni and The Leisure Class, a rock-n-roll bar band that "raised a ruckus" for decades. Jack's love of the written word eventually led him to pursue the craft of writing. In 2013 he began serving as the Writer-in-Residence and house manager at The Noepe Center for Literary Arts in Martha's Vineyard. He was there until 2015, and it was at Noepe that he found inspiration for the novel *Sagamore*. Research for *Sagamore* brought Jack to Taylor, Mississippi, where for the remaining years of his life he made his home within a community of artists, writers, musicians, chefs and bartenders. He created and hosted a *Newsweek* podcast that featured an eclectic mix of talented guests, comprised both of new local friends and connections from Jack's storied life, which exemplified the gift he had of bringing people from one part of his life into camaraderie with others. He also streamed a nightly broadcast titled "Jack Sonni Guitar Radio" where he shared his favorite music with a worldwide audience. Jack was passionate about many things. His family, his friends, music, food, cocktails, and his writing. *Sagamore* is the result of passion, perseverance, and his love for art and the power of words. Jack passed away on August 30, 2023, leaving behind a legacy that will not soon be forgotten.

www.ingramcontent.com/pod-product-compliance
Lightning Source LLC
Chambersburg PA
CBHW021327190825
31354CB00008B/543